Nate grinned, no half smile about it.

The two sides of his mouth matched in upturned delight.

Julie almost fell over. That full grin. She'd never seen it before. It boosted him from handsome to gorgeous. He should smile like that all the time. Strike that. If he smiled like that all the time, he'd be irresistible. To women. To...her.

Deep inside her something shifted; something fit. And it fit as easily as her thumb on Nate's worry stone. She looked away, refusing to name it or acknowledge it or think about what that something was.

But that grin. It made her wonder.

Dear Reader,

Welcome to Harmony Valley!

Just a few short years ago, Harmony Valley was on the brink of extinction with only those over the age of sixty in residence. Now the influx of a younger generation is making life in Harmony Valley more fun than afternoon television for its gray-haired residents.

Sheriff Nate Landry had a tough childhood that made him reluctant to have children of his own, so when he met a woman who had faced her own challenges and wouldn't be having children, it seemed like a sign. But things fell apart on his wedding day. Now, more than two years later, his ex-fiancée's sister, Julie Smith, shows up with a toddler she says is her sister's baby and *his*, and she's got custody papers that she wants him to sign. After all Nate's been through, his decision to let go should be easy.

I hope you enjoy Nate and Julie's journey to a happily-ever-after, as well as the other romances in the Harmony Valley series. I love to hear from readers. Check my website, www.melindacurtis.com, to learn more about upcoming books, sign up for email book announcements, and I'll send you a free sweet romance read, or chat with me on Facebook at MelindaCurtisAuthor to hear about my latest giveaways.

Melinda Curtis

HEARTWARMING

Support Your Local Sheriff

———

USA TODAY Bestselling Author

Melinda Curtis

Recycling programs
for this product may
not exist in your area.

ISBN-13: 978-0-373-36855-6

Support Your Local Sheriff

Copyright © 2017 by Melinda Wooten

This edition published by arrangement with Harlequin Books S.A.

For questions and comments about the quality of this book,
please contact us at CustomerService@Harlequin.com.

Printed in U.S.A.

Award-winning *USA TODAY* bestselling author **Melinda Curtis** is an empty nester still married to her college sweetheart, despite raising three kids, flipping houses and writing full-time through many live-in remodels. Having been raised on a remote sheep ranch with grandparents who built houses from scratch made Melinda the perfect match for Mr. Curtis, who was raised by a family of contractors. Just don't ask her to operate a drill, because she always seems to reverse the setting.

Melinda writes sweet contemporary romances as Melinda Curtis (Brenda Novak says of *Season of Change*, it "found a place on my keeper shelf"), and fun, sexy reads as Mel Curtis (Jayne Ann Krentz says of *Fool For Love*, it was "wonderfully entertaining").

Books by Melinda Curtis

Harlequin Heartwarming

Dandelion Wishes
Summer Kisses
Season of Change
A Perfect Year
Time for Love
A Memory Away
Marrying the Single Dad
Love, Special Delivery

For more books by Melinda Curtis,
visit her Author Page at Harlequin.com.

This book is dedicated to my sister-in-law, Lynn DeMerritt, who was the inspiration for April. Both Lynn and April went through cancer treatments that left them sterile, only to be blessed with a child after they'd lost all hope and their relationships fell apart. Lynn, you knew your fate and still showed the world love and grace. Your daughter is a blessing to me. I'm so happy that part of your story is being told in a book released on the first anniversary of your passing.

CHAPTER ONE

"WHAT'S THE EMERGENCY?" Sheriff Nate Landry, fresh from chasing chickens at Clara Barra's house, took a seat on a creaky wooden pew in the back of the church. "Spring Festival meltdown?"

"The emergency is next," Flynn Harris said in a hushed voice so as not to wake baby Ian in his arms.

Nate's entrance met with turned heads, warm smiles and nods of recognition. The Harmony Valley Town Council was in session, better attended than some small-town basketball games. The meetings were held in the historic, steepled church downtown, being led from folding tables and chairs set up on the pulpit. That was the way of life in the remote northeastern corner of Sonoma County—casual, a bit of making do and a bit impromptu.

Flynn managed to brush reddish-brown hair from his eyes with his shoulder without disrupting his newborn's sleep. "The emergency is Doris Schlotski."

A little black rain cloud formed above Nate. As the only lawman in town, he prided himself on figuring out what made each resident tick. Doris Schlotski. She'd moved here four months ago and was a conundrum.

About three months ago, Nate had issued Doris citations for violating both the noise and pet ordinances. She bred Chihuahuas and her ten adult dogs barked 24/7. She'd argued that they were only small dogs and quieter than a neighbor's Saint Bernard. A few weeks after that he'd issued her a citation for permanently parking her never-used fishing boat on the street. She'd argued that her driveway wasn't wide enough for both her car and the boat. Just last week, he'd pulled Doris over for speeding. She'd argued that the speed limit hadn't been updated in fifty years and was therefore invalid.

Nate was still trying to determine what made Doris tick, but he was done arguing. He bet Doris wasn't. He bet she was here to argue about speed limits or public right-of-way or pet regulations.

Ian squirmed, rolling his head until the blue

puppy blanket dropped unnoticed from his head and over Flynn's arm.

The door behind them opened, bringing a nip of evening air. Harmony Valley was near enough to the Pacific Ocean to be cooled nightly by ocean breezes and thick fog.

Nate tucked the baby blanket snugly around the tufts of red-brown hair on Ian's head.

Footsteps and whispers from the newcomers were covered by Mayor Larry recording a quorum on a request to rezone some property in the south part of town. The pew behind them groaned as someone sat down. At the front of the church, heads turned to see who'd entered. Inquisitive stares and nudges of neighbors followed.

Nate began to turn to see who had come in when Flynn nudged him and said, "Here we go."

"Next on the agenda..." Mayor Larry squinted at his notes through black rectangular reading glasses. *"'Sheriff elections?'"*

Abruptly, everyone faced forward, perhaps as shocked by the agenda item as Nate was.

The little black rain cloud above Nate's head thickened. Doris wasn't here to talk about speed limits or public right-of-way or pet regulations. She was here to talk about him!

Nate leaned closer to Flynn, keeping his

voice down. "We don't have sheriff elections." He'd come to Harmony Valley nearly three years ago because the town was plain and simple. He'd been hired, plain and simple. He'd renewed his contract, plain and simple. Less than two hundred residents lived in town, most of them pleasant, law-abiding, elderly. Plain and simple.

At least, until Doris had returned to the area, breathing fire.

Doris approached the speaker podium like she was going to bulldoze it. She was shaped like a fireplug—short, compact, the promise of energy behind every step. Her gray hair didn't dare curl or frizz, not even in the fog. Barely an inch long, it stood on end. She was a fireplug, all right. Only instead of spouting water, Doris spouted words. That woman could out-debate a presidential candidate.

Nate sucked back a grin. She hadn't been able to talk her way out of those citations.

Something bumped the back of Nate's pew just as Doris began to speak. "Mr. Mayor—"

Nate's grin slipped free by half, poking holes in his rain cloud.

Mr. Mayor? Everyone called him Mayor Larry, at the mayor's request. The aging hippie and tie-dye business entrepreneur was unorthodox, from his long gray ponytail to his tie-dyed attire and his penchant for naked yoga down by the river.

Doris continued to address those on the dais. "Madames Councilwomen—"

Nate's war to contain the grin became more challenging. The three councilwomen weren't into formalities either.

"Ladies and gentlemen," Doris continued in her high-pitched, grating voice. "We should be proud of many things in our community. The wonderful festivals we have. The resurgence of new businesses. And the low crime rate. But that isn't good enough."

Not good enough? The little black rain cloud sucked the oxygen from the old church.

"In this age of police misconduct, the people need a voice." Doris had a death grip on the podium.

Nate thought it might be his death she planned.

"Can't see," came a little voice from behind Nate.

That innocent voice. It broke through the cloud.

Clop-clump.

It sounded like the tyke stood on the next pew back.

"That better, Juju."

Doris wasn't only upsetting Nate. On the pulpit, the town council murmured and shifted in their seats. Those in pews in front of Nate exchanged significant glances and whispered commentary.

"The people have a voice, Doris." Councilwoman Agnes Villanova drew the microphone she shared with the other councilwomen closer. "Residents vote for representatives of our town. Your representatives then vote on issues of health, well-being and safety. Why, just this last year your town council hired two firefighters and renewed the sheriff's contract."

Short, spunky Agnes ran the town from her seat to the mayor's right. Next to her sat Rose Cascia. Rose looked like a retired ballerina with her thin frame and her crisp white chignon. She might have pulled off New York sophistication if she didn't tap-dance her way into rooms. At the end of the table sat Mildred Parsons. Mildred could barely see, despite her thick lenses. She was made of soft angles, from the snow-white curls in her short hair to her plump frame.

Nate loved those old ladies. They'd chase away storm clouds on a rainy day.

"Beg pardon, Madame Councilwoman." The

smirk in Doris's voice carried to the back of the church without her having to turn around. "But I was talking about *removing* a layer of politics from the process."

"A layer of politics?" Spritely Agnes had the heart of a saint and silver hair as short as Doris's, except Agnes's hair relaxed on her head. "Are you questioning our dedication to this town? Are you questioning our...*ethics*?"

The crowd murmured in disapproval. The mayor and town council had been serving for decades. They were wise. They were beloved. They always ran unopposed.

Nate drew a calming breath. Whatever agenda Doris had, the town council would thwart it.

"What I'm saying is clear enough that everyone in this room understands," Doris said with the pomp of the self-important. "Everyone but you!"

In the midst of horrified gasps, a small hand landed on Nate's shoulder.

"Hi." Hot breath gusted in Nate's ear.

Nate glanced over his shoulder into a pair of large gray eyes framed by a dark mop of hair. He'd never seen the toddler before, but the boy was cute and most likely the reason for the curious stares a few minutes ago.

Across the aisle, Old Man Takata beamed at the tyke and tapped the shoulder of his neighbor Snarky Sam, who owned the antiques/used goods store on Main Street. Sam's smiles were rare. And yet he gave the kid a toothy grin.

The little boy touched his forehead to Nate's and repeated, "Hi."

"Hey," Nate said softly, unable to resist returning the boy's impish smile. "Be careful."

Feminine hands curled around the boy's torso and drew him back. Nate began to twist around to see who the hands belonged to when Flynn spoke again, halting him. "Do you think Doris would be more respectful of you if you wore a uniform?" Even in a whisper, Flynn sounded like he was enjoying this more than Nate. Of course, Flynn wasn't the sheriff. He was part owner of a winery.

"I don't need a uniform," Nate whispered back, not enjoying this at all. He'd rather be chasing chickens. "I have a star on my truck and a badge in my pocket."

Doris wasn't the whispering type. In fact, she was practically shouting now. "I'm saying that *we the people* and only *we the people* should decide who serves our community. Otherwise, we'll be stuck with a sheriff—" without turning, Doris pointed behind her, toward Nate "—who badgers our residents, berates citizens for their lifestyle choices and bullies the elderly with citations and tickets they can't afford to pay!"

"Freaky," Flynn said louder, causing the baby to stir and loosen the blanket again. "It's like you and Doris are psychically connected. She knew exactly where you were sitting."

"She saw me come in." Nate could solve that mystery more easily than the one involving what made Doris so bitter. "She can't be this upset over tickets."

Doris held up a sheaf of papers. "I have here twenty signed reports from residents about Sheriff Landry's behavior."

Nate didn't think he'd given out twenty tickets in the past year.

"Twenty reports stating that Sheriff Landry gave them warnings rather than a citation with a fee attached. Whereas I…" Doris had worked into huff-and-puff mode. "Whereas I have received three citations in the past three months! I demand we let the people decide who protects us. I demand we fire the sheriff and hold an election!" She dropped the stack of papers on the podium like a rapper dropped a mic at the end of a show. Except she kept talking. "I demand—"

"In my defense—" Nate tucked Ian's blue blanket more securely around his tiny shoulders "—the only way to handle Doris is to give her a ticket and drive away."

"Now, Doris..." Mayor Larry made a rare appearance in an argument. Normally, he delegated trouble to the town council so he could remain as neutral as Switzerland. "These are serious allegations. Please approach with your notes so we may look them over."

Clod-clump. Clod-clump.

"Notes?" Doris snatched up the papers again, clutching them to her chest. "This is my *evidence*!"

Clod-clump. Clod-clump.

The gray-haired residents of Harmony Valley had probably never done the wave at a sports stadium. But their heads turned in the same rippled effect to stare Nate's way, starting from the back of the church and moving forward. Grins and coos rippled through the assembled, almost as if—

The little hand returned to Nate's shoulder, followed by a hot-breathed, "Hi."

Another mystery solved. Residents were doing the neck-craning wave to watch an angelic toddler putting on a show behind Nate.

When Nate turned his head, he received another gentle forehead bump. "You're an awesome little dude." Nate ruffled the boy's hair.

The boy's gray eyes widened in delight. "I Duke." He tapped his skinny chest and grinned.

The majority of the assembled chuckled. The majority being over age sixty-five and being grandparents or great-grandparents who appreciated precocious children.

Behind Nate, someone emitted a heavy sigh. Feminine hands drew the toddler out of view once more.

"For years—" Doris half glanced behind her as if sensing she was losing her audience "—you four have ruled Harmony Valley. Well, no more! The people want to be heard. The people want a say. The people want to vote for a sheriff of our own choosing!"

Nate sat back against the pew. He wasn't the hand-shaking, promise-making, run-for-office type.

"Now, Doris..." Mayor Larry hated discord and looked as if he was ready to break Robert's rules of order and escape out the back. He started again. "Now, Doris—"

"Don't you *Now, Doris* me. I want action and I want it now!"

"She slipped up there," Flynn noted. "She said *I*."

"The people..." Doris was quick with a correction. *"The people* want action now!"

"I'm going to remind the speaker," Mayor Larry said carefully. "That there is a review process written in the town bylaws—"

"By you." Doris scoffed.

The mayor tilted his head down and stared at Doris over the rim of his rectangular readers. "Written by the town council over seventy years ago."

"Hi!" Duke shouted, completely stealing the limelight and bringing some much-needed laughter to the proceedings.

Doris spun, so upset at being upstaged her short hair seemed to tilt forward and take aim at the upstager.

The few residents not enamored of little Duke straightened and quieted like school children caught misbehaving. The rest kept on smiling and scrunching their faces in funny ways designed to encourage the boy, not calm him down. He really was a cute kid. Not even Doris was immune to his charms. Her expression seemed to soften.

"We should wrap this up so we can all meet that adorable young man in the back." Agnes spoke into the microphone. "These are all good points, Doris. Therefore…" Agnes waited until Doris faced her again. "I move we hold a sheriff's election as soon as possible. Say…this week, so as not to hinder our Spring Festival plans."

Voices disappeared beneath a rush of sound, as if Nate was passing a semitruck on the highway with his windows down. His position was an inconvenience to the Spring Festival? His livelihood? His future?

The assembled were just as shocked as Nate. The church had fallen into a stunned silence. There wasn't so much as a peep from Doris or Duke.

During the lull, Agnes elbowed Rose.

"Uh…" Rose looked as confused as Nate felt.

Mildred, who had a slight resemblance to Mrs. Claus, pushed her thick lenses higher up her nose and sighed. "I suppose… I second?"

Anticipating peace, the mayor beamed at the council. "All in favor?"

All three town councilwomen said, "Aye."

"Motion passed." The mayor closed out the meeting.

"An election?" Nate's plain and simple world was suddenly not so plain and simple.

"Don't sweat it." Flynn stared down at Ian with a whole lotta love in his eyes. "You signed a new contract and you're the only qualified candidate in town. In a week, you'll win by a landslide."

Nate's future was out of his control. He didn't think he'd sleep for a week.

"I Duke." The little dude gripped Nate's shoulder.

The woman's hands drew him back.

"Juju," the boy scolded.

In the past eighteen months or so, there'd been an influx of younger residents to Harmony Valley and a baby boom. Nate turned more fully in his seat to see who held his new friend.

Familiar gray eyes collided with his.

The storm cloud returned. And flashed with lightning.

"HELLO, NATE." JULIE SMITH put nearly three years of disdain and disappointment in those two words.

"Julie." Nate shot to his feet, steady as always, guarded as always. If Nate was the sheriff, he was off duty. He wore a brown checkered shirt and blue jeans, not a service uniform.

Duke was balanced on her thighs, his small hard-soled sneakers digging in for purchase as he reached for Nate once more.

Couldn't Duke loathe Nate as much as Julie did?

Couldn't Nate look as if the past few years had been one big heartbreak?

No on both counts.

Duke's fingers flexed as he reached for Nate.

And Nate? It was annoying how good he looked. His black hair might have been in need of a trim and his chin shadowed with stubble, but his teeth hadn't fallen out, his broad shoulders weren't bullet ridden and, worst of all, he didn't look sleep deprived.

The mayor and town council were still on the pulpit surrounded by animated residents with loud voices. Chaos had arrived in Harmony Valley, just not the way Julie had envisioned it.

The man next to Nate came to his feet. He wore a wedding ring, held a swaddled newborn, had spit-up on the shoulder of his yellow polo and New Dad bags under his eyes.

Julie gave him a sympathetic smile. Duke despised naps and could be a restless sleeper at night. Not as restless as Julie lately, but still...

The man with the baby cleared his throat, shaking Nate out of tall, dark and stunned mode.

"Flynn," Nate said. "This is Julie, my…"

And there it was. That awkwardness Julie had been waiting years for.

She pounced. "I'm the sister of Nate's *ex*-fiancée."

Flynn slid a questioning look Nate's way.

Her moment had arrived. Julie stood, scooping Duke to her hip with her left arm. "Didn't Nate tell you he was engaged? He left my sister at the altar." That wasn't all he'd left, but Julie didn't want to waste all her ammunition on the first volley.

Flynn didn't look as shocked as she'd hoped. She blamed Nate. He inspired loyalty wherever he went. Even after being dumped, April had forbidden Julie to confront him. But that ban had been lifted. It was open season on the sheriff.

Duke toppled forward, letting his full weight drop between Julie and Nate, unexpectedly shifting Julie's center of gravity. She slurped in air like it came through a clogged milk shake straw. The stitches beneath her right collarbone pulled sharply, tugging at nerves that quivered up and down her neck and shoulder.

Mom was right. The doctor was right. It was too soon.

And too late to back out now.

Julie drew on years of resentment, drew Duke back and drew down her chin against the pain. She was here for justice. She was here to make Nate suffer. Surely that wouldn't take long.

Nate hadn't been shamed by her announcement that he'd backed out of a wedding. He didn't scowl or frown. He didn't put his hands on his hips and try to stare her down. She'd forgotten he was a man of few words.

Julie was itching for words. Fighting words. "My sister, April, defeated cancer and the idea that it might return gave Nate cold feet." She glared at Nate, daring him to contradict her.

"Not exactly," Nate said in a gruff voice, not riled enough to fully engage in battle.

"What a pleasure to see a new babe in our neck of the woods." It was the miniature old lady from the town council, the one with the relaxed pixie-cut silver hair. She bestowed Duke and Julie with a friendly smile, and then gave Nate the kind of smile grandmothers bestowed on favored grandkids before turning to Flynn. "Can the council borrow you for an assignment?"

Flynn accepted the job and edged past Nate, who was staring at the ceiling as if searching for divine intervention.

Julie hoped April wasn't smiling down on him. Her younger sister had always been the forgiving type.

"Who is this adorable young man?" An overly wrinkled woman with unnaturally black hair and a severe widow's peak stood behind Julie and ruffled Duke's hair.

"I Duke," Julie's nephew repeated, thrusting his shoulders back. He loved attention.

"More important, who are you?" A pale elderly woman wheeled an oxygen tank to Julie's pew and adjusted the cannula in her nose.

"Oh, heavens, no. The important question is are you here to stay?" This from a rotund gentleman waggling a smile and bushy white brows.

At least ten elderly folk clustered around Julie's pew, clogging the aisle. They leaned on walkers and canes and the pew itself, waiting for Julie's answer.

"Is this how we treat visitors to Harmony Valley?" Nate asked them in a voice infused with patience.

For a moment, no one answered. And then someone said, "Yes," which made the group laugh.

"Her name is Julie," Nate said, still in patience mode. "And you can ask her questions some other time. Now, does everyone have a ride home?"

They dutifully nodded and pointed to their rides, or volunteered to take others home.

Amid the subsequent shuffle toward the door, Julie studied Nate some more, trying to figure out how he won everyone over.

He had that ramrod-stiff posture that signified confidence and a history of military service. His black hair was parted to the side where a cowlick prevented the hair over his forehead from lying flat. His brown eyes were serious more often than not, and when others were grinning he only allowed a half smile. He was bottled up and wound tight, keeping his emotions close to his chest. Even after he'd met April.

Which was weird. Everyone had loved April. She handed out smiles the way sample ladies handed out free food at Costco. She'd been the kid least likely to get in a fight and most likely to shed tears over sappy television commercials. She'd grown up to be a kindergarten teacher, of course. And she'd taught dance and tumbling to little ones for the recreation department. She was the opposite of

Nate, who'd been a sniper in the Middle East, and Julie, who was now a sniper on Sacramento's SWAT team.

Julie eased her aching shoulder back, ignoring the growing feeling of exhaustion. She nodded toward the podium. "Stirring up trouble, I see."

"Trouble's always had a way of finding me," Nate said with a half smile.

Julie's aim was off. Nothing was ruffling him. Nothing was satisfying her need for revenge. She'd have to hunker down for the long haul. She'd never been good at the long game, at chess or Monopoly. This time, the stakes were higher than bragging rights or a pile of paper money. This time, she had to be patient.

"Want Mama." Duke collapsed against Julie's shoulder, his forehead pile-driving into the only tender spot on her body.

Her sharp intake of breath caused Nate to dip his head and stare at her more closely. She smoothed her expression into her game face, determined that he only see what she wanted him to see—a strong woman who despised him.

"You got married." Nate's gaze was gentle.

She didn't want his gentleness. She wanted his anger. She wanted to argue and shout and have him argue and shout back. "You think I'm married because…"

A small crease appeared between Nate's brows, only for a moment. "Well…this little guy…"

A surge of satisfaction shored up sagging dreams of revenge. "You think a woman has to be married to have a child?"

The crease returned, deeper this time. "You're a cop. Female cops don't —"

"You're a police officer?" asked the woman who'd been putting up a stink at the podium. She'd stopped at Julie's pew. Doris didn't smile. She didn't coo over Duke. She eyed the pair like a cattle rancher at a bull auction.

Julie didn't put much stock in the woman's claims. Nate was many things, but he was a good cop. And Julie wasn't keen on being sized up. But she wasn't here to cause a ruckus about it either, so she said, "Yes, ma'am," and ground her teeth at the interruption in her attempted takedown of Nate the Unflappable.

The woman stored that information with a brisk nod, and then moved toward the door.

"Mama." Duke crooned softly.

Nate glanced around, perhaps catching on to where this was going, perhaps assessing how much privacy they had. Or how much they'd need.

The more public his humiliation, the better.

"I'm not married." Julie's smile felt the way it did when guys on the force made a crude remark and deserved reproach. "And Duke isn't my child."

CHAPTER TWO

AND DUKE ISN'T my child.

The bottom dropped out of Nate's world and his stomach plunged to the center of the earth.

"Who..." He washed a hand over his face and planted his feet more firmly on the church planks. "Whose child is he?"

"Look at him."

Nate had been looking at Julie, at the delicate lines of her face and the stubborn tilt to her chin. She'd dressed as if she was prepared for a SWAT maneuver——a long-sleeved dark blue utility shirt, belted black utility pants and sturdy boots. But she held a toddler.

She should have been wearing faded blue jeans and a soft T-shirt. Her blond hair should have had bounce, not hung limply to her shoulders. The skin on her face should have glowed, not been washed-out. And the bags under her eyes... Had she spent too many nights on duty?

"Look at him," Julie commanded.

Nate obeyed.

A roaring filled his ears. His heart began to thump faster than it had at the sight of Julie.

The little boy had the Smiths' gray eyes and wide smiling mouth. Like most kids his age, he had thin, lanky legs. His sprouted from a pair of khaki shorts. The friendly sparkle to his eyes was all Smith. But the dark, unruly hair was hard to mistake as anything other than a Landry gift. And as for those ears...

Nate tugged one of his own.

The kid would grow into them.

The kid. His kid.

Nate felt as if he'd been shoved from behind, a blow that threatened to topple him. The only things holding him upright were the curled toes in his boots.

"You're saying he's mine," he whispered.

"I'm saying he's *April's.*" If Julie had been born a man, she'd have been a fighter. Her chin jutted, daring him to take a swing, to pick a fight, to defend himself for leaving April at the altar when she'd obviously been pregnant with his child.

Take a swing? He could barely draw a breath. "How old are you, Duke?"

The boy—*his son!*—held up two fingers.

Nate breathed in. Breathed out. Fought a torrent of emotion—guilt, joy, anger—that further weakened his knees.

The guilt… Guilt was familiar. It rode in his back pocket every day, like his wallet. He had a past, one not suited to fatherhood. Then joy… Joy was a rare emotion for him. It tried to dance through his veins with the virility of being a father. But he wasn't a dancer. And the anger… It was anger that plowed past guilt and joy. Anger that marched behind his eyes with pounding steps, prickled his skin and straightened his backbone. "The chemo sent April into early menopause. The doctor said she'd never have children." The doctor had said no birth control was necessary.

"A miracle." So smug. Julie had been waiting for this.

"It's been three years." News of miracles usually traveled faster than that.

Every step he'd taken. Every vow he'd made. Nate set his feet in a wider stance, straddling the abyss filled with shattered expectations. It was all he could do not to shout, not to shake the back of the pew, not to reject fatherhood because he'd never aspired to the job. "Where's April? Why didn't she say anything?"

"April didn't want you to know until…" Julie's jaw clenched and for the first time since he'd turned around, there was a crack in her bravado. "April passed away three months ago."

Nate's heart plunged to the floor and into the tilting abyss that had sucked normal from his world. No one had told him that either. And by no one, he meant Julie. "I'm sorry about April." She'd been in remission on their wedding day. "Was it—"

"Yes, a brain tumor. Yes, cancer. She..." Julie swallowed, squeezing his son as if the boy was a beloved teddy bear. "It wasn't easy."

But she'd been there. Of that, Nate was certain. While he...he hadn't been. Not for April. Not for Julie. Not for his son, who'd asked for his mother a few minutes ago.

Nate washed a hand over his face again, staring at Duke. "You should've told me. April should've told me."

"Why are you so upset? You always said you didn't want kids." The fight was back in Julie's tone and the flash in her gray eyes. "Besides, you lost the right of parenthood when you jilted April."

Nate's hands fisted at his sides. "A man has a right to know."

"Why? You said you don't want—"

"No mad words." Duke put his small hand over Julie's mouth.

Nate and Julie's gazes locked.

No mad words.

It was something April used to say when Julie's good-natured bickering with anyone turned into hot debates.

Nate shoved his hands in his back pockets. "Why are you here? Why did you come? Why *now*?"

Julie's mouth formed the kind of hard line that made speeders like Doris sweat. "April wanted you to have custody, but I have the right to challenge if I can prove you're unfit to be his father, which is where the Daddy Test comes in."

A test. One he didn't have to pass. Nate should feel relief. He should thank Julie for the information, reiterate his position about children and tell her to keep his son safe. He'd send monthly checks for Duke's care, for birthdays and holidays. In the once-bumpy road that was his life, this could be smoothed over with the right words.

The right words didn't come to mind. Nate leaned forward, hands gripping the back of the pew. "My parental rights won't be judged by a bitter sister-in-law."

"I was *never* your sister-in-law." She turned slightly, putting herself between father and son. "And I have every right to judge you. You were my friend. I trusted you with my sister's heart."

He wanted to say that was her mistake, but it hadn't been. It'd been his.

He and Julie had been in the same class at the police academy and had been hired by the same police force. She was attractive and smart, but off-limits since they were both focused on their careers. Besides, a woman like Julie would want to have kids and Nate had sworn the opposite. They'd hung out off duty with a group of law enforcement friends. She had a formidable presence and had become a cop because her father was a fallen highway patrolman. She put 100 percent into everything she did, whether it was a game of poker or pulling over a speeder. He liked that she did what was right and stood behind her decisions.

And then one day he'd been at a backyard barbecue with a bunch of their friends. He'd heard Julie laugh. He'd looked up to find Julie towing a delicate blonde across the lawn to meet him. "This is my sister, April. I made you two dinner reservations at a restaurant on the river. Don't argue."

"Ignore my sister," April said in a voice as easygoing as sugar on toast. "I've been doing it for years." And then April had looked up at Nate with Julie's gray eyes and Julie's wide smile.

Only she wasn't Julie. He didn't work with her. And April had won a bout with cancer, but wouldn't be able to have children.

"Oh, I don't know." He'd given April a soft half smile. "I think your sister is onto something."

"So HERE'S HOW it's going to go," Julie said firmly, trying not to flinch when Duke dropped his head to her injured shoulder again. "I'm taking a couple of weeks off to see what kind of dad you'll be." That was a bluff. She wanted Nate to sign over custody of Duke to her tonight. The papers were in her backpack.

"A couple of weeks?" Nate's dark gaze drilled for the truth. "How did you get that much time off?"

"It's a combination of bereavement and vacation time," she lied. Why wasn't he focusing on what was important? Why wasn't he squirming out of being a dad? "I've booked a room at the bed-and-breakfast in town." For one night. When she'd walked into the church, she'd doubted she'd need to stay at all.

Nate drew back as if he'd gotten a whiff of dirty diaper. "Why don't you stay with me?"

"With..." Nate's offer jammed words in her throat. He should have been saying there was no reason to stay. That he didn't want to be a dad. "Not a chance." Bunk with the enemy?

Duke yawned. It was nearly eight o'clock, past his bedtime. Julie was spent, too, more energy draining every minute.

Nate placed a tentative hand on Duke's wild curls. "He's really... I can't believe it."

"Up." Duke, being April's kid and having never met a stranger he didn't like, reached for Nate and fell forward in that all-in way of his. He'd leave with the mailman if Julie didn't watch out.

He'd leave with Nate if Julie didn't watch out.

Nate caught him, placing Duke on his hip as if he'd been carrying rug rats around all his life.

The town council, mayor and Flynn spoke softly on the pulpit. The last of the attendees filed out the door with friendly smiles their way. Julie's hopes for a deep stab of revenge and a tidy wrap-up of loose ends went out with them.

"I tall." Duke gazed around, yawning. He dropped his head to Nate's shoulder and closed his eyes.

Nate stood very still. His lips were pursed, but his jaw worked, as if he was wrestling words that wanted to be given voice.

Julie gave him time to reject the little boy in his arms, time to stand by his rote words from years gone by.

Seconds ticked by and still nothing.

"Give me his jacket," Nate said finally, settling Duke closer. "I'll walk you out."

CHAPTER THREE

"YOU DIDN'T HAVE to follow us over." Julie's tone was as nippy as the evening air.

Nate deserved the cold shoulder for the choices he'd made regarding April. Deserved, yes. Enjoyed, no.

This was not how he'd envisioned seeing Julie again. Oh, he'd imagined her trying to rip him a new one. And he'd imagined himself standing and taking it. But a kid...

It wasn't that he didn't like kids or didn't spend time around them. In fact, he'd just returned from a weekend with his sister, Molly, and her toddler. But one of his own? The answer should be *no, thanks*.

Julie undid the straps on his son's safety seat.

He wanted her to hurry. He wanted to have his son in his arms once more. It made no sense. He wasn't like Molly or even Flynn. He hadn't longed for a child.

He stared up at the stately forest green

Victorian that was the bed-and-breakfast, and Harmony Valley's only hotel. "Have you checked in yet?"

"No."

Unable to wait any longer, Nate edged Julie aside and picked up Duke.

"Want bed." Short, sturdy arms wrapped around Nate's neck.

Nate hugged him closer, drinking in the smell of toddler—sweat and dirty clothes and the essence of his son.

Julie had moved to the rear of the red SUV. She unloaded an open bag of diapers with a tub of wipes stuffed in it. A dinosaur-print bedroll came next, followed by a duffel bag and a backpack. She closed the hatch, groaning almost as much as the hinges on the hatch. Was she recovering from the flu?

"Let me carry those," Nate offered.

"No," Julie snapped, but it was a weary snap.

"Juju." Duke leaned toward her, small arms outstretched, near tears. "Want bed."

"Soon." Julie slung the duffel over a shoulder (a sharp intake of breath), held the bedroll under an arm (a wince) and clutched the bag of diapers in her hand (looking like she might topple).

"Let me help you." Nate lowered Duke to the ground and snagged the backpack.

Wailing, the toddler staggered dramatically to Julie and latched onto her leg.

"Duke." Julie looked like she wanted to wail, too.

Without a word, Nate took the duffel, bedroll and diaper bag from her.

The front door opened. Leona Lambridge, the original proprietor of the bed-and-breakfast, stood in the doorway. Her thin-bladed features were sharper than surgical knives. She wore a simple navy dress that cast the gray in her tightly bound hair an eerie blue. She stared at them—an overloaded sheriff, a spent-looking aunt and a hysterical child—clasping her hands as if it helped her withhold verbal judgment.

Leona wasn't a people person. Why she'd opened a bed-and-breakfast was a mystery to Nate.

Julie knelt, gathered Duke with her left arm and muttered, "The music from *Psycho* is playing in my head." Cop humor. Meant to diffuse stress.

"Pay no attention to my grandmother." Reggie, Leona's granddaughter, edged past the old woman and hurried down the stairs to greet them. "I'm running the Lambridge B and B now." Poor Reggie. She had to be working her fingers to the bone. She looked thin and haggard. Her long brown hair listless and her pert nose less than pert.

"She'll run it until something better comes along," Leona quipped. "She's left me once already."

"Your patrons missed me when I was gone." Reggie took the diaper bag from Nate and smiled hard at Julie. "She's friendlier than she'd like you to believe."

Having known Leona a few years, Nate withheld comment.

Reggie scowled at him when he didn't back her up. "Grandmother has friends in town. She's retired. It's not like I have to force her out of the house."

"Oh, she forces me, all right. In hopes I'll take back my ex-husband." Leona retreated into the foyer where her hair seemed less blue and her countenance less sharp. "Or join one of Harmony Valley's many causes."

"Too much information for our guests," Reggie muttered.

"My offer of a place to stay still stands," Nate said to Julie. He had a studio apartment above the sheriff's office.

"I'll face the music of my own making, thank you." Lugging Duke, Julie followed Reggie up the steps. "You'd best do the same."

Nate noted Julie's slow, measured steps. Her uneven breathing as she ascended the stairs. Her rigid posture and the tender way she held Duke. What had torn her apart?

Cancer?

She'd been favoring her left shoulder.

Breast cancer?

Nate bounded up the stairs, suddenly afraid Julie might collapse.

"I could like Ms. Smith." Leona gave Julie a knowing smile. "She has a way with the sheriff. But—" she tilted her head and filled her expression with cheerful remorse "—the reservation was for one."

"Casa Landry has room for two," Nate said, if he slept downstairs on the cot in the jail cell.

"Poaching my business." Reggie tsked and tried to look like there was much business to poach. "Bad form, Sheriff. Children under six stay free, Grandmother."

"Want bed," Duke crooned.

"As soon as we check in, little man." But Julie didn't move toward the door in her usual take-no-prisoners style. She blew out a labored breath and planted her boots on the porch as if it was an accomplishment just to make it that far. "Reservation for Smith."

"Reggie needs your credit card." Leona tried to smile, although it made her look as if she was having indigestion. "I need your assurance that your party won't disrupt other guests."

"By other guests, she means herself." Reggie softened the remark with a more natural smile. "Thankfully, without her hearing aids she can only hear you if you scream. She hasn't been disturbed at night yet."

Julie was a woman of action, but she was loitering on the porch as if this was a social call and she wasn't swaying with fatigue. Why? Because cancer was making a buffet of her strength. Nate was certain of it now. His certainty hollowed him with a sense of impending loss.

"Excuse me." A man's voice reached them from the sidewalk. "Is this the Lambridge Bed & Breakfast?"

"It is." Reggie shoved the diaper bag into Nate's chest. "Grandmother, show the Smiths to their room."

"Yes," Nate said firmly. "Show us now."

WHEN JULIE WAS a kid, she'd had boundless energy. It was as if she'd gotten her share of energy, plus April's.

April had asthma. April had painful growth spurts. April had flat feet, poor eyesight, lactose intolerance, skin that burned, toes prone to warts. You name it, April suffered through it. Not with Julie's spunk, but with a gentle smile and a well-meaning joke.

Five days ago, Julie had been shot in the soft flesh near her shoulder. She'd lost a lot of blood.

Standing and carrying Duke. Fighting with Nate. Being out of bed. How quickly it all drained her reserves. She wanted to collapse on the chair just inside the front door. She didn't want to carry her nephew and follow the Bride of Frankenstein up the stairs to a bedroom.

Seriously. Leona was a dead ringer for the black-and-white film icon. Give her a couple of neck bolts, tease up her hair, and she'd be ready for Halloween.

She was out of place in the house, which was beautiful and serene. It was like stepping back in time. Bead board. Wood floors. Old fixtures. Antique furniture. All lovingly cared for. By Reggie, no doubt.

"I'm curious." Nate stared at Reggie and the man on the sidewalk. And then he turned to look at Leona. "You're singing in Rose's production of *Annie* for the Spring Festival?"

There was a shift in Leona's posture, a preening. "Rose said no one else could play Miss Hannigan."

Nate's half smile twitched. He adjusted his hold on the load he carried. "Can you give us a sample?"

"I don't do requests." With a toss of her head, Leona led them with slow steps that made the creaking stairs wail as plaintively as Duke had outside.

The music from *Psycho* played once more in Julie's head, but this time she was smiling as she climbed.

The pain meds are making me loopy.

Or they would be if I'd taken the pain meds.

When they reached the second floor, Leona gestured to an open door. "This is your bathroom."

It was completely tiled and completely white. Not the best choice for the dirt little boys tended to bring inside.

Blessedly, a few steps later they were at a bedroom. The four-poster bed was huge, and the room was still large enough for a Tae Kwon Do match.

Julie set Duke down on the bed. Only the presence of Nate kept her from collapsing next to him.

She'd played sports in high school and trained in martial arts. She knew how to play through pain. But exhaustion. Exhaustion was different. Exhaustion took you out of the game.

"Breakfast is from 8:30 a.m. to 9:00 a.m." Leona raised her eyebrows at Nate. "Visiting hours end at 9:00 p.m."

Nate dropped Julie's duffel on the chair near the cherry desk, placing the rest of her things around it on the floor, including the backpack with the custody papers. "That gives me ten minutes."

Leona checked her slim gold watch. "Nine minutes."

A smile snuck past Julie's defenses again. Maybe she and Leona would get along after all. She could probably give Julie pointers on how to put Nate in his place.

Leona gave Julie what might have been a charitable smile if Julie was feeling charitable. "Credit card?" When she had it, Leona left. Her heels clacked briskly against the hardwood.

Nate picked up Duke's dinosaur bedroll and shook it out on top of the bed, surrounding it with pillows. "Don't let Leona get under your skin. She senses weakness like a wolf smells blood."

"I could take her," Julie joked, unable to get her eyes off Nate. She'd forgotten how nice he could be. He was supposed to be a jerk when she told him about Duke. He was supposed to reject Duke as his. He was supposed to be angry and insensitive. Julie could deal with angry, insensitive jerks all day long. It was the nice guys who undid her.

She needed her anger, if only for nine more minutes. "Don't think I'm going to hand Duke over to you and walk away. You still have to prove you'll be a good father."

"Says who?" There was some of the anger she sought. A spark in dark eyes. A set to his jaw.

His reaction energized her. "It was April's last wish."

"Want bed," Duke crooned, crawling toward the bedroll.

Nate stared at his son with wonder in his eyes.

Julie had to turn away. She should change Duke's diaper and brush his teeth. She should go downstairs and sign the check-in paperwork. She should get a key to her room. She shouldn't be thinking that Nate's reaction to Duke made him Dadworthy.

She checked her cell phone. Seven more minutes.

She heard Nate remove Duke's shoes. Heard him tuck Duke into the bedroll. Heard him whisper, "Sweet dreams."

Nice. Nate had always been nice. Nice to those he worked with. Nice to those who obeyed the law. Nice. Until the day he'd asked to speak to April alone in the church vestibule. Until the week after that when he'd quit the Sacramento PD and moved away. Until he wasn't by April's side as she wasted away and whispered her last wishes.

How could a man who was so upstanding at work be so unreliable in his personal life?

Julie drew a labored breath.

"We need to talk." Nate was behind her, being civil.

This wasn't a civil situation. Julie turned on legs as stiff and unyielding as green two-by-fours. "We'll talk tomorrow."

He studied her the way they'd been trained at the academy, looking for signs of stress or emotional imbalance.

She forced her lips to make the journey upward toward superiority. "Tomorrow."

After a moment, he nodded. "Breakfast. El Rosal. I'm buying."

"We have a free breakfast here." Needing something to do, she dug out a diaper from the bag, as if she was going to be a stellar caregiver and wake up Duke to change him.

Nada on that. The little man was hell on wheels when he woke up too soon.

His gaze turned as soft as one of Duke's baby blankets. "It's good to see you, Jules."

"Don't call me that, Landry."

He gave her a rueful half smile, glanced at Duke one last time and then left.

She listened to his footsteps recede. She listened to the front door open and close. She listened to him drive away. Nate thought of himself as a good guy. And good guys sometimes did an about-face and came back to check on someone they thought was in need. Only when Julie was positive he'd left did she sink to the floor, resting her back against the footboard.

She texted her mother to tell her they'd arrived safely, assuring her she was all right. What a liar she'd become.

Leona appeared in the doorway, her eyes slanted with disapproval. "Are you sleeping on the floor?"

"No. I'm about to do my exercises for my back." It wasn't a lie if she was joking, right?

"You can leave the key on the dresser with my receipt."

"You don't need a key." Leona placed a handwritten receipt on the dresser with Julie's credit card. "We don't have locks." She closed the door behind her.

"No key," Julie murmured. No privacy. No way to lock Duke in here with her to prevent him wandering if he awoke at midnight. No pain killers. No revenge. No signed custody agreement. What a bust of a day.

Julie unbuttoned her shirt, drawing it carefully over her injured shoulder. Blood trickled from her collarbone. She peeled the bandage off, opened the diaper and shoved it under her bra strap.

She'd sit a few more minutes to gather her strength. And then she'd take her med kit into the bathroom, being careful not to bleed all over those white tiles.

Just a few more minutes...

CHAPTER FOUR

AFTER LEAVING THE BED-AND-BREAKFAST, Nate drove around town, ostensibly to make his nightly rounds.

But it was more than worry for the town that kept him from bed. His mind was as jumbled as a box of well-used Scrabble tiles. As if being blindsided by Doris wasn't bad enough...

I'm a father.

And April was dead. He'd need to visit her grave and pay his respects, maybe make a donation to a cancer-related charity.

I'm a father.

And Julie looked like she'd been run over by a bus. He'd need to contact a few of their mutual friends on the force and find out how bad her cancer was. He didn't want to repeat the mistake he'd made with April. But that mistake hadn't been one-sided. April had had a lot to say on their wedding day and she'd known...

I'm a father.

As were many of his friends in Harmony Valley. But unlike them, he didn't know his son's middle name. He didn't know what he'd looked like as a baby. He didn't even know his son's birth date. Birthdays meant a lot to kids. They tended to remember birthdays as they got older.

Nate had been given a gun for his eighth birthday. It was a wreck of a weapon. The stock was duct-taped. The barrel scraped and the sight bent forward as if someone had used it for a cane. But it was a real rifle, not a BB gun like Matthew Freitas had gotten for his eighth birthday.

"Time you start acting like a man," his father had said in a voice that boomed in their small kitchen. He'd stared at his wife making pancakes for Nate's birthday breakfast with an arrogant grin. "Duck-hunting season is coming up."

Nate longed to go duck hunting. They lived in Willows, California, where everyone hunted. It was practically a law.

"Bring your gun. Let's go shoot." There was a sly note to Dad's voice that Nate didn't understand.

Not that he cared. He'd played shooting video games at Tony Arno's house down the block. Nate was a good shot. Wait until he showed Dad!

"No." Mom sounded a little panicked, like she did when she didn't have dinner ready and Dad pulled into the driveway. She came to stand behind Nate, drawing him to her with fingers that dug through to bone.

His little sister's eyes were big. She tugged at the skirt of her Sunday school dress.

Nate bet Molly was jealous. She never got to do anything with Dad.

But Nate was eight. He was a man now. That meant Dad would take him hunting. There'd be no more cleaning toilets for Nate. No more dishes. No more dusting. No more butt-stinging whuppings.

Dad glowered at the women in the household. "The boy's coming with me."

Nate had naively stepped forward.

Someone stepped into the beam of Nate's headlights and then leaped back.

A slender African American man stood on the sidewalk in a bathrobe, shuffling his bunny-slippered feet.

Nate slammed on his brakes. The truck shuddered to a halt, but Nate's limbs continued to quake. He rammed the truck in Park and jumped out, bellowing, "*Terrance!* What are you doing out here?"

"Evening, Nate." The tall, elderly man shoved his hands into his burgundy terry-cloth pockets. "You didn't have to stop so… so quickly."

"Of course, I had to stop." Nate was yelling. He never yelled. Blame it on the night he'd had. "You're walking around in your bathrobe and slippers."

Policing Harmony Valley wasn't about controlling crime. It was about keeping the peace. And peace required patience. The patience Nate usually had in deep reserve was at drought levels.

"I can't do it, Sheriff." Terrance's breath hitched and his shoulders shook. His elongated facial features were accented by sad salt-and-pepper brows and sparse chin stubble. "I can't go to sleep without Robin in bed with me."

Nate heaved a sigh. Terrance had recently lost his wife of fifty years.

But this was the third time in a month he'd found Terrance walking around in his pajamas. The old man had been watching the sun rise from the top of Parish Hill when Nate drove by to check on reports of gunshots. He'd been watching the river pass by from the Harmony

Valley bridge during Nate's morning jog. And now...

A porch light came on at the house on the corner.

If anyone saw Terrance in his pj's, Nate would have to do more than chastise him and make sure he got home safe. Doris would want him to issue a citation for indecent exposure. Agnes would want him to take Terrance to the hospital for observation, which might result in pills being prescribed. Pills Terrance wouldn't take, because the antidepressants and sleeping pills his doctor had given him after Robin's death sat unused in his medicine cabinet.

"Get in the truck and I'll drive you home." He'd get the older man something to eat and stay at his place until Terrance dozed off.

Terrance shook his head in a trembly fashion. The robe was worn and did little to keep out the cold. He was shivering all over.

Nate stood between Terrance and the porch, hopefully blocking the view of anyone peering out the front window. He swept Terrance toward the truck with both hands. "If you're going to walk, you need to walk with all your clothes on."

Except to shiver, Terrance didn't budge. "I'm dressed for bed because I try to sleep and I can't." The mournful sound in his voice echoed on the empty street. "I always thought I'd go first. I should have spoiled her more. I should have told her I loved her more. I should have—"

"Get in the truck." Nate closed in. "Turn those bunny slippers around and get in."

"Are you arresting me?" Even the bunny ears seemed to be shivering now. "More important, are you making fun of Robin's slippers?"

He was. Some levity was called for, otherwise he'd never get Terrance off the street. Nate put his hands on the older man's shoulders and gently turned him around. "You're telling me your feet are the same size as Robin's?"

"Robin had long, elegant feet." Salt-and-pepper brows dive-bombed blue eyes as he stared at Nate over his shoulder. "I feel closer to her when I wear her slippers."

Locks turned in the door behind them. Out of time, Nate hustled Terrance into the truck.

"Sheriff? Is that you?" Lilac Miller wore a pink silk bathrobe, heels and what looked like a shower cap.

"Yes, ma'am." Nate walked in front of the headlights so she could see him. "Sorry about the noise. A cat ran out in front of me." He got in the truck, hoping Lilac hadn't seen his passenger.

"I saw Lilac driving Doris to the market this morning out by the highway." Terrance's knobby knees bumped against the old metal dash.

Nate bit back a curse, adding Lilac to his to-do list tomorrow. She was dangerous on the road, and had promised him she wouldn't drive unless it was an emergency. "Thanks for telling me."

Terrance squirmed in his seat. "Should I mention I was walking in my bathrobe and bunny slippers?"

"Only if you want to spend a night in jail under my supervision."

JULIE'S BREATH SOUNDED HOLLOW. Her throat felt dry.

Someone had thrown a smoke grenade. Despite the mask, Julie couldn't breathe. Visibility in the house was like a midnight-thick fog in San Francisco.

A woman appeared before her, holding a baby and a weapon. The assault rifle was trained on Julie.

Julie tried to shout a warning to the officers behind her.

Too late. The woman's finger squeezed the trigger.

Julie fired.

She couldn't see. She didn't know...

Her breath rasped. Her throat burned.

The woman closed the distance between them, pressing the muzzle of her gun into Julie's shoulder. Julie wanted to run, but her legs were sinking into the floor.

Crying out, Julie fired again. Suddenly, it was April who held her. April, who crumpled to the linoleum, her mouth moving as she tried to speak one word: *forgive.*

Julie sat up, shaking and sweating. She'd fallen asleep on the floor of the bed-and-breakfast. The lights were still on, but the chill of the evening had seeped into the room. Into her.

Helpless. She felt so helpless. And sleep deprived. She hadn't been able to sleep properly since she'd been released from the hospital. Not since she'd stopped taking the pain pills. But if she took them she couldn't drive or care for Duke.

It took several minutes for the shakes to subside. Several more for her to trust her legs to hold her.

But peace of mind? That remained elusive.

"Juju." A whisper. A tug on the quilt.

Julie cracked her eyes open. She felt like sun-dried roadkill. Her eyes were gritty. Her mouth dry. And her head…it felt as if her skull had been stuffed with heavy mountain clay. She wanted to roll over and stay beneath the covers.

But there was her nephew. His black hair in a rumpled half Mohawk and his mouth set in his welcome-to-morning grumpy line.

Cheerful. She had to channel April and be cheerful. "Want to snuggle, little man?"

"No. Want milk." He tugged harder on the quilt. "Juju."

Julie squinted at her watch. It was seven thirty, late for Duke. "Okay. Okay." She ran through the list. Shower. Clean teeth. Clean diaper. Clean dressing. Clean clothes. Could she distract a two-year-old for an hour until Leona's official breakfast time?

"Juju!"

"Okay, I'm moving." Julie folded her right arm to her chest and rolled slowly to an upright position. Duke didn't look any better when she was upright. He was still rumpled and grumpy. She caught her reflection in the mirror hanging above the desk. She didn't look much better. She looked ready to audition for a role as a zombie—dark circles under her eyes, hollow cheeks, hair in loopy tangles. "I hope we see Leona on the way to the bathroom. She could use a good scare."

Thirty minutes later, Julie and Duke were dressed in jeans, sneakers and thick black hoodies. She carried a backpack with toddler supplies and the custody contract she wanted Nate to sign. He'd thrown her a curveball last night by not rejecting Duke outright. In all the years she'd known him, he'd always said he didn't want kids. He couldn't change his mind now. She wouldn't let him. If he didn't sign today, she'd put the Daddy Test into play.

"Me walk. Me walk." Duke ran to the staircase.

"Wait." Julie dashed after him, juggling the backpack and the umbrella stroller. "Hold my hand."

Together, they took the stairs one at a time. When they reached the foyer, they peeked into the empty living room. Sunlight streamed across the antique wood-trimmed couch, a delicate coffee table, a Boston fern and the antique rocking horse. The wood floors gleamed. There wasn't a dust mote in sight.

"Breakfast is at eight thirty," Reggie said

cheerfully from the dining room. "There's coffee, milk and juice on the sideboard."

"Milk would be fantastic." Julie tugged Duke's blue sippy cup from her backpack.

"Why do you say breakfast is at eight thirty, Regina, when you don't mean it?" Leona stood at the end of the foyer beneath the stairs. Dark green sheath, low black heels, pearls at her neck, hands clasped at her waist and looking as if she didn't want to let on she smelled something unpleasant.

Julie gave a tentative sniff to make sure Duke wasn't fragrant—he wasn't—before slipping into the dining room to fill Duke's cup.

"It's hard to believe Grandmother's first review of the bed-and-breakfast was positive," Reggie deadpanned, wiping the dining room table as if she only had a few seconds left to clean. "Customer service isn't her forte."

"Chad Healy appreciates good repartee." Leona entered the dining room, stiff as starch. "The art of conversation is dying, being replaced by the Twitter and those hashtags you always mumble about."

Reggie stopped cleaning and grinned, a real, live, genuine smile directed at her grandmother. "Did you joke with your father when the telegraph became obsolete?"

Leona didn't answer, but the corner of her lip twitched. Those two may go at it, but they clearly enjoyed their banter.

"How about Great-Grandpa's horse and buggy?" Reggie leaned on the table, coming in for the proverbial kill, her tone gleeful. "His gas lamps? His…" She faltered and glanced at Julie for help.

"Uh…" Julie drew a blank, having been tag-teamed before she knew she was part of Reggie's team.

"You petty." Duke grinned up at Leona. He wrapped his arms around her spindly leg and gave her a hug.

Leona stared down at Duke. Almost of its own volition, her hand drifted to the top of his head and gave him a pat.

Duke released her, still grinning. "Petty you." He reached out and patted her bottom. And then he caught sight of his sippy cup and ran to Julie. "Milk!"

Leona's cheeks were redder than a ripe strawberry. She walked woodenly out of the room.

"I wouldn't have believed it if I hadn't seen it." Reggie stared at Duke in awe. "The Ice Queen melted. Honestly, I don't think she touched me when I was growing up."

Julie felt compelled to come to Leona's defense. "I'm sure she must have—"

"Nope." Reggie shook her head. "She was… Well, that's not important. It's been a challenge being here and your son gave me hope." Reggie turned mahogany eyes filled with tears Julie's way. "Thank you."

A man appeared in the dining room doorway. "Am I too early for breakfast?"

"No." Reggie clutched her cleaning rag. "Not at all. I just need to put it in the oven and…" She composed herself. "Why don't you have a cup of coffee while you wait? Get to know our other guests and…make yourself at home."

Julie sighed. A cup of coffee sounded like heaven.

Duke stopped sucking down milk and tugged on the umbrella stroller. "Out, Juju. Go out."

"Can't I have my coffee first?" Julie's gaze drifted to the stack of mugs by the coffee carafe.

"Peeeeeze." Duke hugged Julie's leg and gazed up at her with April's gray eyes. "Go peeze."

Julie was a sucker for that sweet face. A cup of coffee would have to wait. Maybe this wouldn't be so bad. She'd take Nate up on his offer of breakfast. She'd start him on the Daddy Test. That'd make him squirm. The idea perked her up.

A few minutes later, having made her apologies to the other guest, Julie pushed Duke through the foggy streets toward the town square in a blue umbrella stroller. For being two, Duke was a solid kid. Pushing him wasn't easy. Back in the day, as an older sister, she'd pushed April in her stroller. She'd whined, of course.

"People like you and me have to take care of others," Dad had said in response to her complaints. As a highway patrolman, he'd been adamant about duty and responsibility.

He'd been her strongest supporter when she'd wanted to try out for Little League baseball instead of softball. He'd argued her case with the school board when she wanted to pitch for her high school baseball team. But in return, he'd made her volunteer for every charity that needed an extra pair of hands. He'd insisted she babysit April and help her with her homework. He'd nourished her competitive streak and her sense of responsibility. A burden and a curse, she'd once told Nate.

Thinking about how close she and Nate had been made her cringe inside. The inward cringe made her wound ache. Aching wounds reignited her need for justice.

"Tree." Duke interrupted her thoughts and his milk consumption, pointing to a large fir tree.

A yellow tow truck drove past. The driver waved at Duke.

"Truck." Duke turned in his seat to grin up at Julie, eyes so like April's that her breath caught.

She forgot about vendettas, twinging gunshot wounds and the past. She let her chest fill with the blissful sight of the gift April had left the world. "Do you know how much your mama loved you?"

Duke's grin deepened and he spread his little arms wide. "This much!" He sat back in the stroller and pointed to the town square, which was all grass except for one large oak. "Tree." And then he pointed to the left, to a blue pickup with a gold star on the door. "Truck."

Nate's truck. Nate was at El Rosal. Julie's steps slowed.

El Rosal was a colorful Mexican restaurant with outdoor dining fenced in by a low wrought iron fence. On the same side of the street a few doors down was Martin's Bakery. Both seemed to be doing a brisk morning business.

Nate sat at an outdoor table with a thin, elderly black man. The sheriff wore a blue checkered shirt beneath a navy sleeveless jacket. He gave his dining companion that half smile she knew so well. Only it wasn't the same half smile of old. Not the one he used to send Julie's way, the one that said he couldn't trust himself to release his feelings. This one said he liked the man across from him and he was comfortable letting his companion know it.

Julie's throat ached with the feeling of loss. It shouldn't. She'd lost Nate as a friend the day he'd left April. But looking at him now, at that open-book smile, she wondered if their friendship had been one-sided.

"You're early." Nate pushed back his chair and hurried to meet them on the sidewalk, the contained half smile giving nothing away. He bent down near Duke's level. "How're you today, buddy?"

"Great!" Duke thrust his cup in the air.

Julie's gaze stumbled over Nate. No uniform. No gun belt. She had no idea who he was anymore.

Nate's scruffy dining companion appeared at his side. He wore a wrinkled orange T-shirt and a dirty green zippered sweatshirt. He had *bachelor* written all over him. "I'm Terrance."

He slanted a frown Nate's way. "Next time you put me in jail for the night, I'd like breakfast in bed." He walked slowly away, as if he had nowhere to go.

"What did you arrest him for?" Julie asked.

Nate's gaze followed the old man. "Annoying me." There was the dry humor she remembered.

"And that's against the law?"

"In my town, yes."

It was Julie's turn to frown at the sheriff. Maybe Doris did have a legitimate claim against him. That cheered Julie, even if she didn't quite believe it.

Meanwhile, Nate's gaze focused on Julie and the lines around his dark eyes deepened. "You should reconsider your accommodations and stay with me."

"No, thanks. Terrance didn't look all that rested."

"Neither do you."

She glanced past Nate to the bakery sign, a little of her confidence returning. She knew how to deal with this Nate—be firm.

"I see you're tempted by the bakery," Nate said, moving closer to Julie. "On the one hand, Martin's will have those pastries you're craving." Nate took her left arm, leaving her no choice but to push the stroller to his table. "On the other, El Rosal has bacon."

From his seat in the stroller, Duke gasped. *"Ba-con?"*

"Yep, bacon," Nate confirmed.

"Are you trying to tell me what's best for Duke and me?" Julie felt overheated in her thick black hoodie. She was sure it was because she resented Nate's touch, his calm, his command.

"They have good coffee here, Jules," Nate said in a soft voice that contradicted the warning in his dark eyes. "And apple fritters."

She hated that he knew her so well. She also hated that three words softened her resolve—*coffee, apple fritters.*

"Ba-con?" Duke searched several tables for his culinary prize.

"We'll get you bacon while Juju parks the stroller and takes a rest at the table." Nate unbuckled Duke and carried him inside. Into his life and away from hers.

Julie felt cold. Not the cold terror when she'd been shot, but the vein-freezing cold she'd felt when April had drifted off in death. The alone kind of cold. Her toes stung with it.

She parked the stroller inside the low wrought

iron fence and took a seat beneath a tall heater, feeling chilled.

The patrons outside were mostly elderly. A few people looked at her curiously.

"You're staying at the Lambridge Bed & Breakfast." The mayor came to stand next to Julie's table. He was wearing tie-dye again today. His sweatshirt was a wild mix of purple and green. "Welcome to Harmony Valley. Whatever brings you to town…" He paused to see if she'd explain why she'd come. When she didn't, he continued, "We hope you enjoy your stay and perhaps stay."

The patrons at other tables beamed at her.

"Oh, no. I'm not staying." Julie put her hands on the table, as if to cradle the coffee cup that wasn't there.

The mayor was nothing if not the town's salesman. "Don't judge so quickly. How many towns can boast affordable living, a winery and views like this." He pointed to a fog-shrouded mountain towering over the trees.

"I'm sure it's beautiful when the fog burns off," Julie allowed, lacing her fingers together.

The mayor pointed at her with both index fingers and backed away. "I won't give up on you."

"I can respect that." Julie fought off the sudden need to yawn.

She couldn't see Nate inside. She couldn't see a waitress with a carafe of coffee. She was out of her element here and in her own skin. Her head felt heavy enough from lack of sleep to fall off her shoulders and there was a knot tightening beneath her right shoulder blade, about the place where Nate had stabbed her in the back years ago.

When they were rookies on the Sacramento police force, Julie had had to prove she was tough enough to fit in. Nate fit in just by putting on the uniform. They'd been working the same shift when they'd received a domestic abuse call. Julie pulled up to the house just after Nate did. It was the first time they'd responded to a call together. The first time Julie had been on a domestic abuse call.

The call looked bad from the get-go. Rundown neighborhood. Dingy white house. Dirt where a lawn should be. The crack by the front door handle indicated it'd been kicked in at least once before. It wasn't the kind of place you sent a patrol officer alone.

"I'll take point." Nate's hand was on his holster as he knocked on the front door. "Police! Open up!"

Inside the house, a gun went off. A woman screamed.

Nate drew his gun and kicked down the door before Julie could report shots fired and request backup. And then she drew her weapon and followed.

"Landry!" Julie tried to control the slight shake to her hands.

There were sounds of a scuffle deep inside the house. At the end of the hall, a woman appeared.

Julie flinched, nearly shooting her.

The woman was unarmed, her face bruised and bloodied. She carried a toddler with a red welt on his cheek. They were both crying.

Crap. Julie's legs had felt as if she'd run the police academy obstacle course one too many times. She'd trained for worst-case scenarios, but Julie had never been in a situation like this before. "Get out," Julie ordered the woman, keeping her weapon and her eyes trained on the end of the hallway as the woman escaped past her. "Landry! Answer me."

Something hit a wall, shaking the entire house. And then there was a thud.

Julie turned the corner of the hall and looked into the master bedroom.

Nate sat on top of a panting shirtless man,

cuffing his hands behind his back. He stared up at Julie, breathing heavily, one eye swelling and his lip bloody. Two handguns were on the carpet near the door. "Read him his rights."

Later, as they'd worked on the report at the station, Julie put a hand on Nate's arm. "That was stupid, running in there like that. He had a gun. He could've—"

"His wife didn't think it was stupid since he was pistol-whipping her." There was a dangerous edge to Nate's voice that Julie had never heard before.

"Do you know them?" He hadn't put that in the report. "Is this personal?"

"I've seen abuse before." Nate's jaw ticked. "It's worth taking a bullet to save someone. He hit that woman and—" his voice roughened "—that little boy." Nate stared at her, but he didn't seem to see Julie.

She'd wanted him to. She wanted him to confide in her.

"Do you know what it's like to feel helpless and trapped?" He did see her then. And behind his gaze was something so bleak, Julie almost couldn't bear it. "Your options are taken away. Your spontaneity… Your personality… You can't show anything. And your freedom…"

His gaze turned distant again. "It's like a storm comes in with dark, heavy clouds, and you have no shelter, no choice but to weather the storm."

"Nate... I'm so sorry." Was this why he never talked about his family? Because he'd been abused?

"Sorry?" Nate had sat back in his chair, suddenly completely in the present and completely angry. "I was talking about the victims." He stood and went to get a cup of coffee.

She hadn't believed him. But what she did believe was that Nate took his work to heart. And she'd respected him for that. Heck, she'd practically worshipped the ground he walked on.

Inside El Rosal, a waiter entered the main dining room through the swinging kitchen door. He held the door for Nate, who carried Duke and a large mug of steaming coffee. Duke clutched a piece of bacon in each hand.

The waiter opened the main restaurant door for Nate, and then followed him to the table. He had a swarthy complexion, thick black hair and a killer smile that probably netted him lots of tips. If he'd brought a coffeepot, Julie might have tipped him well, too.

Instead, she sighed and held up the sippy cup. First things first.

Nate set the steaming mug in front of Julie and sat down across from her, lifting a happy Duke in his lap. Julie's lap felt empty. It was small consolation that Nate suddenly looked as if he'd been taken over by aliens and was just now realizing he had a small boy with him.

"Truck." Duke grinned, pointing at Nate's Ford.

"Truck," Nate echoed.

The waiter leaned both hands on the edge of the table and beamed at Julie. He'd pinned his name tag—Arturo—upside down. "Sheriff Nate wanted to order you the empanada, which he mistakenly calls an apple fritter. He also wants to order pancakes and eggs for his little sidekick." Arturo's gently rolling consonants fell out of his smiling mouth like the cheery notes of a pop song's chorus. "But my mama won't accept the order until you confirm it. She says we don't know you, but we know how bossy Sheriff Nate is." He plucked the sippy cup from her hand. "Milk or juice?"

"Milk. And just this once we'll go with the sheriff's order." She gave Nate a stern look and then mainlined the coffee.

"I know the difference between an apple fritter and an empanada," Nate grumbled.

"The key to happiness is to establish expectations." Arturo moved to a stack of wooden high chairs. "Both in dining and in relationships." He carried one to the table, and then left them.

"Pay no attention to the talking fortune cookie." Nate deposited Duke in the high chair like a pro. At Julie's questioning glance, he gave her the tight half smile. "My sister has a twenty-month-old little girl and I'm one of the few people trusted to babysit Camille."

Deep down, something inside Julie gave a plaintive cry of *foul*. She wanted Nate to be all thumbs with Duke, to generate disinterest and temper tantrums. Nothing was going right in Harmony Valley.

Arturo returned with the sippy cup, placing it in front of Duke. "Milk."

"Milk." Duke dropped bacon bits on the table and reached for the cup, only to stop midgrab and stare at his hands, flexing his fingers. "I dirty."

Before Julie could set her coffee down, Nate was wiping her nephew's hands with a napkin.

"Okay, I get it," Julie groused. "You have experience with little kids." Drat and darn. "Why didn't you tell me last night?"

Nate met her gaze squarely. "Why didn't you tell me you'd been shot?"

She sat back, resisting the urge to touch her shoulder. He must have called someone from the force. "Why would I? We don't work together. We're not partners, friends or in-laws."

He ignored her boundary setting. In fact, he steamrolled over her defenses. "You look like hell. I thought you were dying of cancer."

Julie clung to her coffee cup and held her tongue.

"You're not taking time off to grieve. You're taking time off to heal and awaiting an internal investigation into the shooting." Something passed over Nate's face, a bleakness so fleeting, she couldn't catch its meaning. "I heard it was your first."

Her first kill, he meant.

Sweat traced the band of her bra. Only because the fleece of her hoodie was too thick and the heater above her too warm. Her toes were still cold.

"Don't talk about it as if I was hunting deer." Julie stared into her mug while Duke slurped his milk and black birds twittered and the morning fog dissipated and life went on happily for other people.

CHAPTER FIVE

JULIE WASN'T DYING.

The relief when Nate had received the return text message this morning from Captain Bradford at Sacramento PD had lifted a weight off his shoulders. He hadn't realized how stressed-out he'd been until he'd nearly run out to meet her in front of El Rosal. Only her scowl had slowed his steps and kept him from wrapping his arms around her. Only her scowl and April's assumption on their wedding day that he'd loved Julie more than he'd loved his bride-to-be.

Love Julie? He didn't know how to love someone. That was something you learned by example from your parents.

And so, he'd brushed aside foolish emotions, stopped in his tracks and looked at Julie closely. Blood loss and trauma from being shot took a toll on a body. He'd expected Julie to look rested this morning. But this... She looked worse. Pasty complexion. Dark circles under her eyes. Mouth thinned with tension.

Perhaps his son was partly to blame. Nate's niece was a good sleeper, but that didn't mean Duke was. He knew from his sister that being a sole caregiver was draining. Julie didn't have much energy left to drain. So he'd plucked Duke from the stroller and taken him to the kitchen to give Julie some relief. But when he'd returned, Julie had looked more haunted than before.

The midweek breakfast crowd at El Rosal was at its peak. People were starting their days with a hearty meal. Nate had a long to-do list, rounds to make, people to check up on. It would all have to wait. Unless there was an emergency, Julie was his priority, along with Duke.

Nate's glance fell on his son. The boy had felt right in his arms when he'd carried him back to the kitchen. Long ago he'd decided not to be a father. Fatherhood should be a choice. Last night, he'd vowed to explain to Julie why he couldn't be a father, without explaining anything at all. But first, he had to ease Julie's suffering.

"You aren't sleeping." Nate could relate. He hadn't slept much last night either. "You have to talk to someone about the shooting." Taking a life was taboo. Breaking a taboo could rattle even the strongest person.

"I sleep fine." Julie scowled, but the effect was ruined by the light breeze pushing wisps of blond hair across vacant eyes.

"You can talk to me," Nate persisted. "Just like you used to." When they'd worked together, she'd unloaded emotions with him like she unloaded bullets at the shooting range. It was part of her venting process. She'd talk and he'd listen.

Today, she let silence be her answer.

Nate wanted to lean across the narrow table, slip his hand to the nape of her neck and make her stop hiding, stop bottling up her emotions and tell him about it. About April. About the shooting. About her feelings for him.

Nate rocked back in his seat. Julie was as off-limits as fatherhood.

"Ba-con." Duke picked up another piece, grinning at Julie.

She stopped glaring at Nate and grinned back at Duke.

He'd seen a grin similar to hers often on his sister's face when she gazed at Camille. "You want to keep him."

"Anyone with a heart would." Julie lifted

her chin, daring him to admit he didn't have a heart.

She didn't understand his childhood hadn't been carefree and loving, as hers had been. He enjoyed children, but he was satisfied enjoying other people's children. And yet, if he admitted that…if he signed over rights to Duke, Julie would leave town. She'd go home and pretend to be fine when the life she'd taken would be eating her inside.

Flynn entered the patio wearing faded blue jeans and a ratty T-shirt. He was a dot-com millionaire who dressed like a construction worker. Since he'd become a father, he'd been dressing like an out-of-work construction worker. He'd worn that same ratty T-shirt two days ago. Flynn didn't quite meet Nate's gaze. "Do you have something for me?"

Nate handed a thick envelope that had been sitting on the chair to Flynn. "Those are all the citations for the past six months." Flynn had requested them last night. He was helping the town council investigate Nate's job performance.

Flynn nodded his thanks and wove his way between tables to where the mayor sat in the corner.

Mayor Larry wore black yoga pants, an

oversize sweatshirt and the false smile of a lifelong politician. He held Nate's future in his hands. And not in a tight clasp either.

Would the mayor back him in the race? The breeze shifted, blowing cold air in Nate's face.

"They'll be talking about you." Julie set down her mug, restored enough with caffeine and a change in topic to take a poke at him.

It was a weak poke. "I'm a sheriff, not an administrator." He might be powerless about his career, but he could do something to help Julie's.

"Sheriff Nate." It was Agnes. The short town councilwoman carried a coffee cup from Martin's and a pastry bag that Julie eyed with envy. "I meant to ask for an introduction last night. Who's your friend?"

Nate introduced Julie and Duke. He was going to stop at names, but impulsively, he added, "Duke is my son."

"I Duke," the boy said proudly scratching his head and dragging his hair over the Landry ears. "You Nay." He pointed at Nate.

Unexpectedly, happiness buoyed Nate's cheeks, trying to lift them into a smile.

Duke's words seemed to have the opposite effect on Julie. She was frowning.

"I see the resemblance now. He's adorable." Agnes gave Julie a kind, if shrewd, look. "Sheriff, I hadn't realized you'd been married before."

"He wasn't. He knocked up my sister and jilted her." The frown vanished and Julie's face bloomed with color.

That color, that spark in her eyes. It almost made the awkwardness of his past worth telling.

"To be fair," Nate said flatly, the way he gave testimony on the witness stand. "April didn't tell me she was pregnant." And didn't that still sting.

"Do you mind if I use the town phone tree to spread the word?" Agnes tapped Julie's shoulder with the back of her hand as if sharing a joke. "I'd like to say I'm pulling your leg, but we love gossip as much as we love our sheriff." She gave Nate a fond smile. "Well, off to my meeting." She joined Flynn and the mayor, but fiddled with her phone before engaging in conversation.

The phone tree. Julie had no idea what she was in for.

Nate felt compelled to warn her. "By mid-afternoon, everyone will know your name. But half the population will have gotten the story wrong. They'll say I jilted you, and that Duke is our son."

Our son. His gaze stuck on Julie's gray eyes.

"I'll gladly correct them." Julie beamed.

She hadn't smiled at him like that in years. A feeling long buried in his chest climbed into his throat. He didn't have a word for that feeling. April had tried to call it love. But... Love for Julie? Love for her mercurial moods and her broad smile? For her dedication to her career, her need for justice and her bighearted, slightly naive view of the world? He appreciated all those things about her. He'd missed all those things about her. But love? If he truly loved her, how could he have lived without her for more than two years?

Arturo appeared with Duke's sippy cup refill and three plates of food.

"Ooh." Duke clapped his hands when he saw his pancake and eggs.

Arturo set Julie's plate down last. "I had the kitchen add cinnamon glaze to your empanada."

Julie's eyes lit up. "Arturo, your wife is one lucky woman."

"I'm not married." Arturo clucked his tongue and gave her an appreciative once-over. "And neither are you."

"She's not interested," Nate growled, feeling proprietary. He buttered Duke's pancakes to keep from growling further at his friend.

"Who says I'm not interested?" Julie gave Arturo a calculated smile.

"This is why I'm single. Too many arguments." Arturo laughed and moved to the next table.

"That's not why he's single." Nate narrowed his eyes. "He thinks of himself as a ladies' man."

"The ladies love me," Arturo tossed over his shoulder.

"Ladies over sixty-five," Nate said, qualifying and loading his fork. "Ladies who tip well."

Julie said nothing. Her attention had dropped to her plate. She'd never been much good at multitasking.

There was a lull in both conversation and argument while they dug into their food. Several minutes later, Duke was slowing down on his pancake, eating with his fingers and getting nearly as much in his mouth as on his face, hands and sweatshirt.

Julie was perking up. The empanada was nearly gone. Her coffee cup had been refilled again. But sugar and caffeine couldn't erase the look of exhaustion on her face. She needed someone to care for her. Fat chance of her letting it be him.

Nate cleared his throat. "What was April's criteria for my gaining custody?"

Julie pinned him with an intense gaze. "She called it the Daddy Test."

Just hearing the name made him uneasy. "I take it April made the test up."

"She did." Julie nodded, a mix of superiority and satisfaction in her eyes. She didn't expect him to pass.

The quickest way out of fatherhood was to fail. Little Duke was awesome and deserved a loving home with someone who knew how to provide it for him. Julie had already offered. She'd do an excellent job. So it made no sense that he said, "Your test won't hold up in a court of law."

"I know." Color appeared in her cheeks. Arguing with him seemed to do that to her. "But I also know you won't push the issue. We were friends once. You'll wait to hear my evaluation."

He shouldn't. And he wouldn't have. Except, the longer it took Julie to assess him, the longer she'd stay in Harmony Valley. Worst case, she'd have a chance to find some peace from the shooting. "If I agree, you have to stay for a month."

She frowned. "I don't have to agree to anything."

"You can stay until the doctor clears you for duty." He could make amends to April if he helped her get through this. Troubled and injured as she was, she couldn't properly care for Duke or herself.

"The doctor will clear me for a desk job sooner if I pass my psych eval." Her frown deepened to a scowl. She knew she wouldn't pass anytime soon. "Besides, I can't afford to stay here a month."

"You could stay with me for free." Before she made a decision, Nate's phone chirped and vibrated.

In the distance, a siren split the spring air.

"I have to go." Nate stood, hesitating as he looked down at his son, suddenly loathe to leave. He stroked Duke's unruly black curls and said, "Be good." And then Nate looked at Julie. "You, too."

She scoffed.

Men and women of all ages were coming out of Martin's and El Rosal. The volunteer firefighters were mobilizing, as were the lookie-loos. Nate needed to lead the pack, not trail behind.

"We'll talk later," he said to Julie, who looked like she was eager to join in on a good emergency call.

If it was excitement she was missing, she wouldn't find it in Harmony Valley.

Nate checked his phone for the address, but it was just as easy to follow the volunteers and spectators up the switchbacks to the top of Parish Hill. Having arrived at a thinly graveled, rutted driveway belonging to a crotchety old man, some turned around when they saw the sign—Trespassers Will Be Shot. Rutgar wasn't known for exaggeration.

Nate parked his truck along the two-lane road. He walked to the rear of the property with Gage, the town vet.

"What's this I hear about you being a dad?" Gage wasn't as tall as Nate, but they had the same long-legged stride.

Nate knew gossip in Harmony Valley traveled fast. But this was light speed. "Just found out he existed last night. He's two."

"That must have been a shock." Gage spared Nate a searching glance. "And here I was telling Doc not to spread rumors."

Nate fought the urge to smile, to preen, to

high-five. Those were the responses of a proud and loving dad. Still, he wouldn't lie about being a father. "Let Doc run with the news. It's true."

"Congratulations. I think I've still got some cigars from when Mae was born." Gage slapped Nate soundly on the back. "While I've got you here… I'm still learning the emergency codes. What are we responding to? I don't see smoke."

"Injury."

The closest thing they had to a doctor in town was Patti, a retired nurse practitioner. She was currently enjoying an Alaskan cruise. The first responders would stabilize and arrange transport to medical services in nearby Cloverdale, if necessary.

Nate and Gage reached the end of the driveway and a two-story house sitting on stilts. It was painted a dirty brown and surrounded by towering pines that had probably been saplings when it was built. The town's fire engine was parked in front of the steps leading to the porch, where the home's owner sat and howled his displeasure.

"No! The last time someone wanted me to be seen by a doctor, I spent days in the hospital." Rutgar was a bear of a man, with gray-blond hair that swept past his shoulders and a long gray-blond beard that swept up dinner crumbs. His gaze roved around the gathered emergency workers. "Where's Gage? He can look at my ankle."

"Although you're bullheaded, you aren't a bull." Gage wound his way through the crowd, followed by Nate, until they reached the two uniformed fire personnel. "And I prefer patients who don't talk back."

"What happened?" Nate asked Ben, the fire captain.

"Rutgar missed the top step, fell and slid to the bottom. Tried to catch himself with his foot on the post down here." Ben turned his back to Rutgar and lowered his voice, although the gathered volunteers had no qualms closing ranks to hear better. "He needs an X-ray of his ankle. He says his head hurts and when Mandy tried to get him to stand, he vomited. He might have a concussion."

"I'll take him to the hospital," Nate offered, despite wanting to get back to Julie and Duke.

"I can drive him." Flynn joined them. "I know you've got things to do." The new dad raised an eyebrow, daring Nate to contradict him.

Nate did nonetheless. "Are you sure? What about Becca and Ian?"

"How long can it take?" Flynn shrugged.

Hours, but Nate wasn't going to look a gift horse in the mouth. Rutgar was more demanding than a toddler in the terrible-two stage. "I'll send folks back down the hill so you can get your truck in."

Nate walked toward the road, stopping at each car to convey the basics—that Rutgar had fallen and needed nonemergency medical care. Slowly, cars began to wend their way back downhill.

A classic blue Cadillac convertible swung wide around the switchback, nearly driving the faded green Buick that carried the town council off the road.

Nate flagged down the Caddy driver, who nearly ran him over before stopping in the middle of Rutgar's driveway. "Lilac, you aren't supposed to be behind the wheel."

Lilac blinked behind her large tortoiseshell sunglasses and flung the end of her maroon paisley scarf over one shoulder before answering coyly, "Is that you, Sheriff?"

"If you can't tell it's me," Nate said stiffly, "you shouldn't be driving."

"Pfft." Lilac waved a beringed hand. "No one has twenty-twenty vision anymore."

"Just those who drive legally," Nate muttered. And then he added in a loud voice in case Lilac hadn't put in her hearing aids, "There's nothing to see here. Go home and park your car in the driveway." Where he could see it on his rounds and know she wasn't being a menace on the roads.

Lilac lifted her nose in the air. "Doris says I should be able to drive wherever and whenever I want."

Annoyance pounded in his temples and threatened to flatten what little patience he had left. "The agreement you made after nearly *killing* Chad Healy was you'd only drive in an emergency."

"There's an emergency here." Lilac let her foot off the brake and the Caddy lurched forward.

"Stop!" Nate slapped a hand on a blue bubble fender. "They're going to be taking Rutgar to the hospital any minute. I need the driveway free of vehicles." He'd cleared it enough to get Flynn's truck in a few minutes before her arrival.

Lilac pouted. "I didn't even get to see."

"There's nothing to see." And he doubted she could make out the details if she stood on Rutgar's steps next to him. "Rutgar may have sprained an ankle. No blood. No bone."

"How did he fall? And when? And…" She

pursed her lips. "Never mind. I'll find the juice in the phone tree." She put the car in Reverse, and then stared up at him with renewed interest. "So you're a father?"

"Yes." He snapped, as if the fact annoyed him, when it was Lilac who'd gotten under his skin.

After helping Lilac make a ten-point turn, Nate returned to the house to help load Rutgar into Flynn's truck. It took both Nate and Gage to get him moving with a shoulder under each arm. Even then, when the big man staggered, all three men nearly stumbled.

"Wait," Rutgar said when Nate tried to shut the truck door.

"I found it!" Ben hurried down the front stairs carrying a small red pillow with a cupcake silk-screened on it. Not exactly what one expected a fireman to rescue.

"Don't judge a man by his pillow." Without opening his eyes, Rutgar tucked the pillow beneath his back. "Jessica gave me this."

"Jessica, who owns Martin's Bakery?" Nate asked with a straight face. "Recently married?" Forty years or so Rutgar's junior.

"There's no other Jessica in town," Rutgar huffed. "Do you know how hard it is to find a good woman? And then Duffy beat me to the punch. You've got to be quick when you find The One."

Nate thought about Julie. She'd make some-one The Perfect One. She was the kind of woman you went slow with. Not that Nate planned on going for Julie at all.

Nate closed the truck door and watched Flynn drive away. Only then did he notice the shot-up cans on the fence posts. It looked like Rutgar was holding target practice. Nate hadn't seen cans set up like that in a long time.

Dad had driven far on Nate's eighth birth-day.

They could have gone to the dirt bike track to try Nate's rifle. That's where Bobby Leaf and his dad went shooting, early in the morn-ing before the motocross people showed up. They could have gone to the dump, because it was Sunday and it was closed. That's where Ignacio Maldonado went with his dad.

Instead, Dad drove. They left Willows far behind them. Dad steered them down back roads and drank beer, muttering to himself about how much he hated his life. The shine Nate had felt upon receiving his birthday gift began to fade.

He was older now. He knew how the world worked. You had to hide your emotions from

Dad—the joy, the sadness, the tears. And the smiles and laughter. Especially the smiles and laughter. You had to be good and quiet and sit in the corner where no one noticed you, Dad particularly. When Dad drank too many beers, he passed out. Or he shouted. Hurtful words, his third grade teacher would've said about his father's language. "Let it slide off," Mom would say after a particularly bad day. Mom, Molly and Nate had to take Dad's words in silence or he'd slap someone, usually Mom.

This time, Mom wasn't around to deal with Dad. This time, it was Nate, now a man. Being a man meant Nate had to act like one. He rubbed his cheek where Dad had smacked him a few weeks ago. The sky seemed to darken. Eight didn't seem so old anymore.

"I bet you're a good shot," Ben said from behind him, startling Nate out of his reverie.

Nate made a noncommittal noise and then walked to his truck, still lost in the past.

The spot Dad chose to shoot was isolated—a small grove of eucalyptus trees set away from the road.

When they pulled up, Nate's stomach had growled. He'd been so excited, he hadn't eaten his birthday pancakes before they'd left.

Hunger wasn't the worst of his problems. Dad had stopped drinking. He wasn't loud, but he wasn't happy either. He kept turning his heavy-lidded stare toward Nate. That stare said something wasn't to his liking.

Nate wished he hadn't gotten that rifle. He wished he was back in town, stomach full of pancakes, sitting in bible study and pretending to pay attention.

"Grab those cans." Dad pointed to the six empty beer cans at his feet and then across the field. "Set them up on that fallen log."

"Yes, sir." Nate hurried to do his father's bidding. He'd just placed the last one when a shot rang out. Nate could swear a bullet whizzed past his head.

His father swore. "Missed."

Nate scurried back to his father's side. "Was it a deer? Can I try?"

"Ammo is expensive," Dad grumbled, giving Nate that heavy-lidded stare again.

"But it's my birthday." And they'd come all this way.

Dad squinted at him. "How old are you?"

"Eight. Same age as you when Grandpa gave you a rifle." Nate knew the story well. He picked up the rifle, the new symbol of his manhood. He reached for the box of ammo on the ground and then hesitated, looking up at Dad. "Can I?"

Dad nodded slowly, backing up. He held his gun with two hands, ready to lift and fire, the way hunters did when they knew prey was near.

Nate loaded two shells. He drew the gun up. It was heavier than Matthew's BB gun, heavier still than Tony's video game gun. It took him a moment to find his balance, feet far enough apart to compensate for the weight of the barrel. "Five says I hit that second can." It was a phrase he and his friends used. *Five* meaning *five cents*. Sometimes they didn't even have the nickels to back up the bet.

"Shoot like your life depends on it." Dad's voice wasn't loud, and it wasn't friendly either. "Not for a five."

Nate drew a breath and slowly squeezed the trigger. The recoil knocked him back. The gunshot filled his ears and sent black birds flying from the trees. "I hit it! Did you see?" Nate turned to his father, practically bumping into the muzzle of his gun.

He'd expected to see pride on his father's face. He didn't expect to see tears in his eyes. "Get in the truck."

"But, Dad, I only shot once." And he'd hit the can!

"Get in the truck before I change my mind."

CHAPTER SIX

"I'VE BEEN WATCHING you from inside the restaurant." The short, stout woman sat down across from Julie at El Rosal. "My name is Doris Schlotski and you're a cop."

"Yes." Julie pushed her mug to the center of the table. She'd been thinking it was time to leave and this was her cue. She dipped her paper napkin in her water glass and began cleaning Duke's hands.

"You're a cop," Doris repeated as if Julie hadn't spoken. "But you're also a mother." She patted Duke on the head almost as an afterthought. "It must be hard to be a working mom."

Julie didn't feel like a working mom. She and her mother had been sharing the duty of taking care of Duke. Mom worked at a shoe store in the mall and had more regular hours than Julie did. And they had a flexible daycare provider in the mix.

"There's not much crime in Harmony Valley," Doris went on. "You might almost say the job of sheriff is a cakewalk."

She'd bet not. No law enforcement job was easy.

Duke grinned at their unexpected visitor and said his favorite words in the world. "I Duke."

The old woman ignored him, glancing furtively over her shoulder and around the outdoor seating area as if she was on an important spy mission and she was a very bad spy. And then Doris stretched her shoulders over the table, lowering her voice. "How would you like to be sheriff of Harmony Valley?"

"You mean, work for Nate?" That would drive them both crazy.

Still leaning forward, Doris shook her head. "You were there last night. You know what I mean."

"You're looking for a pawn for the election." But wouldn't running for the job irk Nate? It was tempting. Oh, so tempting.

"I'm looking to surprise the town council with a viable alternative." Doris sized her up. "I can tell there's no love lost between you and Nate. The title of sheriff would look good on your résumé. It's a win-win for both of us."

Julie kept her opinion to herself. She wanted full custody of Duke. She wanted the courage

to suit up for SWAT again. She didn't want
the job of sheriff in a Podunky town where
the worst lawbreaker was retired and a whiner.

She met the retired whiner's gaze squarely.

"Think about it for a day or so, and let me
know." Doris stood and then slunk away, as if
she didn't want to be seen with Julie.

Julie's cell phone buzzed with a message
from Captain Bradford: Psych eval in two days.
Be there.

She replied, assuring him she would be and
then sat, worrying about the test.

I have to pass.

There was too much at stake. Her reputa-
tion, for one.

Yes, she'd pass. She'd push herself through
it the same way she'd pushed herself through
competing against boys in baseball and men at
the police academy, the same way she'd proven
she could do anything a man could do on the
police force. She'd set the goal in front of her
and work for it one step at a time. She wouldn't
question.

Her nightly dreams made her question. The
nightmares made her doubt. All those questions and doubts turned her stomach.

I have to pass.

She imagined herself back on the force.

She imagined the look of respect in her commander's eyes. And while she was visualizing success, she imagined herself having a good night's sleep.

A short time later, Julie pushed the stroller up and down Main Street, checking out the businesses and the bakery. That didn't take long. Main Street had become something of a ghost town since Nate had been called away. She let Duke run off his sugar high on the grass in the town square, while she rested on the bench under the oak tree.

A petite blonde wearing a cute fuzzy pink jacket pushed her stroller across the road toward them. Her toddler had the same wild blond curls as her mother, but wore pink leggings and sparkly tennis shoes instead of blue jeans and boots.

The woman waved. She was about Julie's age and had an infectious smile. "Now that the fog's burned off, isn't the view of Parish Hill beautiful? It's so clear, you can see the granite face." She pointed to the eastern skyline.

Julie'd had a glimpse of it before, through the fog. Now the mountain that rose above the treetops was strong and sturdy.

Like me. Like I used to be.

Julie needed to stop talking to herself.

"Do you want to come to the play park with us?" the blonde asked, stopping at the corner.

Duke slammed into Julie's legs, wrapping his arms around them. "Ye-es!"

Julie was up for any activity that tired her nephew out. She strapped him in the stroller and joined the pair, walking behind them on the sidewalk.

"I'm Shelby," the woman said over her shoulder, keeping up a pace designed to burn calories and kill Julie. "And this is Mac."

Julie reciprocated the introductions.

Little Mae leaned around her stroller to sneak shy glances at Duke. Typical boy, Duke was drinking from his sippy cup and pretending to ignore her.

"Mae..." Julie cast about her memory for why the name rang a bell. "Isn't there a boutique on Main Street called Mae something?"

"Yes. Mae's Pretty Things." Shelby reached down and fluffed Mae's blond curls. "Mae used to own the dress shop in town. She died a little over two years ago. I was close to her before she passed."

"I'm so sorry."

"It happens to all of us," Shelby said in the resigned voice people used when the elderly passed away. She'd probably never lost anyone her own age.

Julie's wound tingled with each dragging step.

"I had to take the day off because my caregiver needed to go into Santa Rosa." Shelby grinned over her shoulder. "Truthfully, I don't mind a day off. Time goes by so quickly with kids. It seems like yesterday Mae was a baby." Shelby marched on, boots ringing on pavement, heedless of the fact her speed was draining Julie. "There's going to be a legion of toddlers at the play park, since most of us share the same sitter and most of us—although we love our babies—need to run down their batteries before lunch so we get a good naptime."

Amen, sister.

"Mama, want pay. Mae want pay." Mae smiled coquettishly at Duke. "Boy want pay?"

Three-word sentences. Other than "No mad words," Duke only spoke in two-word sentences.

Mom Jealousy lifted Julie's feet with renewed vigor. She had to keep pace with Shelby and Duke had to keep pace with Mae.

Unbidden, a memory of April resurfaced.

"Come on, Duke," Julie encouraged, down on all fours with her nephew at one of those mommy-and-baby classes. "Crawl. You can do it. That kid over there is crawling and he's younger than you are."

"Take a breath, Aunt Julie," April said from her chair nearby. She'd been too tired to participate. She wore a knit cap to hide her baldness and a benevolent smile. "Kids develop at their own pace."

"He just needs encouragement." Julie moved one of Duke's fat fists forward.

Duke collapsed on the mat, rolled onto his back and gave her a drooly grin.

"Enjoy him the way he is today," April said with the wisdom of one who'd studied child development in college. "Otherwise you'll view every mom out there as competition. Mom Jealousy will eat you alive."

Little Mae repeated her question. "Boy want pay?"

Duke remained silent, playing hard to get. Typical man.

Julie had to prompt him. "Duke, do you want to play?"

He nodded, a man of few words like his father.

They turned a corner and spotted the playground. The legion turned out to be five toddlers of varying shapes and sizes.

"Kids!" Duke tried to get out of the stroller, but the lap belt held him back. *"Juju."*

"Just a minute. We're not there yet."

Julie was sweating by the time they reached the playground. It was part of the schoolyard, but looked like new with short slides and low towers to climb on. The ground was covered with plastic bark and everything was painted in bright primary colors—red, yellow, blue, green. It was as colorful as El Rosal.

"Are you visiting or moving here?" Shelby parked her stroller near a bench outside the gate, setting the brake.

"Visiting." Julie declined to say who. She freed Duke.

Duke hugged Julie's leg, and then ran to Mae and hugged her. "Fend. Kids." He moved with the exaggerated form of a racewalker to the playground entry—elbows up, booty waddling.

Shelby followed Mae and Duke. Julie hesitated. The only bench was outside the small playground. She should go inside, but she needed the rest. She took a seat. After all, there were six moms inside. Better to sit now than collapse later.

Thirty minutes passed and a blue truck with a star on the door pulled up to the curb. Nate hopped out. He looked like any other dad in the world, if you discounted the military precision with which he moved, the lack of a soft dad body and the way his appearance made Julie's heart beat faster. If only because she was nervous about the papers she wanted him to sign.

The moms greeted Nate by name. Many of the kids waved.

Mr. Popularity had arrived.

Julie gritted her teeth. Nate didn't want kids. He shouldn't be so popular with the toddler set.

Nate came to stand next to her. "When you're done here, we can start your test. I suggest we do it at the jail. Less chance of an unwanted audience."

She crossed her arms over her chest and gave a curt nod, indulging in a little self-pity. None of her revenge dreams were coming true.

"What do I need? A pencil? A calculator?"

"A heart?" She refused to look at him.

"Got one of those," he said, adding less cheerfully and in a voice only she could hear, "Battered and bruised though it might be."

"Somewhere, a cricket is playing a violin," she deadpanned. Like he'd ever had his heart broken.

He stared down at her, that half grin on his face. But this time it was the more open version he'd flashed at Terrance. "I've missed you, Jules."

"The feeling isn't mutual." He would not get inside her head...or her heart.

"Nay!" Duke ran over and pressed his body against the fence as if giving Nate a hug. "Me pay." He pointed to the other children moving about the playground. "Me fends."

"You're playing with friends? That is so cool."

Julie envied his easy way with Duke. Of course, he didn't worry if Duke was talking appropriately for his age. Or eating right. Or sleeping enough.

Nate left her and went through the gate. "Who wants a helicopter ride?" Immediately, he was swamped by children smiling and raising their hands, begging to be picked up.

Nate put them in a line—no small feat as forming a line of toddlers was more like herding chickens. And then he began to pick them up by their wrists, whirling thcm around until their feet flew high above the ground and they squealed with delight.

Shelby leaned against the fence near Julie. "Nate is great with kids. I mean, he rarely talks until he gets around them. And then he's a chatterbox." Shelby's tone turned curious, her gaze speculative. "Are you dating?"

"No. We used to work together." It seemed like a lifetime ago.

"I was wondering if he'd finally get to use the wedding dress Mae left him," Shelby said slyly. "Has he shown it to you?"

"No," Julie choked out, not wanting to know about Nate's wedding dress or why he'd have one. "We're not that close."

"I was only wondering because my grandfather said Nate's girlfriend was in town." Shelby gave a small laugh. "I guess he meant Nate's *girl* friend. You should ask to see it anyway. Mae would appreciate it being shown off." Shelby's smile softened. "She knew how to match a dress with the right woman."

Nate finished giving rides. Toddlers were dropping like flies—sitting in the bark, lying in the bark, stumbling to their mothers and begging to be picked up. They were all worn-out. All that is, except Duke. He climbed the short ladder to the slide, while other moms led their kids to the gate.

Nate returned to her side. "I've got to make my rounds. Come to the jail after lunch."

A few of the moms hugged Nate goodbye,

as if he was a noble knight in shining armor.
He'd sold them a bill of goods.

Julie refused to be sold again. In fact, she
felt a sudden urge to run for sheriff.

CHAPTER SEVEN

"JUST TAKE ME HOME." Rutgar sat in Flynn's big black truck parked in front of the sheriff's office, covering his eyes with one hand. The edge of his red cupcake pillow was visible behind his back, and his right ankle was swollen and taped.

"What's up?" Nate stood at Flynn's open passenger door, having received an SOS call from his friend a few minutes ago, asking him for help with Rutgar, but offering no specifics.

It was after lunch. Nate was expecting Julie and Duke anytime. He felt jittery, like he'd had too much caffeine. He blamed it on the Daddy Test. April may have created it, but it gave Julie too much pleasure. There had to be a catch in there somewhere. A trick Julie would relish pulling from her sleeve.

"The doctor said Rutgar has a mild concussion and a slightly sprained ankle." Flynn had the twitchy look of a dad who'd received a desperate call from his wife. His reddish-brown hair stood on end above his forehead. "Rutgar needs darkness and twenty-four-hour observation. Unfortunately, Ian's been colicky since I left. If I take Rutgar home with me, the old man won't get any rest."

"The old man will walk home, thank you very much, no matter where you put me." Rutgar's words lacked conviction given his ankle was swollen and he couldn't open his eyes.

Flynn leaned over the steering wheel to make eye contact with Nate. "We could get him a room at Leona's."

"Leona?" Rutgar howled. "Just shoot me now. Better yet. Lend me your gun, Sheriff. It's time to end it."

"Sadly…" Nate felt a smile work its way up one cheek. "I don't think I have any bullets."

"What kind of sheriff are you?" Rutgar's voice rumbled though the air like a train on a straight stretch of track.

"The worst kind. The kind who cares." Nate probably enjoyed teasing Rutgar too much, but normally the big man could take it. Most people in Harmony Valley were good sports and Nate enjoyed interacting with them since he didn't speak to his own parents. "If you're good, you'll get ice cream later." Maybe he could use that to entice Julie to bring Duke over.

"I knew I brought him to the right place." Flynn joined in on the fun.

"The jail is the right place to put me?" Rutgar tried to glare through his fingers, but almost immediately shut his eyes tight. "Rock-hard cots. Drafty cells. Bad food."

Flynn grinned. "Why do I get the feeling he's been in jail before?"

A breeze tickled the new leaves on the trees flanking Nate's office as if they, too, were enjoying a laugh at Rutgar's expense.

"I tell you what." Nate took pity on the big man. "You stay in jail for observation and I won't make you wear an orange jumpsuit. And I'll get you coffee and scones in the morning from Martin's Bakery." If Terrance got lonely tonight, he'd have to share the cell with Rutgar.

"Everybody wants to be a comedian." But Rutgar shifted in his seat. "Lead me to this paradise of which you speak so highly."

"Need any help?" Shelby backed a stroller out of the winery's barrel storage facility next door. In the fall after harvest, the entire street smelled like red wine.

Little Mae watched them with sleepy eyes from her stroller.

"Can you open the door to the office, Shelby?" Nate guided Rutgar's feet toward the wide running board. "And then the door to the jail cell. This big guy has a concussion and needs a night of monitoring."

"The horror." Rutgar made a growling noise. "A man of my age reduced to a night in the slammer."

"Rutgar." Flynn's tone was borderline angry. He pushed his door open. "My wife has been alone with a crying newborn since breakfast. Let's not overdramatize. I need to get home."

"Everybody, take a breath," Nate said, and then encouraged Rutgar to extend his good foot another few inches.

Squinting, Rutgar tried to look down. He groaned. "Can't. I'll be sick."

"Not in my truck." Flynn stopped a safe distance from Nate.

"Not on me," Nate added. "Close your eyes. Breathe. Think of the clean taste of apple."

Flynn targeted Nate with a questioning look.

"How can I think of an apple when you told me about ice cream?" Rutgar scooted another inch toward the edge of his seat. "I hope you have chocolate."

"Ginger ale is better for upset tummies." Shelby opened the front door. "I'm going to pull down the blinds so it'll be dark in here."

"Good idea." Nate talked Rutgar through

getting his good foot to the ground. "This is where a squad car would come in handy." Lower to the ground. "Or a stretcher. You're going to have to lean on us to get inside." The crutches in the truck bed weren't an option if Rutgar couldn't open his eyes.

"I'm going to put your ugly mugs on my cans at my shooting range," Rutgar grumbled, sliding slowly to the ground.

Flynn drew Rutgar's arm over his shoulders. "That's the thanks I get for taking you to the doctor."

"That's the thanks I get for taking him into my home." Nate did the same.

Rutgar hobbled along at a good clip, leaning heavily on the two men. "Who loves people and makes a home over a jail?"

"Who loves people and lives alone on top of a mountain?" Nate countered.

"I don't love people." Rutgar scoffed. "People are annoying. Don't get many visitors on the mountain."

Not with that no-trespassing sign. "And I don't get many visitors to my jail."

They passed through the doorway and guided him to the jail cell bed. Once he was seated, Nate lifted the old man's legs onto the cot.

When Rutgar caught his breath, he said, "Ooh. Made it."

Shelby covered him with a blanket she'd found folded on the nearby bench. "I better go," she whispered, pointing to little Mae, who'd fallen asleep in her stroller.

"My pillow," Rutgar said in near panicky tones. "Where is it? It helps my back."

"I'll get it," Flynn said, following Shelby out.

Doris appeared in the open doorway, her voice a shrill shout. "Why are the shades drawn? I can't see in. What's happening here?"

"That voice is torture." Rutgar covered his ears. "Shut up."

Doris huffed, but didn't leave.

Nate came to stand behind the counter, putting him in the position of authority. "Rutgar's got a concussion and needs darkness and quiet. He doesn't have anyone to monitor his condition, so Flynn brought him here." That's right. He was throwing Flynn under the bus.

Rutgar moaned, totally overplaying it, which Nate appreciated.

"What if you need the jail cell?" Doris was nothing if not persistent. She carried a purse big enough to fit the head of any adversary she defeated. It was tan and had a Chihuahua appliquéd on it.

"I need the jail cell for Rutgar," Nate said evenly, struck by the sudden impression that Doris was a worst-case scenario thinker. Was it anxiety that drove her to try and control her surroundings?

Flynn—the coward—hovered on the safety of the sidewalk, checking his phone.

"This isn't a hotel." Doris's entire body trembled as she drew herself up. "What if you need that cell for a criminal?"

Nate could only think of one person in Harmony Valley he wanted to throw in jail. She was short and loved little dogs. He slid his glance away from her and chose his words carefully. "I've only arrested one person in three years."

"My point exactly." Doris slung her dog purse higher on her shoulder. "The people's tax dollars haven't been put to good use."

"Or we haven't had any criminals in town," Nate pointed out.

She harrumphed. "A likely story."

"The doctor prescribed peace and quiet," Rutgar rumbled. "I'll gladly commit a crime if that will make Doris leave."

She'd been pushed too far. Doris narrowed

her eyes and took a small step forward, leaning toward Nate over the four-foot counter. "You're going down."

Nate cleared his throat. "Just to be clear, because threatening an officer of the law is classified as a criminal threat, are you speaking metaphorically or physically?"

Doris drew back slowly, like a snake pulling back to strike. "Polish your résumé. You're going to need it." She stomped out the door, giving Flynn a wide berth on her way out.

"Do women make a habit of threatening you?" Rutgar said in a subdued voice. "If so, I need to hang out here more often."

"Why?"

"I like strong women and I might want to date one." He blew out a breath. "Just not *that* one."

JULIE WASN'T DREAMING of anything.

The nothingness was blissful.

And then there was a knock on the door. "Miss Smith." Leona's voice. She sounded like she was in the room.

"Shhh." Julie sat up groggily, squinting against the bright afternoon sunlight coming through the window. "The baby's sleeping."

The baby wasn't sleeping. Leona stood in the doorway holding Duke's hand.

When Duke saw Julie, he ran to the bed, extending his arms out to her. She lifted him into her lap.

He hid his face against her good shoulder with a fearful, if guilty, *"Juju."*

Regardless of who was at fault, mama bear came out of hibernation with a scowl. "What happened?"

If looks could kill, Julie might not have survived another bullet. "Your child was in my kitchen."

"Oh." She'd slept through Duke leaving the room? Julie was the worst caregiver ever. Still, she managed to muster a weak retort. "That wouldn't be a problem if there was a lock on the door."

"He was looking in my refrigerator." From the horrified expression on Leona's face, she might just as well have said he'd been looking under her skirt.

"I'm sorry," Julie said because the situation seemed to require it. Who knew Leona would be so proprietary about her fridge?

"What if the boy ate something and was allergic? What if he climbed into the refrigerator and suffocated?" Leona's agitation was palpable. Where normally she stood still, her hands shook and rolled and crested midair. "What if..." She left her question unanswered.

"I bad," Duke said miserably.

Duke's admission seemed to calm the older woman. Her sharp features resumed their normal position in disapproval. "Yes, you were."

"I sorry." He buried his head in Julie's good shoulder.

"He won't wander again." How easily reassurances slipped through Julie's lips. Duke was an explorer by nature. Just last week he'd used her kitchen cupboards as a jungle gym while she was in the shower.

Given her raised eyebrows, Leona didn't believe Julie either. She closed the door with a near-silent click.

Julie fell back on the bed with Duke on top of her. "Not good, little man."

Duke scooted to the edge of the bed, turned on his stomach and slipped to the floor. "Want go, Juju."

"Okay. We'll go see Nate." And administer phase one of the Daddy Test.

The Daddy Test. April had been adamant that Julie administer it, not their mother.

"This is important," April had said, eyes closed as she lay in bed looking nothing like the April who'd glowed on the morning of her wedding day. Where she'd once been optimistic, now there was a desperate air about her. "It has to be you. Face-to-face. Nate will be honest with you."

Julie doubted that. April's questions were unorthodox and personal. Nate was the most impersonal man she knew.

And yet, he'd surprised her with his treatment of Duke. He may not have embraced fatherhood, but he hadn't rejected Duke outright. He was warm and kind to him, which wasn't helpful when it came to keeping her hatred of him alive. Here in Harmony Valley, he was the quiet, sensitive Nate, the man she'd called friend at the academy.

They'd tackled the obstacle course on the same day. With her shorter legs, Julie had been struggling to pass under the time limit.

"You gonna do this thing?" Nate had looked down at her with that half smile of his and a challenge in his eyes.

"You'd like to see me fail, wouldn't you?" That was Julie's MO. If she put everyone in the column against her, she didn't let anyone get close enough to make her weak.

"Nope. I'd like to see you beat me." He gave her a tight grin. "Or at least go down trying."

The instructor had called them to the starting line.

"Why would you want to see me succeed?" She crouched at the starting line, unable to hide her curiosity when she should have been clearing her head.

"Because you can take what people here dish out, which means you'd take it on the streets, too. And give back in good measure."

She might not have believed Nate if she hadn't looked beyond the contained challenging. There was warmth and respect in his gaze.

It was her dad all over again. Someone was rooting for her. Someone had her back. Nate may have six inches on her and a wider stride, but she wasn't facing the course as if she'd already failed. Nate had said she could give as good as she got. She had to prepare to attack the course the same way.

Julie removed her sweatshirt and Duke's. She brushed her hair, but it was a lost cause. She still looked as gaunt and washed-out as she had this morning, just minus the tangles. She didn't look strong enough to handle a two-year-old. No wonder Nate had thought she had cancer.

It was going to be hard to hate Nate when he acted supportive, like the Nate she'd entrusted with her sister. But just because Nate was perceptive and kind now, didn't mean he wouldn't betray a trust again.

Forgive, April's voice said.

Julie didn't want to hear it.

"Petty you." Duke stood at the door with his fingers opening and closing as if waiting for her hand to clasp his.

She knew Duke meant it as a compliment, telling her she was pretty, but she felt more petty than pretty. And she'd felt that way since she'd woken up in the hospital. Mom had been there holding Julie's cold hand, Duke asleep in her lap.

"You could have died. You still look like you could." A tear slid down Mom's cheek. "The three of us. That's all we've got left of this family."

Sobering thought, that.

"SWAT, Julie?" Mom's voice had cracked. "Does Duke mean so little to you that you'd choose SWAT? Do I mean so little to you?"

She hadn't told her mother that she'd been granted a transfer to SWAT. She'd applied for the assignment because it was another hurdle to push past. And when she'd tried to defend herself that day in the hospital room—her throat raw from the breathing tube they'd removed, and raw from the emotion of making her mother cry—Julie had been unable to defend her choice and her selfish, petty self.

"You're going to tell Nate about his son." Mom had wiped her eyes with a crumpled tissue. "With our luck, I'll drop dead from a heart attack, you'll get hit by a bus and it'll take months for them to link Duke to Nate."

Still unable to speak, Julie had shaken her head. She didn't feel strong enough to face Nate.

"It's time," her mother had said. "As soon as you recover."

The hospital had released Julie three days after the shooting. Not one to procrastinate once she'd made up her mind, she went home and packed a bag for Harmony Valley. She'd taken the custody papers April had had her draft months ago out of the fire safe and stared at them. She didn't want to let Nate back into her life, but she knew he wasn't the type of man to deal with a lawyer. He'd want to deal with this kind of thing in person.

She stopped the stroller outside the sheriff's office, now, not quite ready to face Nate.

The shades were drawn over the plate glass window as if it was a business closed for the day. Julie tried the door and was surprised to find it open.

"Must be my day for visitors." Nate sat at his desk, which was behind the counter separating the office from the jail cell. He'd shed the sleeveless jacket. His gaze was friendly. His attitude relaxed.

Julie felt warm. Not uncomfortably warm as she had earlier when they'd been together, but cozy warm, welcome warm. Must be the fact that she stood in a jail.

"Nay!" Duke burst out of the stroller the moment his belt was unbuckled, running for Nate.

"Who is it this time?" a voice boomed from the cell, although the door stood wide open.

"It's Julie and my son, Duke."

Duke gasped, slowing down. "Who dat?" He stopped at the corner of the counter, pointing at the jail cell bars. "What dat?"

"Bars." Nate stood, looking strong and rested, every black hair in place. He walked to the cell bars and grabbed hold of one. "You can touch it."

Duke ran the last few feet to the bars, tentatively stretching out his hand without making contact. "Tree?"

"No. It's a bar."

Nate's kindness for Julie's most precious person touched her.

Duke touched several black bars with one finger. "Bar. Bar. Bar."

"And that's Rutgar." Nate pointed to the large man on the cot. "He fell down and hurt himself."

"He fell down?" Julie leaned on the counter, trying to act casual. "Is that against the law in this town, too?"

"Yep." Nate's gaze bounced briefly from Duke to her and back to Duke.

In that moment when their eyes met—between one breath and the next—the feeling of welcome expanded in Julie's chest to a feeling of belonging. Of belonging here. With Nate.

She rejected the feeling, of course. She didn't belong with Nate or to this town. But the feeling hung on, like a persistent taste lingering on her tongue.

Duke shook the bars with both hands, and then tried to squeeze his body between them.

Nate gently drew him back. "One thing you never want to do is break into prison."

"Because you'll never get out," Rutgar said. The man was large, both in length and in girth. He barely fit on the cot. He had one leg propped on a small red pillow and a red handkerchief draped over his eyes. His long gray-blond locks spilled over his shoulder and his gray-blond beard held up one end of the handkerchief. "Come here, boy. What was his name? Duke? As in Marmaduke? Strange name for a boy."

"He's named after John Wayne," Nate surprised Julie by saying. "His mother and I used to enjoy watching the Duke's Western movies." His voice grew as soft as his memory might have been, as tender as Julie's memories of watching those same films with her father. "April appreciated an honorable man willing to give his life for what was right."

Julie's throat strained to close. He'd left April. He shouldn't have known why April had named her son Duke. He shouldn't have talked about honor as if he had some.

Duke went inside the cell. He patted Rutgar's shoulder. "Hi."

"You've got some big britches to live up to," Rutgar said, his voice as dry as a desert plain. "Wouldn't catch the Duke stealing a girl's lunch money."

"You might catch him stealing a kiss." There was laughter in Nate's dark brown eyes and a tease at the corner of his mouth. He returned to his chair behind the desk, leaving Duke with

Rutgar. "How do you like Harmony Valley's hub of law enforcement?"

"It makes me want to nap." Of course, breathing made her want to nap since she'd been shot. Julie glanced around, taking in the picture on the wall of their class at the academy, keys hanging on a hook to the right of the desk and an empty gun case on the back wall. "What? No weapons?"

"Not anymore." He patted his chest in different places. Only those who'd been in law enforcement would know he was telling her he didn't carry concealed in any hidden shirt pockets. "I don't need a gun in Harmony Valley to keep the peace. I've got my Taser in my glove box, but I've never used it."

Julie was envious of his ability to keep the bad guys at bay with nothing more than a bolt of electricity. She used to be so proud of her marksmanship. She used to feel comforted carrying a weapon.

"I'm ready for your Daddy Test." Nate indicated she sit in a boxy office chair across from him. His desk was tidy. A laptop, a blotter with scribbled notes in black ink, a phone charger, a small lamp and a small wooden bowl filled with smooth stones.

She hadn't expected her plan to veer this

far off course—to her actually administering April's Daddy Test. Her heart pounded.

She grabbed her backpack, sat and pulled out April's small notebook. She paused. The last time the notebook had been opened, April had done it.

"Is there a problem?" Nate asked.

"No." She spread the notebook in her lap. "There are a few questions."

"This should be quick." Nate sat back in his chair, confident yet wary. Everything the Academy taught them to be when interrogating subjects.

She'd be doing the interrogation today. Anger worked its way beneath the thin layer of her composure. Anger that he'd put her in this position. Anger that she'd been unable to crack his veneer yet. She embraced the anger and let it bleed through her words. "I'd take your time. They're more like essay questions."

He frowned. "This test was designed by April? I have to write a paper?"

"Yes and no. She wrote them in the notebook as if you'd get a take-home test." She flipped the page to the first section, suppressing a pang of grief at seeing April's looping handwriting, those *i*'s she dotted with hearts. "Here's the first question. A good father is honest. Honest about his feelings, about the world and about how to be a good man. My father knew that honesty was a double-edged sword. Give two examples of honesty in your life—one you experienced with your dad, and one you experienced with someone you loved."

Nate's expression changed. Or not so much changed as perhaps hardened like the granite face of Parish Hill. "What?" His words dropped to a place filled with darkness and danger. "You're grading me? On answers to questions like that?"

"You don't have to answer anything." Her heart continued its pounding, but it felt more like an urgent, repetitive warning—*Retreat! Retreat! Retreat!*

"You're asking me about my past." His jaw set in rejection mode. "Are you asking these questions for yourself or for April?"

Julie was shocked to discover she wasn't as sure as she should have been. Or was she feeling a gut response to the raw emotion in Nate's voice? Whatever it was, she couldn't weaken. "I'm asking for Duke. And for April. It was one of her last wishes."

"But April isn't here to listen to my answers." His tone was as hard as his expression. A wall seemed to go up between them.

There would be no compromise, no Daddy Test, no lengthy stays in Harmony Valley.

Julie's heart pounded in a different gear—slower, more certain. He was going to veto the process. She was that much closer to having Duke all to herself. She'd choose some-one from the force to be his guardian, just in case. "You don't have to answer anything for either one of us." Julie closed the notebook and tucked it into the backpack's zippered pocket. She withdrew a sheaf of papers from another compartment. "We can stop this here. By you signing over custody of Duke to me."

CHAPTER EIGHT

WHEN NATE HAD served overseas, there'd been days when nothing went right. When the wind whipped dirt and grit, and hurled it in his face. When bullets flew and rockets exploded and when the very air seemed to make him want to give in and walk away.

April and Julie's dad had believed the truth cut both ways. Nate felt sliced and diced.

What happens in this family stays in this family.

Nate stared at Julie, but he didn't see her limp golden hair or her steely gray eyes. He saw his father, leaning over him, shaking a finger in his face. Mom crying softly in the corner. Molly in her arms. Dad's knuckles red.

Since Nate had turned around last night and seen Julie, his thoughts and emotions were in turmoil. Nothing felt right. Not his past. Not his present. Not his future.

The goal of not rejecting Duke outright had been to help Julie gain perspective on the life she'd taken with a bullet, not dig up the skel-etons that used to haunt Nate's nights. What was to be gained by taking the Daddy Test when he didn't plan on being a full-time dad? April was dead and Julie wouldn't think bet-ter of him if he answered honestly.

What happens in this family stays in this family.

Nate stopped staring at Julie and searched his desk for a blue-ink pen.

And then Duke laughed. More like a giggle. A melodious sound that said this was a safe place. This town. These four walls. Julie.

His hand came up empty. "I don't talk about my personal history." Nate's voice sounded gruffer than a trained dog with a prowler in his sights.

"I know." Julie's expression turned smug. It was the face of the smug walking dead, but it was smug nonetheless.

Her face might not have looked so stark if she'd worn a pastel shirt. She'd chosen a muted gray button-down. Its drab color matched her skin tone.

He washed a hand over his face. "How many questions did you say are in this test?"

"Eight sections. A couple of questions in each section."

"I'll answer one section a day." She wouldn't give Harmony Valley a month, but she could spare eight days. And maybe that much would help her. It'd be torture for him. Even now, he wanted to put an arm around her, and tell her everything would be all right. Instead, he laced his fingers together and set his hands on his desk.

Julie's eyes narrowed. She was still going to hate him eight days from now. Signing the papers would make it easier on both of them, but nothing in his life had ever been easy.

Rutgar said something to Duke, too soft to catch beyond the deep rumble of his voice.

Duke giggled again.

Nate waited, heartened.

"I have a psych evaluation in two days." She hadn't said no.

"You won't pass." The therapist would take one look at her and see she wasn't ready to return to duty of any kind. Failing would make it harder for Julie to pass the next time. "Call and reschedule."

"Stay here and hide?" She rubbed her injured shoulder, caught him watching her and scowled. "Appear weak? *You'd* never do that."

He ignored the ploy to change the subject. "Heal, not hide. Eight days from now you'll have your strength back and your head on straight."

"You sound like my mother." Now it was her turn to wash a hand over her face. "You're going to bankrupt me."

"You can stay with me rent-free." When she still didn't capitulate to his terms, Nate put the pressure on. "Those are April's questions. She wanted my answers." He stopped himself short of pressing harder.

"And Duke? What are your intentions toward him?"

If he told her, she'd bolt. "We'll talk after the test."

Nate glanced over his shoulder into the jail cell and then back to Julie. "Let's go outside." Where Rutgar wouldn't hear. The old man might be a recluse, but he was as gossipy as anyone in Harmony Valley, not to mention a member of the phone tree.

Nate led Julie to a bench near the curb. The sun was shining and the sky a clear blue. It was that quiet time midafternoon when folks were at work, busy visiting friends, home watching television or napping. While she settled opposite him, Nate cast about his memories for something to fit her questions.

"My dad was brutally honest," Nate began,

keeping his body facing forward, not to her. It was hard enough to talk about his dad without seeing the horror and pity he was sure would come to her face.

"Was?" Julie picked up on his word choice immediately. "Is he dead?"

"No." Nate couldn't get that lucky. "We don't talk anymore."

The garden club had planted flowers beneath a tree a short distance away. A hummingbird flitted around the red buds. Normal. Carefree.

"My dad used to tell me what happens in the family stays in the family." There was an empty shop across the street with Santa, his sleigh and reindeer painted on the window. Santa's colors were faded and his face had cracked with age. But he, like the myth of Saint Nick, had weathered many a storm. "Dad felt whatever problems we had with each other would only be complicated if we told anyone else." Like the pastor, the police or child protective services.

"Do you think he was right?"

"I think he thought he was right." About teaching his kids to shut up and wipe away tears and lock their feelings away. Sometimes it'd helped, mostly it hadn't.

"And yet, you don't talk about your past,

so you must agree with him." Whereas before she'd been angry, now there was cool interest in her voice.

Good thing Julie wasn't part of the phone tree.

Privacy. It was one of the few things Dad had gotten right.

"And the second example?" she prompted, her gaze registering every tic in his expression.

The only thing that came to mind was his wedding day. Had April wanted him to share his side of the story with Julie? It was clear to him from her accusations last night that Julie didn't know the entire truth. But the truth about his conversation with April on their wedding day would only hurt her.

He suspected Julie would settle for nothing less than an answer that involved her sister and the wedding. "Did April tell you what happened that day?"

"You mean your *wedding day*?" Julie's tone had enough hot sarcasm to propel a steam engine. "Only what you told her. That the wedding was off."

Nate wanted to angle his knees toward Julie, to take one of her hands between both of his. He remained facing forward, facing Santa and the myth of happily-ever-afters. "She texted me, asking to see me before the ceremony. I thought it was a sign. I'd been having doubts."

Joe Messina drove by in his tow truck and waved.

"Hang on." Julie curled her fingers around Nate's arm, unaware of how her touch made his stomach tie up in knots. "April asked you? But when you got to the church, you asked me if you could talk to her."

Only because she'd seen him come in. Or more precisely, he'd seen Julie and been stopped in his tracks. She'd worn a plum-colored dress that traced her feminine curves in a way no patrol uniform had ever outlined. Julie's blond hair had been braided around her head like a crown and when she'd smiled... He'd had no idea why April wanted to talk to him, but he'd known it wouldn't go well by how hard Julie's appearance impacted him. "There was a traffic jam on the highway. I got there closer to the ceremony than I would've liked to. And then you stopped me."

Her hand slipped away. "So you went in to see her and..."

"April started talking. We discussed some things." Nate returned his gaze to Santa. What could he tell Julie about that day? "I admitted

I didn't love April as much as she deserved to be loved."

"You got that right." Julie's voice trembled with anger. "You led her on. You acted like—"

"She said she knew." There was no way to sugarcoat his words as Santa might have done. He had to look at Julie and let her see the honesty in his eyes. She'd see the pain, too. And the guilt.

Julie rocked back, as if struck, shaking her head. "No."

"I loved her," Nate reiterated in case she'd missed that part yesterday. "Just not as deeply as a groom should love his bride. I asked April if she still wanted to go through with the wedding and—"

"She did not say no." Julie's head shaking had become a slow pendulum swing. "She did *not*. April was crushed when you dumped her. She barely talked to anyone, not even me."

Appropriate, given the circumstances. "It was her choice."

"I have to go. I can't—"

"Jules." Nate reached for her hand when he should have let her go.

She jerked out of reach, face contorted with pain. "April wanted to marry you. She told me that morning she was pregnant." Julie drew a deep breath. Her gaze swept the sidewalk, searching for answers Nate wouldn't give. "She said she loved you. She told me she'd make any sacrifice so her baby would have two loving parents. I thought she meant she'd go through any cancer treatment, no matter how heinous, to stay alive." Her gaze landing on Nate with gut-punching intensity. "If you loved her...she would have married you."

The truth tried to cut its way from his heart to his mouth. Nate swallowed it back. No good ever came from knowing the full truth. "I loved her, Jules. I never met anyone so kind and thoughtful, so gentle and open. But it wasn't the absolute be-all-end-all sort of love." Nate still wasn't certain he knew what that was. "And when it came down to it, April didn't want to settle."

Julie's hand went to her throat. Her mouth opened and closed. And then she opened it again and spoke, spitting out the words like buckshot. "Then she did it for you. She made things easy on you." She spun away, and then turned back, color high in her cheeks, tears in her eyes. "You couldn't have hung in there for her? You knew the likelihood of the tumors returning was almost 100 percent. You couldn't have made her happy for the time she had left?"

"It would've been wrong. We both knew it." Nate's throat was choked for a different reason. "She deserved someone who loved her more than life itself."

Julie closed her eyes, and swiped her head from right to left.

"And she got that someone," Nate whispered. "In Duke."

Julie's face crumpled. But she bit her lip and squeezed her eyes tight and resisted tears.

"I don't expect you to forgive me." But Nate wanted her to. He didn't want to admit how much.

Her eyes flew open and she started to shout. "I could never—"

"No mad words." Duke ran out of the sheriff's office and hid his face against Julie's leg.

"You're right, Duke." There were still tears in Julie's eyes. "No mad words. Nate isn't worth the breath. Come on. We're going home." She took Duke's hand and headed toward the door and her things.

Home. She meant back to Sacramento.

Nate pushed to his feet, darting around them to block their path. "You made a promise."

"I don't care." She'd stopped in the middle

of the sidewalk, eyes closed, looking as if she'd topple at any moment.

"Eight days," Nate insisted, reminding himself why he'd made the bargain. "You owe April eight days. Or you'll never have the answers she sought."

I WANT NATE to pay.

Julie's words to April pinballed around her head as she pushed Duke back to the bed-and-breakfast. Maybe the memory had returned to her because she'd told April she'd wanted justice on multiple occasions. Or maybe because April had made Julie promise to give Nate a chance with Duke when she hadn't told Julie everything.

April called off the wedding. Not Nate.

Betrayal roiled in her stomach.

It was hard to go for Nate's jugular when she hadn't known everything that went on between her sister and Nate. Hard when he was so good with Duke.

No mad words.

How would she honor that for another week? She wished April had never come up with the Daddy Test.

"You can't hold a special meeting announcing candidates." Doris was shouting in front of the bakery down the street. If smoke could come out of ears, it would have spewed from Doris's in one angry volcanic eruption. She spotted Julie. "I'm not ready. I will not allow it!"

Agnes followed the direction of Doris's gaze. Her gaze turned thoughtful.

Not wanting to get involved, Julie pushed the stroller faster.

She didn't want to be sheriff of Harmony Valley. There were no threats in town, no criminal element, no troublemakers. She refused to count Doris or Leona. They weren't gun-toting domestic abusers or petty thieves that needed to be brought to justice.

She wanted to see Nate suffer. She wanted to feel unadulterated hatred when she looked at him. But she couldn't. And she hated herself for it. She hated April for it. She'd never have lost her grip on her anger toward him if she hadn't promised to come here.

"No matter what you think of Nate," April had said, propped up in bed. Her body was losing muscle, even in her cheeks. She was looking less and less like the fighter she'd once been. "He's Duke's father. You can't be a part of Duke's life while Nate raises him if you're constantly on his case for what happened between us."

"Who says Nate's raising him?" Despite the venom in her words, Julie gently eased April higher in bed, sliding a pillow beneath her shoulders. "You know he doesn't want kids."

April touched the scar on her bare scalp where they'd removed the tumor the first time. "Men say things they don't mean all the time."

"Like *I love you*?"

April had latched on to Julie's hand. "When you're lying on your deathbed, you won't be thinking about how much you made Nate suffer."

"Wanna bet?" She'd be counting the perps she sent to jail, too.

April dug her fingers into Julie's bones. "You'll be thinking about the gifts you had in life and the gifts you left behind." She tugged on Julie's arm with more strength than she'd shown in days. "You're such a pain in the butt."

Julie worked her fingers beneath April's until she clasped her hand. "You want forgiveness. I'm more about justice, like Dad."

April shook her head. "Don't say justice when you mean revenge."

In Nate's case, what was the difference?

Had Nate lied when he'd said he didn't want kids? It seemed like it.

Julie reached the bed-and-breakfast, winded. She sat on the bottom step and freed Duke from his safety restraint. "Run on the grass, little man." While she gathered enough strength to climb the steps to their room. The evening stretched out before her with too many unanswered questions, none of which were April's.

Duke ran to the thick green lawn and made a slow-motion flop onto his tummy. He tucked in his arms and rolled back and forth, giggling.

Julie's mind drifted back to April and their conversations about the Daddy Test.

"No matter what Nate answers," Julie had said. "I won't approve. He's not good enough for Duke."

"You'll see things differently once I'm gone."

"True that," Julie muttered as Duke ran across the grass. What was she supposed to make of April turning Nate away? Was it pride? Had she regretted it?

A large black truck drove slowly around the corner. The windows were down, allowing the worst music ever known to mankind— a crying baby—to reach Julie's ears. The truck slowed and pulled up to the curb in front of the bed-and-breakfast. Flynn grimaced.

Out of sympathy, Julie risked her eardrums and approached the truck. "That's some set of lungs." Julie had to utilize her own to be heard.

Flynn nodded and shouted back, "Colic."

The baby's car seat was rear facing and in the back seat.

"And now he's exhausted and won't sleep," Julie surmised. She'd been there. And Nate hadn't. A slow smile lifted her cheeks. "Have you been by the jail? Nate seems like he's good with kids." Evil. She was evil. She didn't care.

"Great idea." Flynn gave her a thumbs-up. "I need to stay away long enough for my wife to get in a good nap since I was gone most of the day." He waved and drove off.

Duke tugged on Julie's hand.

Still smiling, Julie looked down. Her smile faded. "What pretty flowers," she said with false appreciation of the yellow daffodil bouquet he offered her. "Where did you get them?"

"Those are mine." Leona stood in the bed-and-breakfast doorway, arms crossed. "Meant to be enjoyed by everyone."

Reggie materialized behind her grandmother. "But we can always plant more."

Leona rolled her eyes.

Duke turned and saw Leona. "Petty you." He hurried toward the front porch steps, holding out his bouquet.

"He wants to give you his pretty flowers." Julie followed, grabbing her backpack and dragging the stroller up the steps without folding it.

"You mean *my* pretty flowers." Leona didn't so much huff as breathe fire.

"When was the last time anyone gave you flowers, Grandmother?" Reggie wore the grin Julie was becoming familiar with, the one that said she was enjoying her grandmother's discomfort. "You should accept them."

Duke stopped a few feet from Leona and raised the bouquet. "Petty you?"

"Thank you," Leona said stiffly, taking the bent-stemmed flowers from Julie's little love. "I'll put these in water."

"Good fend." Duke hugged the elderly woman's leg with little hands that left dirt smudges on her plain green dress.

Before Leona realized she'd been sullied, Julie folded the umbrella stroller, took Duke by the hand and led him upstairs. She had to stop at the top and catch her breath. When she looked back down at Leona, she realized a miracle had occurred.

Leona stood in the foyer, smiling at the flowers.

CHAPTER NINE

"DID SOMEONE RUN over a cat?" Rutgar startled on the cot, sending his pillow to the floor and jostling his ankle enough that he howled like said feline. "What is that noise?"

A noise Nate could only describe as a caterwaul grew louder.

"I have no idea." Nate had been perusing the bulletins regarding persons wanted for questioning in the county. He returned Rutgar's pillow beneath the man's swollen ankle, and then went to the door to find out what the ruckus outside was.

Before he got there, the volume increased as Flynn came in carrying a crying baby in his arms. "Ian has colic."

"No kidding," Nate replied in his outdoor voice.

"Julie reminded me you were good with babies." Flynn handed Ian off to Nate and collapsed in Nate's chair behind the desk. He rested his forehead on the blotter. "Nobody warned me about colic. Not even my sister."

Ian's little face was scrunched and scarlet. His thatch of reddish-brown hair was sweat slicked to his head. And his entire body shook with sobs.

"I don't know what to do besides walk him." Nate imitated Molly's bouncy baby walk, the one she'd used to settle Camille when she'd been upset.

Terrance opened the door, took in the scene and then turned to go.

"Not so fast." Without stopping his rocking pace, Nate halted the widower in his tracks by shouting above the baby's cries. "You raised five kids. We need your expertise."

"You don't need me." But Terrance let the door swing shut. He still wore the wrinkled clothes he'd grabbed from home last night on their way to jail. But the lost expression he'd been wearing for months? That was clearly fading. "What you need is that baby's mother."

They were all yelling now.

"She's sleeping." Flynn lifted his head and glanced at Nate's computer screen. "Oh, man. Tell me this guy with the tattoo across his forehead isn't on the loose here."

"He's not." Nate rock-stepped to the desk

and closed the computer's window with a keystroke.

Ian's cries were interrupted by the hiccups. Nate shifted the poor little guy to his shoulder. "Terrance, please."

Terrance disappeared up the stairs to Nate's apartment. He was probably searching for a beer. Nate hoped he brought back one for everyone.

"I want to go home." Rutgar sat up too quickly. His eyes rolled back in his head and he flopped back on the cot.

Nate handed Ian back to Flynn, grabbed the med kit from behind the counter and hurried to Rutgar's side. The old man still had a pulse, but was out cold. Nate waved smelling salts beneath his nose. "When are we getting a doctor in town?"

"Soon, I hope," Flynn shouted back.

Rutgar startled, and then pressed his palms over his eyes. "I had a dream..."

Ian's cries continued to fill the jail, interspersed with hiccups.

"Someone save me!" Rutgar shouted. "It wasn't a dream."

Terrance returned carrying something that looked like one of Nate's green hand towels. A wet hand towel. He took the baby from Flynn the way you'd expect a father of five to—with sure hands. Covering his index finger with the towel, he pressed it to Ian's lips.

Ian's cries lessened, and then he began to suckle the wet towel.

Silence rang in Nate's ears. No one moved.

"Why would Ian respond to that and not breastfeed or take a pacifier?" Flynn whispered, collapsing in Nate's desk chair.

"Every baby's different," Terrance said in a muted voice fit for a late-night visit to a nursery. "That's why parents need a big arsenal of tricks."

Nate pulled out a chair behind the counter for Terrance, unable to stop himself from pointing out, "Good thing you aren't on walkabout today. We'd still be here with a screaming baby."

"You'd have managed," Terrance said gruffly, not looking up from the spent baby in his arms. "But you'd have managed badly."

Slouching in the desk chair, Flynn considered Nate. "It must be bittersweet to have missed out on two years of your son's life. The panic over colic. The joy over first smiles."

"First smiles are always gas, son," Terrance murmured.

Nate felt numb. He'd been upset last night

because he hadn't been told Duke existed. He hadn't looked at it from the heart, from the emotional moments and milestones that bound a father to a son. Duke was a great kid. The years stretched out before Nate. Duke playing on the school playground, his legs too long for his torso and his ears still too big. Duke bringing friends home to play video games and raid the refrigerator. Duke dating, graduating, choosing a college or a career path. Getting married. All without Nate.

He felt hollow. So hollow. Was this what he wanted?

It didn't matter what Nate might want or long for. Duke needed a father who knew how to navigate the waters of childhood.

"I'm having a hard time imagining you leaving anyone at the altar," Flynn said into the silence.

Terrance looked up sharply.

Nate could've done without Flynn's sudden interest in his personal life. "It's not what you think," Nate began. And then he restarted, "I mean, it's kind of what you think. I was dating Julie's sister. We were talking about what we wanted to do in the future. We both said marriage. And all of a sudden she was hugging me and saying, 'Yes.'"

"There's usually a lot of time between becoming engaged and getting married," Terrance pointed out.

"Plenty of time to stop the wedding," Flynn seconded.

Not to be outdone on rubbing it in, Rutgar added, "You had to have taken her ring shopping, rented a venue, talked to a caterer and a florist, been fitted for a tux—"

"Not to mention you had a thing for Julie." Terrance looked at Nate like he was an unexpected exhibit in the reptile section of the zoo. "That must have weighed on your mind—being engaged to the wrong sister."

"I never said I was in love with Julie." Nate's voice rose to baby-waking volume.

"I have five sons." Apparently Terrance's blue eyes had seen the truth during those brief few minutes at El Rosal. "I know that lovesick stare when I see it."

Whereas Nate had no clue what love looked like.

"Oh," Flynn said, grinning. "That's what that look at breakfast was."

"Enough." Nate cut them off with a slice of his hand. "You've all had your fun."

"And it's always fun," Rutgar said gruffly. "Until someone gets their heart broken."

They were too loud. Nate was too annoyed. Ian waved his arms and whimpered.

Terrance settled him down with a few soft-spoken words, and then he turned his attention to Nate. "You wanted to do the right thing with Julie's sister. But I'm disappointed you let it get that far."

No one but his Uncle Paul had spoken to Nate like that. Terrance's words touched Nate in a way that had him saying, "It won't happen again."

Terrance and Flynn looked at Nate as if he was a public defender who hadn't made a solid case.

This was why Nate didn't talk about his past or his feelings. It made him feel as flat as a boot-squashed bug.

"I have to make my rounds." Nate headed for the door, needing space. "Can one of you stay with Rutgar?"

"I should get Ian home." Flynn stood and took his son. "Thanks, Terrance. Hopefully he'll sleep for a couple of hours." He left with Nate's towel.

Terrance crossed his arms over his chest and leaned back in the chair. "I'll do it, but I insist you go see your son while you're out and that sweet girl you can't stop staring at."

"She was here already," Nate groused. "And I have rounds."

"Rounds." Terrance scoffed. "I can tell you what's going on in town. The widows are meeting at El Rosal, discussing floats for this year's Spring Festival. The bowling team is having coffee at Martin's. Phil's smells like they've been doing too many perms. The science experiment at school was supposed to launch a rocket that would then parachute to earth, but Brad what's his name aimed it at a tree by *accident*." This last Terrance put in air quotes. "Oh, and Eunice convinced Jessica to make horseradish spice cupcakes." He lowered his chin and his voice. "Not for the faint of heart."

"Jessica likes a man who'll try anything she makes," Rutgar said staunchly. "Like me."

Nate opened the door. "I guess I'll swing by the bakery and pick up a cupcake for you, Rutgar." Regardless of Terrance's update, Nate had to see for himself.

Nate made his rounds. He stopped to talk to Old Man Takata, who was sitting on his front porch *not* smoking a cigar—he'd quit after a health scare a few years ago. Nate swung by the Messina garage when he noticed there were more cars than usual outside—Joe was having an oil change special. Nate stopped to see Agnes, who'd texted him about needing to talk.

When he arrived, Agnes was weeding her flower beds. She pulled off her dirty gloves and dusted off her blue jeans. Her normally lively eyes were framed with concern. "I wanted to tell you personally in case you haven't heard. The town council is calling a special meeting tomorrow to announce candidates. We want to deal with this challenge to our power and your position as quickly as possible."

"I appreciate that." The black rain cloud appeared on the horizon.

She patted his shoulder. "You trust me, don't you?"

"Of course." Most of the time. It was Doris he didn't trust. She was like the Rubik's Cube he'd tried to solve once. "Can you tell me why Doris is so…"

"Unhappy?" The wind tousled her pixie-length gray bangs. "Poor Doris. She was never the easiest of girls." At what must be a confused look on Nate's face, Agnes explained, "She grew up here, like many of us." She clasped her garden gloves between her thumb and forefinger.

The black rain cloud hovering on the horizon moved closer, diluting the warmth of the spring sunshine.

"Agnes..." Nate wasn't sure he wanted to ask this question. "What were her parents like?"

Agnes closed her fingers around her gloves; her expression switched to disapproving. "They were strict. Stricter than strict."

The rain cloud floated above Harmony Valley, somewhere in the vicinity of Doris's house.

"And she was married?"

"For too long." The garden gloves were bunched in her fist now. "Maury was more closed off than her parents." Agnes leaned in and lowered her voice, as if they were at a cocktail party and at risk of being heard. "There were rumors. Like Maury controlling the finances. Some said he gave Doris cash to buy groceries and made her return with the receipt and exact change."

Nate glanced skyward. He didn't want to know anything more about Doris, about her pain or her past. She'd won her freedom from her parents and her husband. Now he understood why she considered any rule constrictive. Her vindictiveness wasn't fair, but it had little to do with Nate.

"Nate." Agnes stared up at him with the same

tender smile many Harmony Valley residents gave him, the one that made him long for a different kind of childhood. "You have nothing to worry about with this election."

Nate disagreed. He had plenty to worry about. He wanted nothing more than to belly up to the bar at El Rosal and order a tall cold beer. But he continued with his rounds, checking on some of the town's shut-ins and driving the roads to make sure no one had broken down.

Finally, after he'd circled the Lambridge Bed & Breakfast three times, he admitted that he wanted to check on Julie and Duke. Terrance would say it was because he loved Julie. Nate would've countered that it was because he was simply worried about them.

Leona opened the door before Nate had set foot on the front step. It was eerie how she watched the neighborhood. "Sheriff Nate. To what do I owe this pleasure?"

"We." Reggie muscled her way past her grandmother to the front porch. "To what do *we* owe his pleasure?"

Leona released a long-suffering sigh.

Nate stopped on the porch. "If you must know—" and who in Harmony Valley wasn't curious about business that wasn't their own?

"—I'm here to ask Julie and Duke to dinner." Might just as well admit it. If he only had a week with Duke and Julie, he wanted to help them out as much as he could.

"Nay!" Duke shouted excitedly from the second-floor landing. He wore a clean white T-shirt. His hair had been combed, revealing those Landry ears. He hurried toward the steps.

"Wait for me." Julie took Duke's hand and escorted him downstairs, glancing up occasionally to frown at Nate.

"Looks like she's given her answer," Leona said, still standing in Nate's way.

"Nothing personal, Grandmother, but you know nothing about people," Reggie said, softening the ruthless remark with a hug that was so unexpected, it widened Leona's eyes and stilled her tongue.

"Just so you know, Jules…" Nate jumped into the void with the most logical reasons they should have dinner with him. "Most places in town roll up the carpet at about four. I thought I'd make dinner at my place."

"How sweet." Reggie herded Leona into the foyer.

Recovered from the shock of Reggie's hug, Leona harrumphed. "A word of warning, Miss

Smith. I've never heard anyone say the sheriff is a good cook."

"That's because I've never cooked for anyone here." But he'd picked up a couple of steaks and potatoes at the grocery store out by the highway, and horseradish spice cupcakes for Rutgar from Martin's. "What do you say, Jules? Steak and baked potatoes? Cold beer?"

Julie's gray eyes were cool. "We'll get something at El Rosal."

"You can have El Rosal any night," Reggie said, stepping in front of Leona, who looked as if she had a different comment in mind. "It's not every night a man offers to cook for you."

Nate gave Reggie a grateful smile. "I'm cooking for Rutgar, so making extra is no trouble. You can put your feet up and Duke can run around the jail. That should wear him out enough that he'll sleep late in the morning."

Julie's eyes sparked with reluctant interest.

The key to compromise with Julie, Nate realized, was offering to help with Duke. Keeping his son occupied and wearing him out so that Julie could rest was as appealing to her as a chocolate doughnut with cream filling.

"Well," Julie said with all the enthusiasm of a cat faced with a bath. "If you burn anything, El Rosal will be our backup."

JULIE SHOULDN'T HAVE accepted Nate's invitation. Despite the day's revelation about April, he was still the enemy. But here she was, sitting in a chair in his office, feeling as cranky as a hall monitor in a school filled with free passes.

Nate should've been the cranky one. She and April had stolen two years of Duke's life from him. Instead, in between turning the steaks Nate was barbecuing in the back alley, he played hide-and-seek with Duke. April would have been ecstatic.

Julie should be happy for Duke, too. He was gaining a father. But what if this, too, was short-term? What if Nate couldn't commit to being a regular presence in Duke's life?

But what if Julie was letting her need for justice stand in the way of what was best for Duke?

April, get out of my head.

Nate lived above the jail. It was no place to raise a little boy. Not that Julie's apartment was much better. It was a one-bedroom fourth-floor unit, no playground or park nearby. But she had Mom and her backup caregiver. Nate had no family in town to help.

"Why does the boy keep hiding under my cot?" Rutgar wasn't fooling anyone with that put-upon air. The old man was loving the attention from Duke.

"Juju." Duke ran over and sprawled across her lap. He was done playing. And given her little man hadn't taken a nap today, he'd go to sleep early and sleep late, just as Nate had promised.

"I think I'm going to sleep instead of eat," Rutgar said. Almost immediately, he began to snore.

Nate had set his desk as a dinner table. He put plates loaded with food on it. "If I'd have known Rutgar wasn't going to join us, we could've eaten upstairs."

In his apartment. *No, thanks.* "This is fine." She'd set limits. She'd refused a tour of his personal space above them. She'd declined a beer.

They ate in near silence, exchanging pleasantries about the weather, their favorite football teams, mutual friends.

After cleaning his plate, Duke climbed into Julie's lap and fell asleep as quickly as Rutgar had.

"I never was one for scintillating conversation." Nate gave Julie that tight half smile. "But I've never put so many people to sleep before."

"I'm so full, I might have to join them."

That was the biggest meal she'd eaten since being shot.

"Go ahead and snooze. I found Terrance napping in that chair when I got back from afternoon rounds." Nate stacked the dishes and carried them upstairs. When he returned, he pulled his chair closer so that he sat next to her.

For several minutes, they said nothing. They might just as well have been an old married couple staring at the world from their front porch, not the open door of the local jail. April would've been happy to sit with her thoughts and the man she loved. Julie was unsettled, unsure how she felt about Nate.

"Since you've been talking about a test to determine what makes a good father," Nate said into the lull. "I've been thinking about my dad."

Julie stopped rubbing Duke's back and tried to rein in her need to interrogate. Maybe if she knew more about Nate's history, she'd understand why he'd had doubts about April and why April had backed out of the wedding at the last minute.

"My dad's the reason I chose to go into the army." Nate's words sounded as if they were being forced out past gravel. "And then into the police academy."

"Your father sounds like a good guy." So why didn't Nate talk to him anymore? Why did he look like someone had died when he talked about him?

He was slow to qualify his statement. So slow she thought he wasn't going to answer. "My dad wasn't any prize. His father wasn't any prize either." Nate stroked Duke's hair the way April used to, as if he couldn't believe he existed. "I guess on some level, I don't think I'm a prize, not as marriage or father material."

Julie did a double take, needing to make sure she was still talking to handsome, successful Nate. "Spare me the tale of your insecurities."

"Jules, I—"

"You were asked three years running to be in a calendar benefitting the widows' fund." He was that good-looking.

"But I didn't—"

"No one on the force had a bad word to say about you."

"Jules, I—"

"And you've never been shy or uncertain around women in your life. You see a woman coming and you open doors and pull out chairs and basically act like a prince." Julie was anything but a princess. She intimidated men with her bold attitude. "So don't try to excuse your behavior by blaming it on your nonexistent insecurities."

"I wasn't," he said when she stopped for breath.

Rutgar's steady snore turned into a snortfest before he settled into sleep again.

Julie let her head fall back so she could stare at the ceiling and perhaps receive divine guidance from April. Did her sister really want Nate to have a shot at full-time fatherhood?

"I realize this is hard on you." His deep, calm voice simultaneously riled and soothed. "I'm sorry."

"You should have said that to April."

"I did." Everything about him communicated his sincerity—his posture, his tone, the way he didn't squirm when she went on the attack.

Had April known how hard this would be? Had April developed the Daddy Test as punishment for Julie because she refused to forgive Nate? Or had April wanted to know the truth about Nate and known she was too weak to ever obtain the answers herself?

Uncertainty chilled her veins. Julie traced the bandage at her shoulder.

"It'll heal." Nate claimed her hand.

Her hand fit in his. The chill faded.

Uncertainty didn't fade. It increased.

His hand was strong and sure. *He* was strong and sure. "And the memories," he said. "The ones that keep you up at night. They'll fade."

The air suddenly seemed too thick. Her body too heavy. "How do you know?"

He didn't say anything. He didn't move. She glanced at him to make sure he was breathing.

Nate met her gaze, his eyes the rich color of dark chocolate. She'd always been a sucker for dark chocolate and for men with jet-black hair, broad shoulders and—

Julie had to look away and remind herself who Nate was and what he'd done.

"Some people think if you carry a gun to make a living, you should be able to handle the consequences of using it." His words drew her gaze back, like a moth to a flame. Nate half shrugged, but there was nothing casual about the movement, nothing casual about his viewpoint. "Others will tell you counseling will make it better—a psychologist, a minister, a mentor." He stared at their hands. She hadn't realized they were still joined. "I'd tell you that after taking a shot, you don't sit in limbo. You try something until you find whatever it is that makes you feel better." He shrugged again and gave her a sideways look.

Chocolate and warmth and comfort, oh, my.

Julie was afraid Nate was making her feel better. Julie didn't want to be afraid of the feelings Nate created.

"You aren't the kind of cop who lets things happen to her," Nate continued in that slow, steady cadence. "Stop being a victim. April wasn't."

He was right. April might have shed tears, but she faced every setback head-on.

"Jules." Her name on his lips. His voice. It tried to soothe. It tried to settle. And where it settled was a place deep inside her. "What did April do when things became too much for her?"

Nothing had ever been too much for April until…

Julie freed her hand from his, missing his warmth the moment she did so. "You mean when April knew she was dying?"

He nodded, without any indication her change in tone bothered him.

Julie was bothered by memories she carried like gunshot scars. Memories of April in those final months.

April's gaunt face, bleached of color. Her gray eyes listless and drained of hope. Her small hands bony and lacking flesh. The more frequent nonsensical ramblings. The rare moments of clarity. The word she'd latched onto, repeating at odd times, rising from the bed to clutch Julie's hand and whisper, "Forgive."

The past clamped on Julie's throat, cutting off air and speech. Cutting off the here and now. Cutting like a knife until Julie wanted to curl her body around Duke's and gasp for air. She missed her sister.

"Jules." Nate's hand found hers again.

She hated him for what he'd done to April. She hated that she couldn't remember her sister's healthy face. She hated herself for finding solace in his touch.

"Let it out," Nate said softly. "No scab ever healed by you picking at it in the darkness."

"She cried." Julie held herself very still, blinking back the sting in her nose and the tears that threatened to spill. "Sometimes she wanted to cry alone. Sometimes she wanted to cry on my shoulder." Being strong for April had been one of the hardest things she'd ever had to do.

"It's important to talk. It's important to have someone listen." He removed his hand from hers, reached into the bowl on his desk and withdrew a small black rock. "I know I'm the last person you want to talk to. But if the world feels like it's closing in, I'd be there for you." He pressed the stone into her palm. "And if you can't stand the sight of my face, hold on to this stone."

It was smooth and warm. The size of a large watch face with an indentation in the middle just the right size for her thumb. There were other rocks in the bowl, other stones worn smooth.

"My mother gave that to me when I was a kid." Nate stared out the front door as a car drove slowly past. "It's a worry stone. Rub it when you feel the need to find peace." He continued to stare outside. "I took it to the other side of the world with me. It helped."

He'd taken a rock to war. To killing.

Julie rubbed the smooth surface with her thumb. He'd found balance in a rock?

Could she?

The idea didn't seem as foolish as it should have been.

CHAPTER TEN

NATE CARRIED A sleeping Duke across the town square.

Julie pushed the empty stroller beside him.

Anyone driving by would think they were a family walking home after dinner or visiting friends.

Nate couldn't let himself be swayed into thinking this was normal. Duke deserved someone great to raise him. Julie deserved a man who was better than Nate. And Nate deserved...

It didn't bear thinking on.

Besides, no one drove past. No one saw them and wondered or reported their walk with the phone tree. The breeze had died down after dark, just as Julie's anger had cooled down with their conversation.

When they reached the Victorian, Julie said, "I'll take him from here."

Nate walked past her, his arms filled with a weight that wasn't a burden. "I've got him."

But for how long? April's questions were designed to make Nate look bad. His past—the one he'd never shared with April—was being dredged up for Julie's review. The whole process was painful and would continue for another week.

Reggie played doorman this time. "Welcome back. How was dinner?"

"No one complained about my cooking," Nate said, carrying Duke past her and up the stairs to bed. "I'll change his diaper." He knew enough about little ones to know they shouldn't go to bed without a dry pair of pants.

"I'll do it. You've...you've done enough." Looking nervous, Julie put the worry stone on the bedside table.

He'd talked. She'd listened. He'd held her hand. She hadn't pulled a gun on him. He'd given her that stone the same way his mother had all those years ago—as a peace offering.

Nate tried to stop himself from being satisfied that Julie hadn't thrown the rock at him, that she might actually see its value. But deep down, he wanted her to see the value in him.

The thought took him aback. What a dead end that was.

Nate turned and left them to walk away alone. He took the long route around to the sheriff's office. Couples and families were inside El Rosal. Gage and Shelby ate at a table with their daughter, Mae, in a high chair. Arturo was tending bar, laughing when his mother poked her head out of the kitchen to say something to him. Slade and his fiancée, Christina, laughed along with him.

Their closeness. Their camaraderie. Their love. It wasn't meant for him. Nate could have friendships but no one had taught him how to love. He'd dated April. They'd been a couple. But it had been a comfortable thing, like Terrance wearing Robin's slippers.

"Who's there?" Rutgar asked when Nate entered the sheriff's office.

"Just me." Nate turned on a small light on his desk and bid Terrance goodnight. "How are you feeling?"

"My ankle hurts more than my head, if that's what you mean."

Nate went into the cell and lifted the handkerchief from Rutgar's face. "How many fingers am I holding up?"

"All of them," Rutgar said, squinting before snatching the handkerchief back. "You have a fine boy. You'll make him a good father."

"Will I?" Nate glanced at the two fingers he'd waved in front of Rutgar's face.

"Don't go thinking you're special," Rutgar grumbled. "Every man who's ever been told he's going to be a father has the same doubt. You're either thinking how can I be as good of a dad as I had, or how can I be a better dad than I had. Or maybe you're pondering the worst option, which would be you thinking you shouldn't be a dad at all. Which is ridiculous."

Nate swallowed thickly. "When did you become—" a mind reader "—so wise?"

Rutgar finger-combed his beard like a prophet who was considering his words carefully. "You'd like to think it was when I hit my head today, wouldn't you?"

"That would be more comforting than thinking you'd been a fountain of wisdom all this time and I'd missed it." Nate returned to his desk, running his fingers through the smooth stones in the bowl on top. He'd given Julie the worry stone he associated with the dark thoughts of his childhood. The other stones he'd picked up here and there over the years. A stream in Colorado. A beach in South Carolina. A ruin in Mexico.

Perhaps he'd chosen the wrong career path. Perhaps he should have become a baker or a carpenter. Someone who made things that people enjoyed. Perhaps then he'd have been more comfortable with people, more at ease expressing his feelings. Instead, he'd chosen law enforcement. A field that required him to detach his emotions and compartmentalize his emotions. When faced with his first crisis on the force, a domestic violence call, he'd reacted on instinct. He'd taken all the frustrated emotions from his childhood and channeled them into positive action in a way he'd been unable to do when faced with a crisis as a kid.

Late on the night of his eighth birthday, crisis had arrived with a big bang, shaking Nate's bedroom wall.

He'd startled awake. It was cold in the house. His nose stung from it. The smart thing to do would have been to roll over and burrow beneath the covers. He had school in the morning.

But something banged against his wall again. And something whimpered in the hallway.

They didn't have animals. Mom had said it wouldn't be fair. She'd never explained why.

But there was a noise and Nate was a man. Still only eight, but a man nonetheless. Men got out of bed when they heard a noise. They checked doors and windows. He'd seen men do that on TV.

Nate crept out of bed, wishing for his gun.

Dad had taken it away when they'd returned from shooting. They'd been pulled over on the way home because Dad was speeding. He'd blamed Nate and threatened the whole time to blister his butt. Only when they'd gotten home, Mr. Chilton from next door had been talking to Mom in the front yard. Nate had run inside and begun to do his Sunday chores, dusting and cleaning toilets. Dad had put away the guns, settled on the couch and drunk more beer. Thankfully, nothing more was said about whuppings.

The wall shook once more. Nate got up and opened the bedroom door a crack.

At the end of the hall, Dad had his hands around Mom's throat, her head against the wall. Blood trickled down one side of Mom's face. Her lip was purple and puffy. Dad had hit Mom before, but nothing like this.

Both his parents focused in his direction. Dad's stare had a dangerous gleam; Mom's widened with horror.

Nate wanted to run. But they stood between him and the front door.

What to do? What to do?

Nate's body tingled with fear.

Dad released Mom and charged toward him.

Nate ran for the master bedroom. He slammed the door and punched the lock.

Dad crashed into it a moment later. "I owe you, boy!" The door handle shook.

He owed him a whupping. Nate's legs shook so hard, he almost collapsed. But he didn't and he grabbed the cordless phone, ran into the bathroom and locked himself in. Then he climbed into the bathtub and dialed 911.

"My dad is trying to kill my mom," Nate said breathlessly when the operator came on the line.

The memory of the bullet whizzing by Nate's head returned. He yelped. "And my dad is trying to kill me!" He huddled in the bathtub, shaking.

By the time the police arrived, Dad had kicked in the bedroom door and was working on breaking down the bathroom door. Nate heard the police tell Dad to freeze. He heard Dad refuse. He heard the slap of bodies and the grunts of a fight. And then the click of handcuffs. No sound had ever rung sweeter in his ears. A policeman told him it was safe to come outside. Nate was shaking so hard he couldn't unlock the door. Some man he was. Mom had hugged him tight and Molly hadn't made fun of his tears.

Later, after a trip to the police station, after

a trip to the hospital for Mom, after being
taken to a safe house in another county, and
after weeks of Mom going through therapy,
she'd pressed the worry stone into Nate's palm.
"Keep this under your pillow. When you can't
sleep at night, rub this stone and know that you
saved my life and I love you for it."

Had she known he'd been feeling guilty for
making that call and sending his father to jail?
Or had she known he'd need it even more in
the years to come?

"I'll take my dinner now," Rutgar said meekly.

"Sure." Still, it took Nate a few more minutes to move.

He'd given Julie his rock. She had no idea
what it meant to him.

JULIE KNEW SHE was in a dream.

It didn't matter.

She couldn't move. Shadowy shapes stalked
her, carrying guns.

She couldn't move. But she carried a weapon.

She couldn't move. But she was able to fire.
To shoot and shoot and shoot until her fingers
cramped and her shoulder ached and her throat
cracked from screaming.

"Stop that." Bony fingers gripped her right
shoulder above her stitches.

Julie grabbed the arm attached to those fingers, twisted and pulled. Fingers fell away. Pain fell away. A body fell on top of her.

A dead body?

This wasn't how it had happened.

"Miss Smith," Leona said in a choked voice. "Miss. Smith."

Light from the bed-and-breakfast hallway illuminated the shadowy figure sprawled across Julie. Leona wore a green velour robe over a white flannel gown. Her streaky gray hair was looped as loosely as a used Brillo pad. Julie's arm was around her thin neck cutting off her air supply.

Julie gasped and released her. "What are you doing in here?" It was better than asking herself what she'd been doing.

Leona scrambled off the bed and to her feet, picking up the white terry slippers that had dropped to the floor during their struggle. "You were crying for help."

Julie sat up, clutching the neck of the Raiders football jersey she wore as a nightgown. "I wasn't... Was I?" She had been. Her throat was raw from it. She rolled over to check on Duke. He slept peacefully within the confines of his pillow wall, worn out by his big day.

"I think the answer to your question is obvious." Leona had the slippers on and was straightening her robe. "It isn't safe for the boy here."

She hadn't added, "With you." But Julie knew she should have.

"What's going on?" Reggie clung to the door frame. "I heard shouts."

"I…" Julie swallowed. She couldn't argue. And it was a relief, really, to be given a reason to leave town. She wouldn't have to stay the week Nate wanted. She wouldn't have to soften her stance on him. But she also wouldn't have a signature on those custody papers. "I'm leaving in the morning."

"She had a nightmare," Leona said, pushing her granddaughter to the hallway. "Go back to bed." She waited until Reggie retreated before turning in the doorway. "I lost a little boy once." The coldness in Leona's sharp features turned as desolate as a snowy peak in the Sierras. "Children are fragile. Be careful with him." And then she closed the door behind her.

Fear coursed through Julie's body. Doubts bubbled up. Would it be better for Duke to be in Nate's care? It was selfish to say no.

She had to beat the nightmares. Julie picked up the rock Nate had given her. It was cool and smooth in her palm. It was calming. She could almost hear his voice saying everything would be all right, almost feel his fingers cradling hers.

It didn't matter. Julie didn't sleep the rest of the night.

CHAPTER ELEVEN

THERE WAS NOTHING like the smell of coffee in the morning when you hadn't slept the night before. Add in the aroma of fresh-baked sugary things, and Julie could believe she was capable of caring for her nephew again.

It was barely seven in the morning. There'd been no sign of Nate at El Rosal as she'd pushed the stroller past. She was glad. He'd take one look at her face and he'd know something bad had happened.

Julie wrestled open the door to Martin's Bakery and wheeled the stroller inside, breathing deeply. Coffee and sugar. Two of her favorite things.

Not only did it smell like heaven, Martin's Bakery looked charming. There were several old wooden tables and chairs in the bakery, most of them mismatched. Framed yellowed photos on the wall displayed who Julie presumed were previous generations of Martins.

"Hey. Don't scare the customers." A woman

wearing an apron and a cheerful smile behind the register snapped her fingers. But she wasn't snapping at Julie.

Julie hadn't realized all eyes had turned her way, or that all conversation had stopped. She recognized the town councilwomen at a table near the counter. A woman with purplish-gray hair sat on the bench seat in the window, pinning together quilt squares. The toddler at her feet was one of the boys they'd met at the playground. At a table against the wall, a scarecrow of a man played checkers with an elderly Asian man with a walker. In the back corner, Nate, Rutgar and Terrance watched her, coffee cups midair.

Nate's gaze was cautious. His smile almost nonexistent. Busted. He knew she'd had a bad night. She looked like she'd been hung on a flagpole during a weeklong hurricane.

Those in the bakery knew whose son Duke was. They looked back and forth from Julie to Nate.

She gave them her cop smile. Polite. Unflappable. Mirthless. Combined with the scary way she looked, they should all give her a wide berth. And space was what she needed given her visit to Harmony Valley so far could be labeled as one big fail after another.

"Peeps. Return to your regularly scheduled lives." When customers began to converse again, the barista waved Julie toward the display cases. "Sugar fix? Coffee fix?"

"Let's start with the necessities. Coffee. Large and black." Julie eyed the sugary options and wishing they weren't so large and each didn't hold so many calories.

"Want dat." Duke pointed to a large muffin closest to him and imbibed his words with the threat of a toddler tantrum. "Dat. Dat. Dat."

Julie read the flavor card. "Horseradish spice muffin?" It didn't sound kid friendly, which meant it wouldn't rid her nephew of the morning grumps.

"It's kind of like—" the blonde flashed an infectious smile "—carrot cake. Without the carrots."

That didn't sound bad. "We'll take one of those and a bear claw."

"Milk for the little guy?"

"Yes." Julie set Duke's sippy cup on the counter.

"Yoo-hoo!" The elderly woman with short purplish-gray hair waved to them. Her hot-pink tracksuit was more eye-opening than the mug of hot coffee the barista was pouring. Her window seat was flanked on either side with smaller tables. The toddler Julie had recognized sat near her neon green sneakers, playing with blocks. "Join us over here. The boys can play while you drink your coffee."

"Fend." Duke strained at his seat belt at the sight of the other boy.

"I accept." Julie unbuckled him, relieved she had an excuse not to sit with Nate. "That's sweet."

"Hi, fend." Duke ran to the toys and got to his knees, scooting himself closer to the action with his hands.

"First time here, the coffee is on me." The blonde loaded their order on a tray. "I'm Tracy. And they've been wondering about you." She gestured to the room at large.

"Great." Julie paid for the pastries and joined the woman at the window seat, latching onto her coffee when she'd sat down. Caffeine took precedence over sugar.

"Don't be shy with Eunice," Tracy said. "And we have free Wi-Fi. You can read our blog."

"Horseradish Is the New Superfood." Eunice set her reading glasses on top of her red and yellow quilt squares in the window seat. And then she fluffed her purplish-gray bangs.

"That's the title of the blog today. It's about horseradish. It grows on Parish Hill."

"On my property," Rutgar said in a too-loud, too-grumbly voice.

Nate almost grinned with both sides of his face. How odd it must be to live like that— anchoring half his smile as if he didn't deserve a full measure of happiness.

"Horseradish makes the bakery unique." Tracy might work the counter, but she ruled the room with a knowing glance, a friendly smile and—in Rutgar's case—a horseradish spice muffin. "No matter where we find it. Or who brings it to us."

"Yes...well... Horseradish grows wild along the road, too." Eunice blushed and blinked at Julie the way people do when they've been caught with their hand in the horseradish patch. "Local vegetation aside, Gregory is a handful. I hardly have a minute of peace until naptime."

Duke and Gregory stacked blocks between them. So good-natured. So peaceful. Julie didn't trust it to last.

Julie angled her body to Eunice's, putting the colorful old woman—and only the colorful old woman—in her line of sight. "Is he your grandchild?"

"Godchild. He's Jessica's. She owns the bakery." Eunice opened her violet-brown eyes wide and then blinked in big swoops of mascara-dredged eyelashes. "I thought it was such an honor until the poopy pants got... well...poopier."

"We all get out of diapers someday," Julie said, mesmerized by the wide-eyed blinking.

Eunice smiled and fingered the cotton fabric of her quilt squares. "I shouldn't complain. I never had a chance to be a mother. But no matter what I do, his parents are always his favorite."

Julie's stomach churned at the truth of Eunice's statement. She'd always be Juju to Duke. She could never take away the mommy title from April. If Nate signed the custody papers, she'd be taking away his parental rights. The thought didn't settle her stomach. It should have. Hadn't that been the point in coming here? In taking the time off? And to appease her mom.

Her gaze drifted to Nate once more. To the shoulders that could bear many burdens and the steady gaze that never seemed to judge. How would he react to know she'd clutched his worry stone all night long? Inexplicably, having Nate near her now eased the need to hold the worry stone in her hand.

But that was a false sense of security. Nate wasn't the type to stick by anyone through thick and thin. And she needed more than a rock or a half smile to beat the nightmares. And she had to beat them. Or she had to give Duke up. To Nate.

Her stomach roiled again.

Duke stopped playing with blocks and stood, peering at the plates on the table. He reached for the bear claw.

"Hey, little man." Julie rearranged the plates so his muffin was within reach. "This is yours."

"Not dat." Duke made a face, apparently not as sold on horseradish as he'd been earlier. He pointed at Julie's bear claw. "Want dat."

Eunice gasped dramatically. "You don't want your horseradish spice muffin? That's based on my mother's recipe. It's very good. If you don't want it, I'll take it." She reached for the plate with a delicate hand, an age-old ploy designed to get Duke to defend his treat.

Julie respected the effort even as Duke let the elderly woman take possession of the muffin.

"That didn't work out the way I'd planned."
Eunice returned the muffin to the plate.

Nate appeared next to Duke in his blue jeans
and blue checked shirt, which seemed to be his
sheriff uniform. "Instead of calling it the ter-
rible twos, they should have called it the fickle
twos." He sat on the floor, folding his long
legs and eliciting sighs of appreciation from
the bakery audience. "I have cupcake pops."
He handed each boy a stick with a small round
cupcake on it. "Later, we'll stop by El Rosal
for some bacon."

"I should kick you out for that," Tracy said
from behind the counter. "This is the home
of carbs."

"Ba-con," Duke crooned and leaned his
head briefly against Nate's arm, the picture
of a strong father-son bond Julie had been certain couldn't possibly exist.

"Real men eat meat and protein for breakfast," Nate said to Julie with a straight face.

Eunice fluffed her hair and fluttered her
eyelashes. "I've always appreciated a man with
an appetite."

"I suppose real men also cut green vegeta-
bles," Julie said, finding it easier to point out
Nate's weaknesses than admit her own. "Although I didn't see you cooking any last night."

"We had a vegetable." Nate looked offended, but the effect was ruined by the twitch of a smile at his cheek.

Julie had to fight a smile of her own. "Potatoes are starch. And starch goes directly to a woman's thighs."

"I wouldn't know," Nate said primly, giving Duke a playful poke in the belly. "Not being a woman."

Laughter filled the bakery, but it couldn't fill the shadowy places in Julie's heart.

"Hey. Fend." Duke leaned into Gregory's space. "Pay? Park?" And then he turned big soulful eyes to Nate. "Nay? Pay? Park?"

He'd asked Nate, not Julie. She slumped and hid her face in her coffee cup.

"You want to go play at the park?" Nate grinned, nothing half about it. The two sides of his face matched in upturned delight.

Julie almost fell over. That full grin. She wasn't sure she'd ever seen it before. It upped him from handsome to gorgeous. He should smile like that all the time.

Strike that. If he smiled like that all the time, he'd be irresistible. To women. To...to...to her.

Deep inside Julie's chest something shifted, something fit. And it fit as easily as her thumb on Nate's worry stone. She slurped her coffee and looked away, refusing to name or acknowledge or think about what that something was.

But that grin. It made her wonder. What made Nate so reserved? April couldn't have known or she wouldn't have created the Daddy Test, which was designed to make Nate reveal his past. So far, all Julie had learned was that Nate and his father didn't get along.

"The park," Eunice said wistfully. "I love how tired Gregory gets after going to the park."

Gregory stood on sturdy jeans-clad legs. "I go park." He was a little older than Duke and had the three-word sentences down.

Julie felt a twinge of Mom Jealousy. She wished Duke would leap to his feet and repeat Gregory's sentence.

Duke picked his nose.

Leaning over to wipe the evidence away with a napkin, Julie wished she wasn't so competitive.

"I'll take them to the town square." Nate's grin became almost angelic as Duke hugged him. "Terrance can come, too. That way you and Eunice can finish your coffee."

Julie stared into her half-empty coffee mug, feeling the cold nip of loneliness. Nate was blossoming with Duke, while she was withering away inside.

"How sweet of the sheriff." Eunice leaned

toward Julie, but didn't lower her voice. "That's the sign of a keeper."

"I'm not fishing," Julie said quickly, unable to look at Nate for fear he'd still look full-on handsome.

Another wave of laughter filled the room. Julie was beginning to see the appeal of El Rosal. Conversations weren't as public there.

"Somebody didn't sleep well last night," Nate said while Eunice went to get Gregory's stroller and sweatshirt from the back, and the boys jumped around enthusiastically. "And I don't mean Duke."

"I don't sleep well in strange beds," Julie lied and immediately felt bad for doing so. "We have to go home today." Panic managed to creep into her voice.

Nate's smile vanished as he picked up on her angst. He angled closer, lowering his voice. "Why?"

"Maybe she's homesick?" someone hypothesized.

"Maybe Leona raised her prices again?" someone else suggested.

"She got kicked out of Leona's," Agnes said, unabashedly eavesdropping from a few tables away.

"No, I...I have an evaluation today. They

moved it up. I can't miss it." Julie tried to lie, but the universe was apparently done with her fibbing. She flinched when her phone chirped with a message, one that took away her alibi, as it turned out. She tucked the cell into her pocket. "My eval was just postponed until next week."

"Therefore, you need a place to stay." Nate's face was so near her own that Julie felt his warm breath on her cheek. "My offer still stands. Rutgar's going home today. I'll have an extra bed. I'll even let you choose—jail cell or my apartment."

Duke would love sleeping in jail. Julie's imagination went a little wild as she pictured Duke growing up here and living with Nate. Her nephew's sleepovers would be the most popular in town. What little boy wouldn't want to play cops and robbers with a real jail cell? Julie couldn't compete with that.

Eunice bumped Gregory's stroller against the table leg. "I love a man who isn't afraid to proposition a woman in front of others."

"I should go home." Julie could get her mother to sleep over until the nightmares faded. If they persisted, she'd…she'd…

"You made a promise." Nate brushed a lock of hair from her forehead.

"You've made promises you didn't keep," Julie countered, breathless from his touch, wishing she felt as righteous as she had when she'd arrived in town.

Doris burst into the bakery, her gaze falling on Julie. "Thank heavens I caught you. I heard you were homeless. I insist you stay with me. Free of charge."

"Don't do that to yourself, Jules." Nate pulled back, staring Doris down. "Even if I locked you in my jail cell, you'd be happier."

"Sheriff, that's just one reason why you are completely unfit to serve." Doris didn't waddle so much as chop her steps. She parked herself next to Julie and put her hands on her Chihuahua-covered hips. She wore a red tunic with black Chihuahua heads dotted across it.

Until she'd met Doris, Julie had never realized how big Chihuahua fashion really was.

"The air in this place suddenly turned stale." Rutgar worked his way to Nate's side on his crutches, looking clear-eyed and steady. He spared Doris a disdainful glance. "Nate, give these women a break and take those boys for a walk."

Nate's gaze pinned Julie, trying to trap her to the promise she'd made to stay. Her only

hope was that he'd fail the Daddy Test. Today.
If only she knew exactly what was pass or fail.

"I'll stay one more night," Julie allowed.
"With Doris." She'd put Duke in a bedroom
and sleep on the couch.

"Ha!" Doris smirked at everyone in the bakery, but mostly at Nate.

Too quickly, both toddlers were being taken
away. Julie sat in the window seat and watched
Duke leave her. Her arms felt empty, the warm
coffee mug cradled in her hands a poor replacement for a warm, loving boy.

"I know how you feel." Eunice picked up
her glasses and quilt squares. "Arms empty.
Alone." She patted Julie's thigh, surprising her
with her perceptiveness. And then she added,
"I know how you feel because I'm an old maid,
too."

"I'm not a baby whisperer," Terrance said as
he and Nate pushed strollers toward the town
square. He'd shaved today and his gray polo
shirt looked to have been ironed. "Nor do I
want to be the town's backup babysitter, much
as I like these young gentlemen."

"Everybody's good at something." Nate's
reply was half-hearted. Concern for Julie

gnawed at his insides. He'd hated to leave her at the bakery.

She looked like death. She wanted to leave Harmony Valley? She'd be asleep at the wheel long before she reached Santa Rosa. If he hadn't had an audience, he'd have taken her off to jail and locked her up so she could sleep.

"What's Julie good at?" Terrance asked.

"Righting wrongs." Although she couldn't seem to right herself.

"Ba-con," Duke crooned as they passed El Rosal's dining patio, eliciting an echoing sentiment from Gregory.

"Once we play tag in the park," Nate reassured him, pausing only to order two coffees and an order of bacon for their return trip. "You didn't go on walkabout last night, did you, Terrance?" After seeing Julie to the bed-and-breakfast, Nate had stayed at the jail, watching over Rutgar instead of making his rounds.

"I was tucked in my bed like a good boy." Terrance sounded as annoyed as Doris often was.

They crossed the street onto the grass in the town square. The lone oak tree stood tall in the middle. In a few weeks, the Spring Festival would be held here. Nate wondered if he'd still be sheriff. His chest constricted. He'd become more attached to the town than he'd realized.

"Admit it." Nate turned his attention back to Terrance. "You *knew* I wouldn't be making late-night rounds last night."

"Or your early-morning run this morning," Terrance said with mock sadness, mischief in his eyes. "How did you get to know me so well?"

"I think you might have been stalking me." Nate allowed a half grin. "No one else claimed to have seen your pajama strolls."

"Enough." Terrance rolled his eyes. "You should be anxious about the meeting tonight. Doris will do anything to make you unemployed."

Nate gazed down on Duke's dark unruly hair, at the ears so like his own. He was worried, yes. But there were other more pressing things to be worried about.

"You're agonizing over Julie's health." Terrance sat on the wrought iron bench beneath the oak tree. "You should be. She looks as if your son kept her up all night."

Nate knew that wasn't true. Duke looked rested and ready for action. It was the shooting. He'd looked the event up on the internet last night. Details had been slim. A domestic violence case, which wouldn't be unusual, except the abuser had been a woman and she'd locked herself in her house with two children for hours, threatening to kill them.

Terrance looked at Nate as if he was a public defender who hadn't made a solid case against a thief caught red-handed. "That woman needs your help."

"She doesn't want it."

"She would if you charmed her a little." The old man's expression turned more sympathetic. "You have no moves. Did your father never teach you how to woo a woman?"

"No." He'd taught Nate other life lessons. "No wooing."

"Woo-woo!" Duke turned the word into a train whistle. "Woo-woo!"

"Woo-woo!" Gregory echoed. The two boys shared the same thick dark hair, but Gregory had the sturdy frame of a future football player.

The two boys giggled and did the train whistle until Nate released them from their strollers and showed them how to fly like an airplane, arms outstretched, mouths making airplane sounds.

The boys circled the tree gleefully, negating the need to play tag.

Nate sat next to Terrance on the wrought iron bench. "Why did you want to be a father?"

"Because I loved Robin so much I wanted the best of both of us." Terrance was only on the serious topic for a moment, before returning the conversation back to Julie. "If your father didn't tell you how to get a girl, I will. You have to treat a woman right. Flowers. Food. Fun." He gestured toward the boys. "The fun is the important part."

Nate shook his head. Growing up, there hadn't been much laughter in his house.

"You have to make Julie laugh," Terrance went on. "She looks like she could use some laughter." He gave Nate a quick once-over. "Now, I know you're not big on words or jokes, but that smile you gave her back at the bakery was a good start."

That smile. It had burst out of Nate like a firecracker. That's what Duke did to him. He reached inside Nate with his innocence and his trusting nature and he found things Nate had buried deep.

Logically, Nate knew there was no harm in smiles. Not now. Not like there'd been when he was a child and showing any kind of happiness around his father had been a risk. But the way he displayed emotion was as deeply entrenched inside him as his early memories of what a father was.

Oblivious to Nate's train of thought, Terrance continued reciting his mantra of how to be a man. "You have to enjoy silences together and plan for a future."

"And have kids." Might just as well get that out in the open. It seemed like Terrance was leading up to that.

"Don't roll your eyes." Terrance gave Nate's shoulder a gentle backhanded swipe with his hand. "You could have this." He pointed at Duke. "Every day. Doesn't looking at your son fill your heart with joy?"

Nate held his tongue.

Terrance lowered his salt-and-pepper eyebrows. "And I thought my youngest son was stubborn." He crossed his arms and increased the stern tone of his lecture. "Start with dinner. Maybe a little romantic music. Some impromptu dancing."

Nate could've argued away his attraction to Julie, but what was the point? Terrance had already called him on it yesterday. "I made dinner for Julie last night."

"And? What did you do wrong? When she came in this morning she looked at you as if you'd tried to steal second base."

"She would've broken my nose if I'd tried to steal any base." Of that, he was certain. "And we had chaperones. Duke was there. And Rutgar." Snoring. "Julie would be shocked to realize I was interested in any bases."

"Do you think love appears out of thin air without any work?" Terrance shook his head. "Why, if Robin were alive we'd be laughing about this."

Nate bit back a retort, because it was the first time he'd heard Terrance speak of his wife in such positive terms since she'd died.

The old man's gaze shifted to the tree-lined horizon. "We were friends first, you see. And I very foolishly waited for her to realize we could be more than that. Wasted time, that's what it was." His voice drifted away like a wisp of cloud on a windy day.

The boys slowed down, airplane motors stalling.

If Nate didn't do something, things in the park would drift toward unhappiness. "How do you know if it's…"

Terrance pulled himself out of his reverie. "How do you know if it's love?"

Nate nodded.

"There are signals. You smile more. She smiles more. There are tender touches and long

gazes. And then…somebody steals a base."
Terrance was on a roll.

Nate had held Julie's hand last night after
dinner. She'd only allowed him to do so because he'd broached the subject of the torment
she'd been feeling from the shooting. "Well, it
can't be that." That being the *l* word.

"Love grows. It isn't just not there one day
and there the next."

"Love isn't going to grow. Julie's grieving
over her sister and dealing with the fallout
from a situation at work." Nate stood, drawing the attention of the toddlers. He raised his
hands to the claw position at his shoulders and
growled at the boys. "I'm gonna get you!" That
was Camille's favorite game, being chased by
her uncle.

The boys squealed and circled the tree as
Nate followed with slow, stilted steps. They
climbed onto the bench and into Terrance's
lap, wrapping their arms around him like love
nooses.

"There's no perfect time to fall in love."
Terrance reveled in being caught. He gathered them close and blew raspberries on each
cheek, increasing their giggles tenfold. "I don't
care if your father never taught you anything
about women." The older man had to raise his

voice to be heard over the glee. "This is worth all the awkward moments of getting to know a woman."

There was no harm in sweeping one boy in each arm. No harm in laughing along with their chortled shouts of joy. There was no harm in living in the moment.

As long as Nate remembered that moments like this didn't last.

IT FELT ODD not to have Duke in her arms, not pushing him in his stroller.

Could this be my life soon?

Julie didn't want to think about it.

"Juju!" Duke shouted from Nate's arms as they crossed the street toward her.

Nate pushed the stroller and carried her nephew. She envied his stamina.

And then Duke looked at Nate with complete adoration. "Ba-con!"

Nate smiled back. No half measure there, although it wasn't the showstopper from the bakery.

With the same dark hair color and broad grins, no one could mistake them for anything but father and son. No one could look at the pair and think they didn't belong together. No one could feel the warmth of their smiles and not want to be in their happy circle. Even Julie felt its magnetic pull.

Nate glanced up. Their gazes connected. For a moment, it was as if she'd never seen his tight half smile. For a moment, she never wanted to see it again. This was Nate. Openly happy and sharing that happiness with her.

Her breath caught. She smiled back. She smiled as if she and Nate exchanged cheerful salutations every morning over coffee.

And then the power of Nate's grin caught and held her.

Unsteady, she had to hold on to the railing around El Rosal's dining patio.

He was… She felt… This couldn't be…

That smile. Nate was handsome. Obviously, she knew that. She knew he was intelligent and had a good sense of humor. She admired his approach to law enforcement and his shooting skill. If she was seeing him for the first time… If they'd just met… She might have considered dating him.

Her butt sagged against the railing. She stared at the toes of her sneakers.

Date Nate?

She couldn't… He wasn't… He'd left April in a lurch. She couldn't look at him and see…

A man she might consider a future with. A man she could lean on and lean into.

She snuck a glance at Nate again from mere feet away. Broad shoulders. Patient demeanor. A steady presence.

Her heart gave a pounding vote of confidence.

Julie demanded a recount, forcing her knees to lock and her legs to hold. She would not make the same mistake April had. She stood tall and smiled at Duke, ignoring Nate completely. "Hey, little man. Are you ready to go?"

"No." Grumpy morning Duke was back after having been spoiled by his father. "Want ba-con."

"No." She had to go. There would soon be toddler tears because Julie couldn't sit across from Nate feeling an attraction for him. She needed breathing room or someone to shake some sense into her.

"Juju." Her nephew's tone was a reprimand.

Arturo set a plate of bacon on a table nearby along with two mugs of coffee and received a glare from Julie for his efforts. Didn't faze him. He smiled.

"I'll take Gregory back to the bakery." Terrance strolled past.

She hadn't noticed him beside Nate. She'd

only seen Nate. She was a cop. She was supposed to see everything. Julie traced the edge
of her shoulder's bandage.

"That'll leave you three some time together,"
Terrance said in falsely innocent matchmaking
tones that did nothing to settle Julie's nerves.

Time together? As if they were family? As
if Nate hadn't broken April's heart? As if he
couldn't break hers?

Julie dragged in a breath and snuck a glance
at Nate.

The tight half grin was back. It filled her
with relief.

"You can ask me another question on the
Daddy Test." Nate didn't move inside the dining patio. He waited on the sidewalk for her
to make a decision.

Stay or go?

There were too many decisions for her tired
brain to deal with. And that was it, wasn't it?
She was tired. That's why she was looking at
Nate as if seeing him for the first time. Her
exhaustion was coloring her world. She didn't
want to date Nate.

Julie glanced to the corner patio table where
the mayor sat. He had a wiry frame beneath
a red tie-dyed sweatshirt. He smiled at her,
creating a network of wrinkles across every

inch of his face. He was datable…in a take-a-grandfather-to-coffee-as-a-nice-gesture kind of way.

Now she looked at a man objectively? Julie huffed and pulled her gaze away. There had to be someone else at El Rosal she found attractive. Where was Arturo?

"Come on." Nate left the stroller on the sidewalk and took her left hand.

And Julie let herself be led. She let herself take a seat across from him. She let herself look at him. At Nate. She let herself feel a longing she hadn't known existed. It confounded her, this longing. It muted her, this longing. It made her feel feminine and fragile and nothing like the loud brash cop she knew herself to be.

Two days ago, life had seemed so simple. Get Nate's signature and get out of town. He'd know he was in a backup position to care for Duke if anything happened to Julie, but he wouldn't want custody. She hadn't planned on him showing an interest in Duke. She hadn't planned on this feeling of attraction. Her awareness of Nate as a man energized. It made her heart thud in her chest. It made her feel like she was dancing on the ledge between happiness and heartbreak.

"Jules," Nate said softly.

"What?" She blinked at him the way Eunice had blinked at her earlier.

"The test?"

Oh, right, the test. She'd been staring at Nate like a lovesick teenager. Julie found the small notebook in her backpack, opened it to the appropriate page and stared at April's words, which blurred, but then came into sharp focus. "A good dad is willing to make sacrifices for those he loves. Give an example of how your father sacrificed for you. Then give an example of a time you sacrificed for someone else."

Nate stared into his coffee cup for so long Duke had time to eat one whole piece of bacon.

He lifted his gaze to Julie's. There was pain in the slant to his eyes and uncertainty in the way his fingers roamed his mug.

Last night he'd said he didn't talk to his father anymore. She'd been so lost in the revelation that April had cancelled the wedding that she hadn't registered its significance. "Every question in the test is about your father."

His jaw shifted to the side and he gave a curt nod.

She wouldn't feel sorry for him. She locked her fingers around her mug.

Nate ran a hand through his hair, over his

face, under his chin. "My dad worked long hours so my mom could stay at home." Was that his voice? It sounded so rough, so dark, so pained.

"It was nice that he helped your mom stay at home."

Nate's lips pressed together. He glanced at Duke, who was busy eating bacon. The slant on his eyes changed, softening to sadness. But it wasn't the pity-me kind of sad. It was the outside-looking-in and. The resigned-to-loneliness sad. The never-have-that sad.

Julie's heart panged and she wished April had never come up with the Daddy Test.

Finally, Nate looked over at her, but the sadness was gone. "I'm assuming you want an honest answer."

Despite being curious, she wanted to say no. She'd heard enough heartrending tales while on patrol that she was sure she'd regret hearing Nate's. She nodded her head anyway.

"There was nothing nice about my dad. He was manipulative and abusive." Nate's dark gaze flared with anger, his voice with injustice. "Letting Mom out of the house would have meant she had a chance at a life of her own, that she'd realize what a rotten home life she had, that she'd find happiness."

Nate had no visible scars. But his voice. It told of deeper pain. It told of raw and open wounds. It made Julie's nightmares seem trivial by comparison.

Nate cleared his throat and continued, no less angry. "I suppose the one thing my father did that was a sacrifice was when the police arrested him, he pled guilty." Nate's hard gaze banked across the street. "Or maybe he thought by pleading guilty he'd save himself time in county lockup and get out that much quicker."

"Is that why you didn't want to have kids? Because children of abuse are more likely to abuse their own spouses and children?" Julie resisted the urge to drag Duke's high chair closer.

"I could never do the kind of things he did to us." He cloaked his anger, locking it behind that tight half smile. The veneer was back in place. "You and April had happy holidays. You played soccer and joined clubs. You had freedom and fun." His gaze drifted back to Duke. "When you think of your childhood, what do you remember?"

That was easy. April. She remembered April. And then came other memories. "Family traditions, like baking cookies at the holidays, road trips to my grandparents' house or playing poker with my dad when we went camping." There was more—holding April as a baby and rocking her to sleep, decorating Christmas trees, staying in her pajamas all day on New Year's. But Julie didn't want to rub her normal upbringing into his scars.

"When I think of my childhood, my stomach turns. The memories...are hard." He looked across the street once more. "That's why I refused to imagine myself as a dad."

"But now you have no choice." The words fell from her lips before she realized what she was saying—that Nate had a right to parent, a right to a say in how Duke was raised, first dibs on custody.

"But now there's the Daddy Test." Nate stood. "I'll be right back." He walked across the street, cautious but confident.

"Nay!" Duke yelled in a demanding tone, but Nate kept going.

A sedan backed up and drove away, revealing a large cardboard box on the sidewalk. Nate circled the box. And then he bent to open it.

"No." Julie hadn't realized she'd stood and shielded Duke with her body.

"Juju." Duke pushed at her injured shoulder.

She flinched backward. How did the boy always find her tender spot?

Nate carried the box back to them. "It's kittens."

Julie sat with a bone-jarring thud. "I thought it was something bad."

"You've been working in the big city too long." Nate set the box at his feet. "It wasn't ticking. It was mewing." He took out his cell phone and called someone named Felix, telling him about the kittens.

He'd watched the street. He'd seen something wasn't right. She hadn't seen anything.

Exhaustion. She blamed exhaustion.

The kittens were crying, a muted sound.

"What dat?" Duke leaned over to peer at the box.

Nate plucked Duke from his seat, set him in his lap and then gently picked up a small fluff of fur. It was orange and white, its eyes still closed. "This is a kitten. A baby cat. Do you know how you have to be with babies? You have to be gentle." Nate cradled the kitten to Duke's chest. "Pet it gently so it doesn't break."

Duke made lovey noises, touching the kitten with his hands and snuggling it with his face.

Julie was struck again by the rightness of the pair, by the vast emptiness in her chest.

"You wanted to know about a time when I sacrificed for someone else?" The breeze ruffled Nate's black hair, but he was otherwise composed. "After the wedding, I left the force because I thought it'd be easier on you if I was gone."

And just like that, she was angry with Nate all over again. Blood rushed in her ears and filled all her empty places. He considered running away after behaving poorly a sacrifice? "You left because you were embarrassed."

Nate shook his head. "Our friends would've had to pick sides. You would've had to be civil to me or look like a fool in front of the department."

He was wrong. Annoyingly wrong. She leaned in and lowered her voice. "You think I couldn't be civil?"

"Juju, shhh." Duke put his finger to his lips. "No mad words."

Nate arched a brow. He had no need to say a word.

Julie gnashed her teeth. She'd proved his point.

CHAPTER TWELVE

"WHERE HAVE YOU BEEN?" Doris stood guard on the top porch step of the bed-and-breakfast with a well-dressed elderly woman when Julie approached. "I got a coffee refill at Martin's and you were gone."

Julie's already-slow stroller pace slowed to snail speed. Birds sang in the big pine tree by the driveway, happy for the spring breeze and the warm sunshine. They sang despite Doris and her vinegary attitude. Despite threats from cats and hawks.

"Birdy." Duke angled his face up until he met Julie's gaze. He grinned.

As long as he was fed and rested, Duke smiled at everyone. Julie didn't feel like smiling. How dare Nate say he'd left the force because of her. How dare he imply she couldn't work with him and conduct herself with dignity. She didn't feel like smiling, but she lifted her lips toward Doris anyway, waiting to answer until she was closer.

Julie reached the bed-and-breakfast porch steps, her hands shaking so hard it took her three tries to release Duke from the stroller. *Darn you, Nate.* "We went to El Rosal."

"We? We?" At Julie's nod, Doris sharpened her tone. "As in you and the boy? Or you and the enemy?" Doris's attitude was the caustic kind that earned drivers speeding tickets, not warnings. "Leona serves coffee and breakfast here, you know."

Speaking of the devil, Leona opened the door and stared down at them all. "Are you expecting to come in?"

"Two of us are." Julie made for the door, riding the energy of anger, hefting Duke, the backpack and the stroller up the stairs. "We need to check out. We're leaving town." She meant it this time.

Reggie bounced on her toes behind Leona, spouting an apology.

But Doris sputtered and cut her off, flinging her arms about. "Julie, you have to listen to what I have to say first."

"I don't, actually." Julie tried to edge past Leona, but the battle-ax wasn't letting her inside or Reggie out.

"Don't go. Your friend Nate is a horrible lawman." Doris crowded into Julie's space and gestured to her elderly friend. "He forbade Lilac to drive around town."

Nodding, Lilac slid her big round sunglasses into her short and stylishly streaked silver hair. She looked competent enough. Clear-eyed and steady handed.

"I see Nate all over town, working on people's houses." Doris hooked Julie's arm with fingers that dug into flesh. "While he's being paid to do police business."

That caught Julie's attention. "As a side job?"

"He abuses his power." Doris increased the volume, so caught up in the moment she didn't realize she was yelling in Julie's ear. "He's holding this town ransom."

"That's not true," Reggie said, her voice echoing in the empty foyer.

Julie exchanged a glance with Leona, while Duke covered his ears.

"What you believe is up to you," Leona said flatly.

"Leona doesn't take sides on anything." Lilac tossed a teal crepe scarf over her shoulder.

"I don't take sides, but I do enjoy a good town shake-up." Leona's words were as hard as the hair spray lacquer on her salt-and-pepper beehive hairstyle. She was not a happy woman.

"We need a second candidate for sheriff." Doris scooted between Leona and Julie.

Julie didn't answer. Duke was getting heavier in her arms. He had his head tucked into the crook of her uninjured shoulder. Soon, he'd feel rested enough to run around some more. She wanted to pack up before he got rambunctious.

"I see the way you look at that boy." Doris pointed to Duke. "You don't want to give him to the sheriff to raise, and I don't blame you."

"A cute boy like that, why…" Lilac smiled with calculated sweetness, moving past Julie to join ranks with Leona and Doris. "The sheriff will ruin him."

Julie knew she was being played. But the prize of the game tempted. She could keep Duke. She could stay in Harmony Valley and never point a gun again. She thought of her father, standing tall and proud in his highway patrol uniform. He'd approve of her being sheriff. She thought of her mother, holding vigil at Julie's hospital bed. She'd approve of her being sheriff. She thought of April's face when she told them there'd be no wedding. Would April approve?

The bear claw turned in her stomach.

She refused to imagine how April would feel. She'd come here to make Nate pay. He loved it here. If he lost...

FLYNN AND NATE sat at the back of the church in their usual seats. This time they were flanked by other men in the community. In their pew, every man but Nate held a baby or toddler in their lap.

Flynn held Ian.

Will held Felicity.

Slade held Liam.

Gage held Mae.

Duffy held Gregory.

Nate's arms were empty. He looked over his shoulder toward the door. No Duke. No Julie. He hadn't seen them around town all day. And he'd driven by Doris's house twice. He slouched in his seat.

"She'll be here," Flynn said.

Nate wasn't so sure. The air in the church felt thick, heavy and heralding a fast-moving storm.

"Nay!" Duke stumbled at the end of the church pew.

Nate gathered Duke into his lap and suddenly the cloud over his head dissipated.

Julie appeared at the aisle, looking SWAT ready in her khaki cargo pants and black utility shirt.

"Scoot over," Nate said to the men in his row.

The pew creaked and groaned as the dads made room for Julie. She sat slowly, without looking at Nate, giving off a vibe weird enough to get that cloud forming again.

Her mood, like his rain cloud, was probably a figment of his imagination. "How are your accommodations at Doris's?"

"I don't know. I went to Cloverdale for diapers after breakfast, so I haven't been by." She was babbling. Julie never babbled. Her rapid-fire words only increased Nate's stress level. "They had a nice park. We had a nice lunch. I took Duke to a Disney movie."

And here he'd thought Julie might be off with Doris plotting to win the sheriff's race. Had Julie slept during the movie? It didn't look like it. "I could have driven you."

"During your shift?" She frowned, sparing him a glance rimmed with dark circles under her eyes.

"My shift is 24/7," he murmured.

The mayor called the meeting to order with a bang of his gavel that startled the babies. "This is a special meeting to address the challenge to the public safety decisions the council has made. Rose, please read tonight's agenda."

"Reviewing public safety performance and registering candidates for sheriff elections," Rose said. And that was all she said. For fast-talking, tap-dancing Rose that was an accomplishment.

Nate hunched his shoulders beneath the thick, dark cloud overhead.

"Don't worry," Flynn whispered, shifting a fussy Ian to his shoulder. "It's not like anyone else in town is going to run."

"We conducted an inquiry of sheriffs in other towns our size." Mildred didn't refer to notes. Given the thickness of her glasses, she wouldn't have been able to see them. "Sheriff Nate has given out fewer citations than in those towns—"

"I told you," Doris interjected from the front row.

"—but their demographics are different. Younger populations tend to lead to higher incidences of things like speeding, disturbing the peace and such."

"All of which we also have here," Nate pointed out to Flynn under his breath, while Doris huffed.

"Not all sheriffs are elected," Mildred was saying. "And satisfaction with the sheriff wasn't based on him being appointed or voted in."

Rose drew the microphone closer, her tidy white bun gleaming in the light. "And no sheriff had 100 percent backing in any community."

"We didn't follow *Robert's Rules of Order* the other night." Agnes had taken possession of the microphone next. "Based on committee findings, and the fact that we have a termination clause in Sheriff Landry's contract, I move we employ a sheriff who is elected by popular vote, with qualifications the same as for other council positions." Agnes's gaze found Nate in the crowd. She smiled. "Election to be held as soon as possible to avoid interfering with the Spring Festival."

"Second." Mildred nodded.

Awakened by the meeting noise, Ian began to whimper.

"All in favor?" Mayor Larry said.

The entire town council said, "Aye."

Nate forced air in his lungs. Agnes had told him to trust her. In some part of his mind, he'd been thinking the election would go away. He should have known better.

"Motion passed." The mayor pounded his gavel. "Nate Landry. Are you willing to run for sheriff?"

Townspeople turned.

Nate stood, bringing Duke to his hip. "I am."

Several people smiled at Nate. It was gratifying to know he had some support.

"Does anyone else wish to run?" Mayor Larry looked around.

The pews shifted and creaked. Some of the tension Nate felt eased. Flynn was right. No one else wanted the job.

And then Doris stood from her seat in the front pew and turned around. She looked right at Nate, brows lowered.

No. She wasn't looking at Nate. She was looking at—

There was a noise nearby. Boots planted firmly on the wood floor. Pew creaking as someone stood.

"I do," Julie said.

On occasion, when Nate let his guard down, he imagined hearing Julie say those words to an entirely different question. Betrayal sucked at the back of his knees until he had to sit down or risk falling with Duke in his arms. Doris's interest in Julie at breakfast. Julie being unable to meet his gaze when she came in. He'd discounted her as a candidate because she was wounded and had only just achieved the position of SWAT.

"She can't run," Rutgar boomed from the pew behind Nate. "This town's never had a female sheriff."

Half the town stood up with a rumble of anger—the female half. Everyone began talking at once.

Julie sat back down. Duke scrambled to her lap.

Nate's black rain cloud was back, flashing with lightning. "You could've told me. We could've discussed this."

The fighter was back. Her chin thrust out. "You wouldn't understand."

Betrayal gave way to the flush of anger. Did she think he was stupid? "I wouldn't understand what a great place this is to raise a kid because you're not planning to give me custody? Or I wouldn't understand that you hate me so much you'd sabotage my career? Or I wouldn't understand how afraid you are to return to active SWAT duty?"

She blanched.

"Well, this changes things." Flynn stood, smiling apologetically at Julie—at Julie, not

Nate. And then he said to Nate, "You're going to need a campaign manager."

"I'll do it." Rutgar banged the back of Nate's pew with his crutches. "Printed signs, speeches, kissing babies, making friends and influencing people. It's right up my alley."

The black cloud descended, funneling Nate's vision. His campaign was doomed before it ever began.

"You've got my vote." Lilac came up to Julie, a gauzy teal scarf knotted at her throat. She tugged on the knot as she spared Nate a deadly glance. "With you in charge, I will never receive a totally undeserved speeding ticket again!"

She'd deserved every driving citation she'd been given. She'd practically run Chad Healey down last year, and nearly killed Truman Harris's dog the year before.

"I'm going to work to get you elected, missy." Clementine Quedoba appeared next. She gave Nate a dirty look. "My son's in jail because of the sheriff. A woman might've gone easy on him."

Nate supposed it wouldn't help his cause to say he'd caught her son Carl stealing copper from vacant buildings and homes in town. Carl may have gone to prison, but he hadn't made financial restitution for the damage he'd done to the property of others.

The elderly women whisked Julie and Duke out of the pew and away from Nate just as the elderly male residents of Harmony Valley crowded toward Nate. They didn't so much want to talk to Nate as to strategize to the group at large.

"I'm in charge here." Rutgar pounded his crutches on the floor, trying to take control. "We'll need to use every trick in the book for this."

"The sheriff is sneaky. He'll be fine." Wilson Hammacker should know sneaky. He'd hid his drinking for years.

"I'm telling you…" Rutgar argued, but the other elderly men outtalked him, tossing out ideas in a jumble of indecipherable noise.

The men Nate's age made their way out of the other end of the pew with their babies and toddlers.

Flynn caught Nate's gaze as he made a break for the door. "We'll talk tomorrow."

Betrayed by Julie. Abandoned by his friends. Hung out to dry by the town council. How much worse could it be?

"Who's making signs?" Old Man Takata

banged his walker against the pew. "You can put one in my yard."

"What we should do is have a contest, like we do for the Pumpkin Queen." This came from the mayor, of all people. He'd finally found a cause that made him abandon neutrality.

"Who can handcuff a perp the fastest," Wilson suggested. "Or who does the best traffic stop."

"Our sheriff should be the best shooter." Rutgar got to his feet and leaned on his crutches. "We need a shooting competition."

"What about a chicken capture?" Old Man Takata got on the crazy suggestion bandwagon. "I've seen the sheriff wrangle chickens. He's very good."

"These are all fantastic ideas." Mayor Larry beamed. "They need to be presented to the town council."

The elderly men hurried to the front of the church, presumably to present their ideas to the women surrounding Julie and the town council.

Nate couldn't sneak out as Flynn had, not when the gist of the meeting involved his livelihood. He leaned back in the pew, listening to suggestions, but not hearing anything more, not wanting to listen. For better or for worse, he had an election ahead of him.

By the time the chaos died down, it'd been decided that the brief election season would include a series of contests and events, ending in a vote.

It was all looking worse.

THE BARKING BEGAN with the first car door slam. Doris's.

It intensified when Julie closed the SUV door in Doris's driveway.

She removed Duke from his car seat in the back. "Are you sure this is okay?" Nothing had felt right since she'd entered the church. She should have celebrated pulling the rug out from under Nate by running against him. But when she'd announced her candidacy, the shocked look on Nate's face hadn't given her any pleasure.

The yapping didn't stop. Duke began to bark, too.

"Let me put the dogs up." Doris opened the door. More barking ensued. Louder barking. Little dog barking.

Little dogs? Chihuahuas perhaps? This shouldn't have come as a surprise given Doris's wardrobe choices.

The next-door neighbor was returning from the town council meeting. He shook his head and hurried inside, muttering something Julie couldn't catch.

Julie slung the diaper bag over her good shoulder and picked up Duke in case some little dog saw the toddler as a doggy treat. "This has mistake written all over it." She'd return for the bedroll and duffel bag once she scoped out the situation inside.

"The coast is clear." Doris waved to her from the front door. She lived in a small ranch house painted coral with white trim. The shrubs in front were as stunted as Doris. A bass-fishing boat sat on a trailer in the street in front of the house, which was technically a violation. Did that account for one of her tickets?

Duke was quiet as she carried him inside.

The floors were a dark laminate. A small pink love seat and two teal high-backed chairs that looked uncomfortable were arranged around a low pine coffee table. There were pictures of dogs on the wall. Framed pictures. Sometimes an extreme close-up. Sometimes a dog posing on a table next to a trophy.

So what, if Doris loved dogs? Julie supposed someone who wasn't in law enforcement would think her apartment was odd. She had black-

and-white still photos of lawmen of the West hanging on her living room wall.

The barking was muffled now, but no less intense and possibly accounted for another one of Doris's citations.

The house smelled of dog, and not just dog hair. Responsible aunts only stayed in a place like this as a last resort. Women running for sheriff shouldn't be living a life of last resorts.

"I'll put you in the guest room." Doris scurried down the hall. "Have you had dinner?"

"Yes." Having lost her way to responsible aunt status sometime in the past forty-eight hours, Julie followed.

The smell was better in the guest room. It had a full-size bed with a blue log cabin quilt on it. Dog crates were stacked along one wall. Dog food bags, bulk packages of potty pads, boxes of dog chews and treats, and folded portable dog pens were stacked in front of the window. If there was a fire, there'd be no escaping through the window. Not to mention if Duke got inquisitive, there'd be an avalanche of dog supplies. Julie could remove the top layer of stuff and put it on the floor. It'd still be a jungle gym, but only a three- to four-foot jungle gym.

Julie didn't think she could stand to sleep

230 SUPPORT YOUR LOCAL SHERIFF

in the living room with that smell. She'd have Duke sleep on the bed and she'd cram herself on the floor somewhere in case she had a nightmare. "How many dogs do you have?" She set Duke on the bed.

He began barking again.

Doris smiled as if Duke's barking was the cutest thing. "I only have a few breeders and some puppies."

It sounded like more than a few. If Julie had to guess, it was the doggy dozen.

After showing Julie the kitchen and bathroom, Doris bade them good-night, claiming she fell into the "early to bed, early to rise" camp.

Julie brought in the rest of their things and cleared a small space on the floor at the foot of the bed. Duke was already asleep. She dropped some pillows on the floor, lay on Duke's dinosaur bedroll and removed her shoes and socks.

For what seemed like hours, she listened to Doris's TV and the frequent chorus of barks—at passing cars, at cat fights, at loud commercials with doorbells from Doris's room. It seemed as if she'd never fall asleep, but she must have dozed, because she woke to the memory of gunshots and blood. Her hands were shaking and it took her a moment to remember where she was—in Doris's guest bedroom.

The house was finally silent. She dug in her pocket for Nate's worry stone.

Nate had told her to take charge of her life and heal. He'd been nothing but helpful and kind since she'd come to Harmony Valley. And how had she repaid his kindness? With a knife in the back. What would her dad think of that?

For nearly three years, she'd dreamed of ruining Nate's life. She should feel happy or vindicated or at peace with the world. She felt sickened.

Her mouth was dry. She got up, intending to get a drink in the bathroom, closing the door behind her. But even roughing it and drinking from the sink didn't quench her thirst or settle the tumultuous feeling in her gut that something wasn't right.

She wandered out to the kitchen and found a glass in the cupboard above the sink. Light from the full moon spilled through the kitchen window so she didn't have to turn on the light and risk waking Doris.

Nails clacked across the laminate. A shadow approached from the living room. A short shadow. One about eight inches high with four legs and a tail.

"Nice doggy," she whispered, willing it not to bark.

It didn't bark. It lunged and nipped Julie's ankle. Once. Twice. Not hard enough to break the skin, but stinging, angering.

"No!" Julie said in the growly voice the canine unit used, which set off a round of barking somewhere in the house. She reached for the light switch, turning on the garbage disposal instead. It growled more fiercely than the pint-size dog that bit her again. She drew back into the corner of the kitchen and shouted this time. *"No!"*

The dog latched onto her pants leg and growled.

Lights blinded her.

"Freeze." Doris appeared in the kitchen doorway, her hair in pink rag curls. She wore a blue checked nightshirt, slippers with Chihuahuas embroidered over the toes, and pointed a handgun at Julie. "Oh." She lowered the barrel, but it was still aimed at Julie's feet. Or maybe the dog.

"Don't point that gun at me." Julie's fingers flexed for a weapon of her own, making her heart beat like it wanted out of her chest. Having a gun in hand didn't make her safe, not if she was unwilling to pull the trigger. "We can't stay here." Now her responsible-aunt gene reared its head?

"But it's the middle of the night." Doris gestured with the gun as if it was an extension of her hand. "I didn't think you'd get up. That's why I let Bruiser out on patrol."

Julie took the gun from Doris and set the safety. She placed it on the white stove which had a layer of what looked like bacon grease ringing the main burner. "We're leaving." She walked down the hall, dragging a growling furry cling-on attached to her pants leg.

"You can't go. You're the perfect candidate for sheriff." Doris followed as close to Julie's heels as she could get without stepping on the dog. "You disarmed me."

"It wasn't that hard." Julie was truly disgusted with herself. She should have known better than to trust Doris. Since the shooting, she'd been making one bad decision after another "Do you have a permit for that thing?"

That thing being the Glock.

"I don't need a permit. I'm not a criminal." There was that holier-than-thou note to her voice that got under Julie's skin.

Julie wanted to thunk herself on the head. She'd thrown in her lot with a woman who didn't think the law applied to her? She'd given

234 SUPPORT YOUR LOCAL SHERIFF

her word in front of the town that she'd run for sheriff? "Everyone who owns a handgun in California needs a permit."

"It's just a piece of paper," Doris explained in the same tone of voice Julie had once used to tell her dad her fender bender had resulted in just a scratch. "Besides, it's not like I wave my gun around. I keep it in my purse."

"That's carrying concealed." Two violations of the law. Julie revised her personal head-thunking wish for a Doris head-thunking wish.

"You really know your stuff." Doris was either thicker than a layer of snow after a Sierra snowstorm or she thought Julie was. "You're the perfect candidate for sheriff."

"So you've said." Nate would have a good laugh over this. Or maybe he'd give her that contained half smile and not say a word.

"Don't leave me." Doris latched onto Julie's hand.

"I can't stay. I can't let Bruiser bite Duke." Julie stood at the guest bedroom door and shook her leg, but Bruiser refused to let go. She shook her arm, but Doris refused to let go. "Get your hands off me and take your dog before I tip off Nate and he writes you enough citations to wallpaper your house, not to mention throws you in jail."

NATE TAPPED ON the passenger window of Julie's SUV.

The passenger seat was reclined and Julie was reclined with it. Duke lay on top of her, covered by his dinosaur bedroll. Neither one of them woke up at his knock.

Nate glanced up and down Kennedy Avenue. He couldn't see far. Fog clung to rooftops and chilled his body to the bone. Julie's windows were mostly clouded over and the SUV's engine was silent. She'd been here awhile. He wouldn't have found out she was sleeping in her vehicle if Terrance hadn't called it in. So much for thinking the old man's pajama-themed walkabouts had ended.

But that wasn't Nate's immediate problem. His immediate problem was sprawled in her SUV like someone on the run from something. This wasn't the woman he'd worked with in Sacramento. This woman needed his patience and compassion.

Patience and compassion weren't what Nate was feeling. No. It was anger. Anger that Julie had exposed Duke to the elements warmed his cold hands. He rapped harder on the window.

Julie startled, opening her eyes. She clutched Duke when she realized there was a man at her door.

"It's me." Nate motioned for her to open the window, holding his temper in check with a thin thread.

It was twenty seconds before the window slid down.

He'd counted.

"You aren't going to win any votes as a homeless sheriff." Nate had to keep this civil or he'd start to yell. He could feel shouts forming in his chest like cannonballs. *Are you nuts? What are you doing? Didn't you think of Duke at all?* "Follow me back to the station." His truck was parked in front of her SUV.

"We're fine," she said inanely, still half-asleep and looking halfway short of fine. She had a bad case of bed head and her sallow complexion in the streetlight looked certifiably corpse-like.

He leaned in the window. "We have vagrancy laws in town. It's within my rights to haul you in." He drew a deep breath, noting Duke shivering, noting Julie shivering, noting Julie made no move to move.

He marched around the SUV, got in behind the wheel, adjusted the seat from recline and drove them home. To jail.

"I put him down in the driver's seat," Julie

said in a dazed voice, holding Duke in her arms. "I thought he'd be safe there."

"With the key in the ignition?" Kudos to Nate for using his indoor voice.

"He climbed into my lap." She didn't seem to register the point Nate was making. "I didn't even wake up."

Nate wanted to shout, "Because you're half dead!"

He didn't think yelling would help matters. So he counted some more. He counted past Madison. Across Harrison. Down Main Street.

When he parked in front of the sheriff's office, he came around to her side of the SUV and relieved her of Duke. "I take it things didn't work out with Doris." He held the office door for her, and then he carried Duke up the stairs.

"We can sleep down here." Julie still sounded half-asleep.

"No. You can't sleep in the jail." He didn't trust her not to walk out at sunrise. Nate opened the door at the top of the stairs and carried Duke to the bed in his studio apartment. "The sheets were clean since yesterday. Don't flush when the shower's running or it'll turn cold."

She sat on the mattress next to Duke. Only

her sit was more like a collapse. "Thank you."
She had something clutched in her fist. She
set it on the bedside table. It was his mother's
worry stone.

Nate bit back a curse and pulled up a chair
from the kitchen table. He took Julie's hands
in his. They were like ice. "What were you
thinking? Why didn't you call?"

"It was horrible. One of her dogs bit me." Julie's mouth worked as if she was fighting tears.
"I should have gone home, but I promised to
run for sheriff. And my dad always said you
had to honor a promise. And I couldn't call
you because I didn't want you to think that I
couldn't take care of Duke."

"That's the exhaustion talking. I would've
respected you if you had called me."

She closed her eyes. "I can't seem to do anything right since—"

"Don't say since the shooting. Don't de-
fine your life that way." He shook her hands,
thought better of it and framed her cold cheeks
with his palms. "You aren't to blame for that
woman dying."

She raised her tear-filled gaze to his. "How
would you know?"

"The woman you shot was cornered, afraid

and angry. She made a choice. She drew her weapon."

"She didn't deserve to die." And there it was. The heart of her sleeplessness.

Nate grabbed her arms, stood and brought her to her feet. "She could have walked out of that house when the negotiators asked. She could have turned herself in. But she didn't. She held her own children hostage. She was trapped and scared and wanted to hurt someone. Or worse. She was trapped and scared and wanted someone to end her pain."

Julie's eyes were huge, desperate to believe she wasn't a cold-blooded killer.

"You protected your unit. You made sure they got home safe to their loved ones."

Her hands crept up his chest. "She haunts me."

Nate glanced at the worry stone. "She doesn't deserve to." He drew her closer and stroked a hand down her back, breathing her in the same way he'd done with Duke days ago. She smelled of daisies and damp. "You have to take care of yourself. If not for you, for Duke."

Julie shuddered. "The nightmares. I can't sleep in the same bed as Duke."

Nate drew her closer still. He'd take away her pain and ease her suffering if he could.

"I…" She sighed and leaned into him. "Leona checked on me last night during a nightmare and I put her in a choke hold."

Now it was Nate who was chilled. He hadn't realized her symptoms from the shooting were that bad. "It'll be all right. I'll get his bedroll. Duke can sleep in the chair."

"Don't leave," she whispered, so faintly he thought he might have imagined it until she stepped free of his embrace, took him by the hand and drew him down on the bed. "He'll be safe with you here. Just…don't talk either. Just…stay with me."

Those words… Longed for, dreamed of… He couldn't have left her if he wanted to.

Nate sat on the bed, his back to the wall. She sat next to him, staring at him with luminous eyes that had taken on more pain than she was ready to handle. She'd arrived in town with vengeance on her mind, but fear in her heart. She'd always fought for what was right. But she'd lost track of the boundary where right ended and wrong began.

Julie took his pillow, placed it in his lap and rested her head on it.

He ran his hand up and down her back with a slow, light touch. He wanted to bring her into his arms and kiss her fears away. But she didn't want that. She didn't want *him*. She wanted a guardian to watch over her nephew.

Her breathing steadied, deepened. How little it took for her to fall asleep. How little it took for his heart to pang with longing.

CHAPTER THIRTEEN

JULIE AWOKE TO the smell of sausage and the gentle feeling of rejuvenation.

She hadn't dreamed, at least, not about the shooting. She'd dreamed she was dozing on a tropical beach. Rested, relaxed, sun warmed.

"Juju," Duke whispered. He crawled into bed next to her and snuggled close.

She expected Duke to tug on her arm or demand to be fed. She peeked at him through half-closed lids. He was smiling. "Is it morning?" Duke never smiled in the morning.

"Juju." Duke made his silly face, the one that said he was blissfully happy. He held up a half-eaten sausage.

Julie opened her eyes more fully and took in the studio apartment. The card table and two folding chairs. The recliner facing a wall-mounted television. The small area built into the short hall that led to a tiny bathroom where his shirts were hanging. The kitchen area where Nate stood cooking breakfast. His dark hair was as rumpled as Duke's every morning.

She started to smile. And then the memories from the night before came rushing back.

The devil dog. The cold SUV. Nate, so angry. Nate, so commanding. Nate, so tender.

He'd held her and she'd slept better than any pain pill could induce. She'd felt safe and protected. She'd felt understood and absolved.

Because of Nate.

Her belly clenched, distressed by the knowledge that she'd failed Duke, that Nate was the reason they were warm and rested and, in Duke's case, fed.

Oh, she'd make a fine sheriff, all right. Cue sarcasm.

"Coffee's ready when you are." Nate's back was to her. He wore blue jeans that hugged his lean frame and a brown long-sleeved T-shirt. His feet were bare.

Julie couldn't remember ever having seen his bare feet. Or maybe she couldn't remember seeing him relaxed enough to go barefoot. She half expected him to turn around and smile at her.

He turned around, not smiling, and dished up eggs and sausage on plates. "If you want your morning sugar fix, you'll have to go elsewhere. Real men eat protein for breakfast."

"So you've said." Julie sat up slowly.

Duke popped up and scrambled to the table.

Her shoulder felt better today. There was less ache and more tightness around her stitches. She sought refuge in the bathroom. She shut herself in and stared at her reflection in the mirror, upgrading her appearance from zombie to vampire. She was still pale, but the bags under her eyes were gone. Her hair was wild, but could be tamed.

She cleaned up and returned to the main apartment, hesitating when she saw something pink in a long plastic bag hanging from a rod in the alcove that led to the bathroom. "Is this Mae's wedding dress?" Further inspection revealed it was a pale rose satin gown with a sweetheart neckline and a mermaid silhouette. It was sweet and flirty and sophisticated all at the same time.

"Yep. That's my wedding dress." Nate stepped into view. The pink in his cheeks matched the soft hue of the dress. "I probably should have donated it or something, but Mae was... She was a character. Her shop used to be next door, where the wine cellar is now.

Mae was convinced that dress would be perfect for the woman I marry."

"She chose pink for you?" A woman would have to be confident in herself to wear such a dress.

"I think she would've chosen anything out of the ordinary." He plucked at the plastic, separating the bag from the shirts and pants hanging around it. "She enjoyed prodding people out of their shells."

While Julie mulled the so-called shell Nate was in, she went to the counter and poured herself a cup of coffee. It wasn't until she poured a packet of sweetener in it that she realized the mug said, Some Heroes Wear Capes. I Wear Kevlar. She brought the mug to the table. "Nice sentiment."

"It was true, once upon a time." Nate sat in the recliner, a travel coffee mug in hand. "My sister and I didn't talk for several years. When we reconnected, she gave me that mug."

The television was on low and tuned to a cartoon. No wonder Duke was silent. He was watching something that had captured his attention.

"Wedding dresses. Cartoons. You've gotten soft, Landry." And yet, the furniture in his apartment projected no permanence.

"Small-town life has a way of changing a person." The half smile again.

The view outside the window was the back of Martin's Bakery.

"About last night…" Julie wanted to say she wouldn't impose on Nate—not by sleeping in his bed, not by sleeping in his arms. But her gaze drifted to his broad chest and she remembered how secure she'd felt last night with him watching over her. She hadn't worried about nightmares or Duke.

"I'll sleep downstairs tonight," Nate said, reading at least some of her thoughts. He nodded toward her duffel, backpack and the bag of diapers. "After you eat, you should get April's notebook and ask me another question."

She didn't want to. Every time she asked a question, Julie was the one who got upset. He'd knocked her for a loop by telling her April had called off the wedding. And then he'd pissed her off with his so-called sacrifice. Granted, she'd been relieved when he'd left the force. Would she have done the same for him? She didn't think so.

"Let's skip the test today." She rubbed at a crease between her eyebrows. "It makes me feel—" dare she admit it? "—petty and shallow."

"You're neither of those things." He didn't hesitate to argue. "You just see the world in black and white. Sometimes I wish I could say the same."

Duke finished eating and crawled back in bed, without taking his eyes off the television.

"The test, Julie."

With a sigh, Julie brought out the notebook, flipping to the third section. "For the record, I don't want to ask you this."

He rubbed the travel mug between his palms as if it was Aladdin's magic lamp. "For the record, I'm sure I don't want to answer."

Their gazes held. There was friendship in his, friendship Julie didn't feel she deserved. This was definitely a gray area.

She returned her attention to the notebook. "A good dad isn't afraid of change or of differences between father and son. As adults, the ability to appreciate each other's differences and strengths draws us to friends and lovers. Give an example of how you and your father were the same and how you were different. Then give an example of differences you appreciate in one of your friends."

Nate's brows lowered dangerously. "How my dad and I are the same?"

"I guess in your dad's case that'd be turning a negative into a positive." She was helping him answer? This wasn't how Julie had foreseen the Daddy Test going. "I suppose you could say your father was determined to do things his way, like you do."

"Wrong," Nate muttered, staring out the window. "He was determined to kill someone."

The air left Julie's lungs as if she'd been sucker punched. Abuse could take many forms and she'd just assumed Nate's abuse hadn't been physical. Now she wasn't so sure.

"Moving on." Julie clutched the notebook to keep from doing something foolish, like drawing Nate to his feet and giving him a consoling hug. "What about differences in your friends? Take Flynn for example."

The lines around Nate's mouth eased. "Flynn can stare at a computer screen and fiddle with programming code for hours on end. I don't have the patience to sit still that long."

"I think you have a lot more patience than I do." No joke.

"You need patience to work with the elderly." His gaze drifted to Duke. "Or with kids."

Julie was feeling woefully unqualified for the job of sheriff and role of aunt when someone called from below.

"Nate?"

NATE CARRIED HIS boots and socks downstairs to see who'd come calling.

The Daddy Test was dredging up his own nightmares. He'd seen the pity in Julie's eyes. She was bound to find a new place to stay by noon. Call him cocky, but she shouldn't move. His care had helped her.

"Nate." Agnes stood by the door wearing grandma jeans and a white sweater. "We brought the schedule for the election." She handed him a sheet of paper with hand-printed dates, times and events.

Rose opened the door for Mildred, who trundled inside with her walker. The town council was now present and accounted for. Once Mildred cleared the door, Rose shuffled off to Buffalo with some kind of tap dance that took her into the jail cell.

Nate sat at his desk and put his socks and boots on while he glanced at the list. "We're going to debate tonight? About what?"

"The issues. Your qualifications." Mildred lowered the seat on her walker and then sat on it. She peered around the room through her thick lenses, much like a mole when it ventured into the sunlight.

Nate tried to make light of the situation. "How many citations I gave Doris?"

"That, too." Rose held on to a bar and did some squats...er, pliés?

Nate perused the list. "And then tomorrow night we're doing mock traffic stops?" He pushed the paper across the desk toward Agnes, who'd taken a seat. "This isn't election week. The circus has come to town."

"Don't put down the circus." Arms raised, Rose spun on her toes as if she wore a tutu and tights instead of loose pants and boots with a low, thick heel. "I was a highflier in one for several months."

"We know," Agnes said indulgently, before turning her attention back to Nate. "Remember that we're allowing our constituents to vote. They also had a say in the events for the week." At his frown, she came around the desk and rubbed his shoulder. "It's not all bad. Don't forget the shooting competition the day after next. That'll be exciting."

"For those of us who can see it," Mildred grumbled, pushing her glasses up her nose.

"You don't see sharpshooters in the circus," Rose pointed out.

"Agnes, you said to trust you." Nate kept his voice down so Julie wouldn't hear him. The last thing he needed was for her to think there was a conspiracy going on.

"Now, Nate." Agnes had a way of smiling at a person that made you want to smile back, even when you were disagreeing with each other. "There's a method to this madness."

"Madness. You got that right." His boots hit the ground. "It's a dog and pony show."

"But you'll come through with flying colors." Living up to her look, Mildred reassured him with a smile and a nod just the way Mrs. Claus might have.

There was a light tread on the stair and Julie appeared. "Am I interrupting?"

"No." Agnes gave Nate a significant look, followed by a nod of approval, to which he rolled his eyes.

"You're not interrupting." Rose was so shocked she walked instead of danced out of the cell. "You're making our day."

"Is that Julie? We were wondering where you'd gotten to." Mildred peered at the staircase. "Why were you…*upstairs*?" She ended her question on a confused note.

"Nate made Duke breakfast." Julie descended, trying to pull off an innocent countenance among a threesome of gossipers. It'd never work. Doris would be on her case in an hour.

"Agnes? Do you still have the phone tree on

speed dial?" Rose was regaining her composure. She held on to a bar with one hand, and swayed back and forth as if it was her dance partner.

"Ladies," Nate warned. "Don't make this into something it isn't."

"It is something." Agnes smiled broader than the Cheshire cat. "You're running against each other. And sharing breakfast. Again."

"Every day this week, from what I've heard," Mildred added. Also smiling. Also not innocently.

"Do you like pink dresses?" Rose said slyly. "Because—"

"Let's get back to the issue at hand." Nate handed Julie the list of election activities before Rose could bring up Mae's wedding dress. "The circus that you call an election."

"You can't just ask people to vote without knowing who the two candidates are." Agnes may have been small in stature, but she was big on fulfilling agendas.

"They know who I am," Nate grumbled.

"But they don't know Julie." Agnes walked up to Julie and hugged her.

So much for Agnes being in Nate's corner. Was his résumé updated?

Julie tugged at the ends of her button-down

and avoided meeting anyone's gaze. "I might not run, after all."

"What?"

Nate wasn't sure who hadn't asked, himself included, but he was the first to say, "Are you sure you want to back out?"

Harmony Valley had a way of boosting a person's confidence. And Julie needed that boost more than Nate.

"You want me to run?" Julie's slender brows drew together.

"Honestly?" Nate couldn't have this conversation with distance between them. He came to her side and placed a hand on Julie's uninjured shoulder. "No."

The peanut gallery chuckled. That was certain to be included in the phone tree.

"But if only one of us can protect Harmony Valley, they've got two good choices." In one sense, Nate meant what he said. In another, he was hopeful Julie would acknowledge this was his turf and drop out.

Julie grinned in that all-in way of hers. "Glad to hear you approve, Nate, because if I'm going to compete, I'm going to play to win."

Nate was simultaneously proud of her and

annoyed with himself. Now if he won, he'd feel guilty.

Doris barged in, catching the gist of Julie's announcement. "From your lips to the heavens above. Of course, Julie's playing to win. Come along, Madame Sheriff, we have a lot to do before the debate tonight." Doris held out her hand as if Julie was a child who'd run away.

Julie shook her head. "I need to shower and change my clothes."

Doris nearly choked on air, her eyes roving the office wildly. "But…but…but…*here*?"

"Yes." Julie was more on top of her game than she'd been in days. "This is a safe place for Duke. Safer than your house."

"Doris," Nate interrupted the old lady's apoplexy. "What's this I hear about one of your dogs biting someone?"

His nemesis waved her hand as if shooing off a fly. "It was only Julie."

"Doris," Agnes chastised.

The rest of the town council wasn't as direct in their disapproval. Rose mumbled something about heartless busybodies, and Mildred might have said she was crossing Doris off her holiday cookie list.

"I'm going to have to make record of it," Nate said without any remorse. "Just so you know—three bites, and that biter has to leave town."

"Only if you win." Doris huffed out.

"I'm with Nate," Julie said staring down at the ankle of her pants, which had a small rip. "Three bites and he's out."

"Is it wrong to wish two more people get bit?" Rose tap-danced toward the door.

Nate sighed. "I'm afraid so."

THE WOMEN OF Harmony Valley had congregated in Martin's Bakery.

Julie sat in the window seat with Eunice, who was no less colorfully dressed today in celery slacks and a violet blouse that deepened the purple in her purple-gray hair. Duke and Gregory played with blocks at their feet.

Doris presided over the chattering women in the center of the bakery in black cargo capris and a blue T-shirt with two Chihuahuas kissing on the front. Presided was probably being kind. No one presided. Everyone was talking over everyone else. Julie heard snatches of conversation, not all of which were pertinent to the election—first woman ever, raise the speed limit, cranberry cake recipe, wrinkle creams.

"Do you have any idea what they're talking

about?" Julie leaned over to show Duke how the blocks interlocked.

He'd been building a castle that kept falling over.

"No." Eunice glanced up from the pink quilt squares she was piecing together. "No offense, but they're more excited to have an excuse to get together than they are about the election. Same thing happened when the barbershop changed to a beauty parlor."

With a squeal of tires, Lilac pulled up to the curb in a classic old Cadillac convertible. The top was down and she looked chicly windblown in her red scarf and large round shades.

"That woman should slow down." Eunice frowned. "Or not drive at all. Everything she needs is within walking distance of her house."

Lilac pushed open her car door. It banged against the silver sedan next to her. Lilac didn't seem to notice. She slammed the door and walked inside with the hip sway of the high-heeled. She made a grand entrance into the bakery, pausing at the door, removing her sunglasses and unwrapping the scarf from her hair.

"Is that a new dress?" someone asked.

"It is." Lilac sashayed her way to Doris's side in magenta floral. "There was a sale."

The crowd erupted again—what sale, how much, how long? Doris scowled at them all and tried to call them to order.

"They're supposed to be helping me run for sheriff," Julie said, picking at a raspberry scone on the small table to her right.

"I wouldn't rely on this bunch to help me run for the exit." Eunice stared at Julie over her readers with a minimal amount of extra blinkage. "If you want something, you have to work for it yourself. That's what my mama used to say."

"Wise words."

Terrance entered the bakery to a chorus of boos.

"Really, peeps." Tracy shouted over them all, bringing silence. "Love thy neighbor or take your business elsewhere."

"But he's a man," Lilac said in a scathing tone.

"A friend of our opponent," Doris added, glaring at Terrance.

"A paying customer." Tracy waved him to the counter.

"I need a break." Eunice stood. "Gregory, let's go see what fun your mama's cooking in the kitchen. Duke, do you want to come see Jessica?"

Duke dropped the blocks he'd been fitting together and stood. "Me fend."

Eunice led the two boys through the swinging doors and into the kitchen.

Meanwhile, Terrance had worked his way to the counter and ordered chai tea. Julie must have caught him on a bad day the morning they'd met. Today his clothes were neat. His shirt clean and tucked in. He was clean shaven. Terrance glanced around the room with interest and a benevolent smile for Julie's supporters, who were whispering and sending him dark looks.

Terrance thanked Tracy for his tea and stopped by Julie on his way out. "I was worried about you and young Duke. I phoned the sheriff when I saw your SUV last night." His gentle smile matched his gentle voice.

"You were out late." Julie's shoulders bunched. She hoped he wasn't going to announce she'd slept in her vehicle. That would cost her votes for sure.

He sipped his chai and gestured to the window seat. "May I?"

"Of course."

He settled next to her, bringing the subtle scent of woodsy cologne. "I was out late because I've been having problems sleeping."

For all his seeming more put-together, he did have bags under his eyes. "Sleeplessness. That's been going around." Thankfully, not last night.

"Heard you were at Nate's later." Terrance kept his voice low. "Good man, Nate."

"He can be," she allowed, noticing she'd shredded her scone to crumbs. She wiped her fingers with a napkin. "Good, I mean."

Terrance chuckled, setting his chai on the small table to his left and producing a handkerchief from his shirt pocket. "We all have it in us to be good. We don't always try as hard as Nate though."

There were several reasons Julie couldn't comment, starting with the original reason she'd come to Harmony Valley.

Terrance blew his nose, a loud trumpet of a sound.

Across the room, Doris seethed, not taking her eyes off Julie.

"You hurt him with this election," Terrance said for Julie's ears only. He tucked the handkerchief back in his pocket and reached for his tea.

Julie was taken aback. "Nate told you that?"

"He didn't have to tell me." Terrance cradled his cup with both hands, but his gaze didn't coddle her. "I saw it last night at the church. After the announcement, his eyes… He expected better from a dear friend."

It was more appealing to focus on the way Nate inspired such loyalty than to dwell on the fact that she wasn't proud of the motives behind her candidacy.

Terrance's blue eyes stood out against his brown skin. Soulful eyes, they didn't judge as much as mourn a disappointment. In this case Julie. "Life isn't about grabbing at every opportunity. You have to want something sincerely before you reach for it."

His words hit their mark. Julie had to look away. She didn't want the sheriff's job. Not really. She wasn't even sure she wanted to make Nate suffer any more than he already had. "I gave these women my word."

"These women?" Terrance recycled his gentle smile. "They stood behind you for no other reason than Rutgar made a sexist comment. They don't know you or what you stand for or how you'd police this town differently from Nate, if at all."

It was the truth. And the truth was if she listened to Terrance long enough she'd be thoroughly disgusted with herself. But she didn't make any effort to stop him.

"Nate has watched over this community for years," Terrance continued. "He cares about people. He's patient with us." The sermon changed tone, lightened. "His patience has been a blessing to me. Fortitude like that isn't oblivious to wounds."

"Nate seemed fine about me running this morning." Julie felt as if Terrance had put her into a small box and then waved a magic wand and made it smaller still.

"Seemed fine." Terrance nodded. "That's the right way to put it. That's what a man does for the woman he cares for. He seems strong and solid when things are coming apart for him."

The woman he cares for?

He cares?

For me?

Julie's heart fluttered as if it had wings.

And then her feet and her heart came back down to earth. She knew Nate cared for her. But he didn't care for her *that* way.

"Did Nate send you?" Doris stepped before them, hands on her hips and a frown on her lips.

"Certainly not." Terrance pinned Doris with a hard look, but it didn't deflate her sour attitude. "I came because Robin would've wanted me to talk to Julie and find out what kind of sheriff she'd make." He cleared his throat and raised his voice. "Have any of the rest of you done that? Do you know what Julie stands for?"

No one said a word.

"Anyone can see immediately what an upstanding person Julie is," Doris said with a grating tone that made Julie wish she was the sheriff and could issue Doris citations for the concealed weapon that mostly likely rested in her purse.

"I apologize for her behavior." Julie laid a hand on Terrance's arm. "You can stay if you like."

"That's all right. I've got places to be." Terrance stood, but Doris remained in his path. Rather than argue, he sighed. "Doris, my wife always said you'd had a hard life, one that made you look at the world as if it was half-empty and you had to guard your half. Robin said you needed our kindness. Me? I think you're a bitter, unhappy woman, not to mention a bully. The only thing bullies deserve is civility." His gaze brushed over the rest of the bakery's patrons. "Don't let Doris think for you. Talk to Julie. I like her, but I also like what Nate has done for this town."

Doris let him step aside, looking as if she hadn't heard that much point-blank honesty in a long time.

The women in the room were murmuring and nodding in agreement.

"We should… We should…" Doris faltered, gaze dropping to the kissing dogs on her shirt. When she spoke again, her voice lacked its usual bluster. "We should practice your answers for tonight."

Julie didn't want to feel sorry for Doris, but she did. The truth was hard to bear, whether you had a big heart or a small one.

Duke pushed the swinging door to the kitchen open a few inches, peeking through and grinning. A tantalizing smell that wasn't horseradish wafted through the front room. He crooked his finger at Julie.

She didn't need a second invitation. "I'm sorry, Doris. I have more important things to do." Like spend time with her nephew and discover what smelled so good.

THE ELECT LANDRY for Sheriff campaign headquarters was abuzz with activity in the late morning.

Well, Rutgar, Terrance and Flynn were buzzing. Nate was feeling the dual weight of supporting Julie in the sheriff's race and wanting to win himself. Harmony Valley was predictable, in its own unpredictable way.

"That forum tonight? It's a trap." Rutgar sat on the bench beneath the front window with his leg propped up. "Don't do it." His sprain was better. He'd switched from crutches to a cane, but he hadn't argued when Nate had suggested he sit and elevate his ankle.

Flynn paced the jail with a bouncy walk and a fussy baby in his arms. "Nate can't bail out of the forum."

"I'm not bailing out of anything." Nate stared out the window at Santa Claus across the street. No matter the weather, Santa always delivered. Nate wasn't going to disappoint. He was going to stand up and answer questions as best he was able, just as he'd tried to do with April's Daddy Test. He worried more about Julie than himself. The Julie of old was capable of putting up a good fight for office. The Julie who'd arrived in Harmony Valley was more fragile.

"You need a message." Rutgar tossed his unkempt gray-blond hair over one shoulder. "So you won't get caught in a trap."

Ian's cherubic face contorted. He squirmed and whimpered.

Flynn flicked a nervous glance Terrance's way.

Terrance didn't notice. "I hate to agree with Rutgar, but he's right about traps." He stared out the door, probably not at Santa across the street. "This is war."

"Guys, this is a friendly competition." Nate felt compelled to act like the adult in the room. "Julie got roped into it in a weak moment. I stand by my record and I'll stand by the vote."

Terrance walked over to the counter and rested his elbow on top. He looked like he'd turned the corner on grief. There was a steadiness about him. "Julie is being played by Doris. Think about what's at stake—*your job*—and fight for it."

Nate paused. "You don't think I can win?" Somehow, Terrance's doubt was worse than his own.

"Let's talk strategy." Flynn paced the length of the window. "You need to stand for something. Why not safety? You can talk about how safe the town is. There's only been one robbery since you've been here."

"Problem." Rutgar raised a finger. "There weren't any robberies for years before he came. That makes him vulnerable to attack."

"Okay." Flynn paced back with a brow as wrinkled as Ian's. "You could talk about how you organized the town when the river flooded and closed the roads. Or how you helped rebuild fences after the windstorm."

"I'm bored." Rutgar yawned, but it was a fake yawn. "Next thing you'll be telling me is Nate's career history. That doesn't win votes."

Apparently, none of Nate's advisors thought he could win. "I'm not telling you anything," Nate said crisply. "Except maybe you're all fired."

Rutgar scowled so hard his gray-blond beard curled beneath his chin.

"Now, Nate." Terrance came around the counter to sit across from Nate at the desk. "Folks in town like you. Be yourself, except maybe talk a little more and…" He gestured to his cheeks. "Smile a little more."

Nate frowned.

"Great advice, especially the smiling part." Flynn stood near Nate's desk, a melancholy look in his eye. "My grandfather chose you to be sheriff." His grandfather had passed away soon after Nate came to town. "Do you know why?"

Nate shook his head.

"Because you're a good person who was in a bad place in life." Flynn stared down at his son. "You arrested the mayor's son in Willows and he didn't like it. Grandpa chose you because you needed a fresh start. He was convinced that's what Harmony Valley did best—accepting caring, talented people for who they are, and letting them move past mistakes and around dead ends."

The hair rose on the back of Nate's neck. That described Julie and what she needed.

"Listen, Sister Mary Sunshine." Rutgar shook his finger at Flynn. "The past doesn't win you any votes. Nate needs to deliver a baby or save a kitten. That'll make all the women swoon."

Nate allowed himself a half grin. "I saved a box of kittens the other day."

"Perfect," Rutgar said. "Swoony women vote for heroic men, even if they do give out tickets unfairly."

"Unfairly?" Nate stood. He'd had about enough of Rutgar's so-called help. "I was serious about firing you."

"Nate, we're only trying to help." Flynn must have clutched Ian too tight, because the baby let out a wail.

"I'm just sayin'." Rutgar spread his arms wide. "I'm a beneficiary of Nate's favoritism. Three weeks ago, I discharged a firearm in city limits."

"You told me it was an accident." Nate tried to pin Rutgar down with his best cop stare.

Rutgar's laughter ricocheted around the room.

Ian wailed again. Flynn walked faster, jiggling the baby with bigger bounces.

"Doesn't matter if it was an accident or not." Rutgar jabbed a finger in Nate's direction. "You didn't give me a ticket."

"Do you want me to cite you today?" Nate dug in his desk for his ticket book. Sad to say it was underneath several wanted bulletins from the FBI. "I will." Nate slapped his ticket book on the desk and sent Rutgar a warning look.

The old man didn't heed the warning. He kept smiling.

"Can we just calm down?" Terrance stepped between the men and held out his hands in the universal sign for stop. "And keep our voices down for the baby's sake?"

"Thank you," Flynn said over Ian's cries.

Terrance took the baby from Flynn, bringing immediate silence. Like it or not, he was a child whisperer. "Maybe we're overthinking this. I mean, Nate's the incumbent. Familiarity and experience count." Terrance's smile turned slyer than a fox. "All the events the town council has planned this week—"

"The *circus*." Nate frowned.

"—are designed to simulate how you'd respond in the line of duty." Terrance smiled down on Ian, who blew bubbles back. "Julie's never tried policing people from Harmony Valley. I like Julie, but we all know how challenging this place is to a newcomer."

Nate felt some of the weight lift off his shoulders.

"And look who's guiding her campaign." Rutgar lowered his big foot carefully down to the floor.

"Doris." Flynn grinned. "She and Julie couldn't be more different. If this thing ran more than a week we might be in trouble, but…"

Nate heaved a guilty sigh of relief. Nothing he'd done before coming to town had prepared him for policing Harmony Valley. Julie would be totally blindsided.

He felt sorry for her.

CHAPTER FOURTEEN

"THIS FORUM WILL open with a statement of qualifications by each candidate." Mayor Larry wore a muted orange tie-dyed button-down. Formal for him.

Nate hadn't dressed up. It was blue jeans and a blue checkered shirt, same as always. Despite the earlier pep talk, nerves bumped around his gut like a Super Ball in a small room. He wanted to do well and he wanted Julie to do well. Just not as well as he did.

No one wanted to miss the circus. The church was packed with residents, divided largely by gender—men on the right, women on the left. Mayor Larry stood at the podium where Doris had made her case against Nate the other night, emceeing the event. The town council sat at their usual table opposite Nate and Julie. Duke squirmed from his seat in Julie's lap.

"We'll begin with our current sheriff." Mayor Larry turned the floor over to Nate.

"Well, I…" Nate felt the town's eyes upon him. Those Super Balls bounced faster in his gut. He hadn't thought much about an introduction. He'd never run for anything before. "I've been your sheriff for several years. We've weathered a storm or two. We've put out fires together. And I…I like to think we all know each other. Trust each other. Like each other." His gaze tripped over sour-looking Doris and moved on to Julie, who sat to his left, nearest her supporters.

Julie looked transformed. Her hair bounced with life at her shoulders. The dark circles were less pronounced. She didn't breathe as if the next lungful of air might be her last. Harmony Valley was restoring her, body and soul.

"Sheriff…" Mayor Larry prompted.

Nate jolted back to the present and the dilemma of what to say. He couldn't talk about fairness. He couldn't talk about his career history. He couldn't talk about the low crime rate. "That's about it."

Duke was sitting in Julie's lap, pounding his head into her shoulder. Seven o'clock was late for a toddler, too late to be out. She was trying to calm him without making him fuss, but his son was tired and cranky. She jiggled him gently on her knees, but she was fighting a losing battle.

The mayor wanted more from Nate. "And before you came to Harmony Valley?"

Bounce, bounce, bounce.

"I was a sheriff in Willows."

Rutgar sat in the front row, frowning and shaking his head. He wanted Nate to say more about himself. Terrance nodded his head, encouraging Nate to go on.

Mayor Larry gestured toward Nate, wanting more information.

They wanted him to share something personal?

What happens in the family, stays in the family.

His gaze connected with Julie's. Tense shoulders, tense lips. She looked as stressed out as he felt.

Bounce, bounce, bounce.

"Um…" Nate tried not to squirm the way Duke was, but there was no getting out of it. "And I spent a few years as a patrolman in the Sacramento Police Department. Before that, I served overseas." He refrained from mentioning he'd been a sniper.

Doris scribbled on her notepad. Across the aisle on Nate's side of the room, Chad Healy typed on his tablet. He wrote a blog about small-town life in Harmony Valley, mostly gentle satire. He was probably hoping to get a lot of mileage out of the town's short election season. Nate hoped it wasn't at his expense.

The mayor hesitated, as if expecting more from Nate. When more didn't come, he sighed and turned to Julie. "And your qualifications, Ms. Smith?"

Duke let out a frustrated cry, and bent over backward. He would've fallen if Julie hadn't had a firm grip on his waist. Halfway into his chair, Nate reached for him, but Julie gave a miniscule shake of her head. She deftly spun Duke around in her lap and handed him a bribe—a cake pop from the bakery.

The women in the audience nodded and whispered to each other, appreciative of Julie's parenting skills.

Rutgar muttered what sounded like, "I knew it was a trap."

Julie drew a breath and began her pitch. "I've served with the Sacramento Police Department for years. First as a patrolman, and most recently on the SWAT team."

"SWAT." Mayor Larry glanced back at the congregation. "That's a very violent job."

"Objection!" Doris rocketed to her feet with

such fervor the church seemed to shake. "Favoritism."

"This isn't a courtroom, Doris." The mayor waved at her to sit back down. "I'm simply stating Ms. Smith serves on an intense unit that uses force."

"Objection!" Refusing to sit, Doris shook her pen at the mayor. "You're interpreting her words."

"No. Mad. Words." Duke's face crumpled and he threw the cake pop on the floor.

The crowd gasped.

"It's okay, buddy." Nate was out of his seat and had his son in his arms before the gasps faded. He began pacing the altar, much as he'd seen Flynn pace with Ian, patting his back, holding him close. "Nobody's going to shout anymore." He sent Doris a stern look.

She sat down.

Rutgar turned his back to the female side of the room and shielded a thumbs up from the opposition's view.

"Sheriff Landry, can you sit?" Mayor Larry's smile was strained. He was a man of peace and tranquility. The natives were getting restless and he didn't like it. "Your pacing is distracting."

"You're not the one trying to keep a child

happy," Nate said in a tone of voice Duke
would approve of.

"Let him walk." Julie picked up the remains
of the cake pop with a tissue. "Can we get on
with the questions?"

"Let's move on to the issues the town council wanted addressed." Mayor Larry perused a
piece of yellow lined paper. "Sheriff Landry,
now that the winery tasting room is open, what
precautions are being taken to keep drunk
drivers off the streets?"

"Objection!" Doris took several steps toward
the podium, stopping when she noticed Duke's
trembling lip and Nate's attempt to calm the
toddler down. "The winery has a suggested
two-glass limit," she continued in a softer
voice.

"The glass limit was the sheriff's suggestion." Mayor Larry took on the rebuttal for
Nate, turning to face the crowd. "As was my
offering a party bus to and from the winery
and Main Street so that downtown businesses
might benefit from the winery's tourism."

"Well, at least the sheriff's suggestion didn't
mean he was riding the coattails of others' suc-
cesses." Doris sat back down. "Mr. Mayor, you
charge for that bus and then pocket the money."

Several women on Julie's side of the room

looked like they wanted to shift allegiances. Nate began to breathe easier.

Mayor Larry turned back to the candidates and used a tie-dyed handkerchief to blot the sweat from his thin face. "The next question is for Ms. Smith. Our town is bordered by a small state highway and a river. In the past, both have been used as a dumping ground for garbage. How would you combat the problem?"

"I'll answer that." Joe Messina, the mechanic who lived and worked near the east bridge and the river, stood on Nate's side of the room. "Since we reopened the garage and set up the permanent outdoor art display, on land donated by Mayor Larry, there hasn't been a dumping problem."

If anyone was winning the debate at this point, it might have been Mayor Larry. He knew it, too. His smile eased. Even Duke relaxed, laying his head on Nate's shoulder. His limbs slackened.

"Perhaps we should move on to questions from the audience," Agnes suggested from the town council table.

"Me first." Doris raised her hand and then without waiting to be selected, she blurted, "Sheriff Landry, are you aware that our mayor does naked yoga in a public place?"

Nate stopped pacing and stood in the middle of the altar, choosing his words carefully. "I haven't witnessed Mayor Larry doing yoga." Everyone knew about the mayor's preference for yoga down by the river, and most knew he was fully clothed unless they were in the warmer months. Regardless, most of those out walking or jogging before work gave that section of river a wide berth.

"He's received no citations for public indecency." Doris was trying to box Nate in, and pretty adeptly, too.

"No one's complained." Mayor Larry spoke without turning.

With a smile plumping her cheeks, Doris turned to the assembly. "Does anyone disapprove of the mayor's practice?"

A few women supporting Julie raised their hands. Nate couldn't blame them.

"I told you it was a trap," Rutgar muttered.

"Moving on." The mayor's cheeks might have been a bit pink beneath his year-round tan. "The next question from the audience is for Ms. Smith."

"Ms. Smith." Rutgar pounded his cane on the floor. "Why are you running for office here? I can't think of any reason other than you want to be on the mommy track."

"Objection!" Doris's voice rattled the rafters. "It's the sheriff's child."

"But she's got custody," Rutgar bellowed back.

Julie blanched and Duke stirred, pushing against Nate's shoulder. He surveyed his surroundings. His chin jutted forward the way Julie's did when she got upset and his lower lip began to tremble.

"Can we keep things civil?" Terrance leaned forward to connect his gaze with Doris, who dialed back her tension, and then swiveled his gaze to Rutgar, who crossed his arms and harrumphed.

Nate resumed pacing, trying to reassure Duke in a whisper that everything would be okay. But Duke was having none of it. The precursor to the toddler's breakdown came in the form of a wail worthy of the siren on the town's fire truck.

"The question is your reason for running for office." Mayor Larry tried to keep up the pretext of normal, but he had to raise his voice to be heard.

Duke began to sob.

"I…" Julie hesitated, glancing at Duke. She passed a hand over her shoulder and then raised her voice. "My father was in law enforcement. Fighting crime is in my blood."

"Sheriff?" Mayor Larry turned to Nate. "Same question."

"I'm here to protect and serve." Nate used his deep voice to project his answer over Duke's sobs. "That includes enforcing the law, settling minor disputes and volunteering to help people like Wilson Hammacker when he needed a ramp built to his front door because his toes were amputated. I'm honored to be a part of this community. I really am, but I'm sorry, folks. That's all I've got to say tonight." Nate walked toward the door. "It's past my son's bedtime."

Doris's mouth dropped open, but she quickly recovered. "That's right. Go, Sheriff. We'll just ask my candidate more questions."

But Julie was following Nate out.

"Well, I guess this forum is over." Mayor Larry sounded relieved as he closed out the meeting. "We'll gather again tomorrow to see how each candidate conducts a traffic stop, and then the day after for the shoot off at the winery. We'll watch from the road just as we did when the barn was brought down. Bring your binoculars."

Nate held the door for Julie. "We're not shooting."

"You're afraid she'll win," Leona said, sitting in the back pew, fingering the pearls at her neck. "Strong women often scare men away."

Julie slipped out and Nate turned his back on Leona to do the same.

He wasn't afraid of losing. He was afraid Julie wasn't ready to shoot again—not physically, not emotionally.

And not against him.

JULIE WASN'T A QUITTER.

Julie wanted to quit.

The debate had been a disaster. She was lucky they hadn't asked her any hard questions, because she hadn't considered what it took to be a good sheriff. Not that anyone in Harmony Valley besides Doris wanted her to be sheriff. Terrance was right. No one knew her well enough. She'd stepped into this mess in a moment of weakness and now she was stuck. Because Julie wasn't a quitter.

She lay in Nate's bed watching the moon rise through the window and rubbing her thumb over the worry stone. As soon as Nate returned, she'd move to the recliner to sleep. Duke had passed out long ago on the bed.

Since they'd come to Harmony Valley, he was sleeping better, perhaps because he wasn't getting any naps, perhaps because they were always on the go.

She heard Nate come in from his evening rounds. She could tell it was him from the slow, steady pace of his steps.

From the moment he'd learned she was running for sheriff, he hadn't treated her any differently. Julie couldn't say she would've done the same. She'd have been defending her turf vehemently. He was steady, like the old oak tree in the town square. She'd been wound up tight, but just hearing Nate come in relaxed her. She should move to the recliner. And she would. In a minute.

Her eyes closed.

Something heavy dropped over her legs. Chained! She was chained.

Julie bolted upright, prepared to fight. Her heart pounded. Her stitches throbbed.

Without waking up, Duke had rolled on her legs.

Julie froze. She could have kicked him. She could have swung a fist. She could have hurt April's precious little boy. Her pulse raced, but couldn't outrace fear.

Nate. She needed Nate.

She eased her feet free and padded to the open door leading to the stairs, taking the steps slowly and on tiptoe. She'd just look to see if Nate was still awake. If he wasn't, she'd return to the apartment and try to sleep in the recliner.

"You don't have to sneak down," Nate said softly. "I'm up."

The blinds on the plate glass window were down, but open, illuminating the room with light from the street.

"Bad dream?" Nate's voice echoed from the jail cell. It was magnetic, that voice.

She drifted to the cell door, anchoring herself by gripping a cool bar lest she drift into his arms.

When she didn't say anything, Nate sat up. "Are you okay?"

In the golden light, there were no hard angles to his face, no tight half smile, no distance in his eyes.

"People don't like you," she blurted when what she really wanted to say was, "Hold me."

"Are you including yourself in that statement?" he asked in a guarded tone.

She didn't think she was. The light from the window wasn't illuminating enough. She couldn't see his face. She leaned forward, still holding the bar.

"Was that what kept you awake?" His words navigated the chasm between them carefully. "Thinking about my dislike rating?"

"People in town who don't even know me claim to like me." She wasn't used to being a pawn. She didn't like it, but it was all her fault.

"And that's what's keeping you awake."

Since he hadn't phrased his response as a query, she didn't answer him with a correction.

"When I was a kid…before I turned eight… I saw the world differently." Nate leaned back against the wall. "I trusted everyone. I believed what they told me about Santa Claus."

Duke had noticed Santa painted on an empty storefront across the street. The jolly old man was cracked and faded, but his smile still had the power to charm a toddler.

Julie gripped the cool metal tighter, because she suspected Nate's experience with Santa wasn't as golden as hers had been or even the one she hoped to provide to Duke.

"My faith in Mr. Claus was one-dimensional, because that's all you can handle as a kid. He was a magical fat man bringing me toys. At least sometimes." Nate tilted his head toward the ceiling. "Then I learned that Santa wasn't real, that it was my mom. And I felt betrayed.

Lied to. At least until I was mature enough to realize she'd done it out of love."

That hadn't been a devastating revelation. Julie breathed easier.

"The sheriff's race isn't keeping you up," Nate said softly. "You're still feeling betrayed by the law enforcement system and feeling guilty for pulling the trigger. Would you have felt the same if the shooter was at a school, aiming at kids?"

Her breath caught. "No... Yes... I don't know." She didn't want to have this conversation. And yet, she was afraid she'd be avoiding the topic until the day she died if she didn't bring it out in the open now.

"Since the day I met you, you've been trying to prove you can fit in as a cop." Nate angled his head her way. How she wished she could see every nuance in his expression. "You did what you were trained to do—protect others. You don't have to prove anything."

She knew he was right. She knew she'd crossed a bridge the night she had ended a life. She just hadn't known how costly the toll would be. "The drive to be a cop is gone." Her legs gave out and she sank to the cold floor. She hadn't realized that either. "I can't go back." Not to SWAT. Not to the police force.

Not even to being sheriff of Harmony Valley. "I can't be a cop anymore, my dad would be crushed."

Nate was next to her before she drew her next breath, gathering her in his arms. "You're wrong. He'd be proud of you no matter what career you chose."

"Would he?" She'd wondered about that, too. "I killed a woman. A mother. Someone's daughter." A defeated sound escaped her throat. "She was carrying a gun and…her baby and…wearing a heart pendant, like the one I got April for Mother's Day."

His arms were strong and steadfast around her. He wasn't letting her go.

She didn't want him to.

"Jules, could you have lived with yourself any easier if you hadn't pulled the trigger? If she had killed those innocent kids? Or if someone in your unit had died because you'd drawn a picture in your head of what bad looks like and she hadn't fit?"

"No." She'd have felt worse.

"Then you have to let that dark cloud over your head go." His hold on her lessened, only for a moment, so briefly she almost imagined it. "In the cold light of day, you'll eventually figure out if you want to stay a cop or not. Or stay in Harmony Valley or not."

He was right about all this, too. She took a few deep breaths, but she still held on to him. She held on and she began to wish she didn't have to ask him a question for the Daddy Test tomorrow.

CHAPTER FIFTEEN

"Hey. Why do I feel like you never sleep?" Julie's voice. The sound of her shifting beneath the covers. The scent of flowery perfume in the air.

This was the second night Julie had slept in Nate's bed. He wondered what it was like in hell today, since it must have frozen over.

Last night, Julie hadn't wanted to sleep alone. He'd dozed in a sitting position on top of the covers once more, her head resting on a pillow in his lap, his hand stroking her back.

"Juju wake." Duke sat on the kitchen counter, eating a sausage link and watching Nate cook breakfast.

"And when I say you never sleep, I mean the both of you." There was no mistaking the teasing in her voice. He'd missed that and the way the humor spread to her eyes and her lips.

Don't look.

If Nate looked, he'd see Julie's sleep-laden eyes and her broad smile. Maybe he'd close the distance between them. Maybe he'd kiss her and never let her go.

Don't look.

He had to let her go, just as he had to let Duke go. And yet...

Don't look.

If hell had frozen over, what harm was there in looking? Nate glanced over his shoulder. Julie yawned and ran a hand through golden locks. And then she smiled. At him.

His emotions were as scrambled as the eggs in his frying pan. He knew she could never see him as more than a friend, nor should she. Julie deserved the best life had to offer. She deserved to be whole and to be able to sleep without someone watching over her. She deserved a job that was challenging and satisfying.

He turned his back on her. "Do you want coffee before or after your shower?" Before or after she interrogated him with the Daddy Test. That test. It dredged up painful memories.

"Before and after." She breezed past him toward the bathroom, stopping only to pour herself a cup of coffee.

A few minutes later, Duke rested his head on the arm of the recliner and watched cartoons standing up. Julie and Nate sat at the table. She consumed more coffee than she ate eggs. She was going to the bakery later. He was sure of it.

"How are you feeling today?" He had to make small talk. Otherwise, the waiting for her to bring out April's notebook would kill him.

"I'm feeling more like me." She set down her coffee cup and poked at her eggs with a fork as if he'd served her fried calamari. She hated seafood.

"Eat your eggs," Nate said gruffly. "You'll live longer."

She set the fork down, clasped her hands and tucked them under her chin. "I don't want to ask you any more of April's questions."

Relief allowed him to breathe easier. But he had to know. Had he failed already? "Why not?"

The sun coming through the window glinted off her golden hair. "What is it going to change?"

She pitied him. He'd barely told her anything and she pitied him. Anger, sharp and reckless, raked his insides. "I don't need you to ask any more questions." He knew he wasn't fit to be Duke's father. He leaned forward, hands braced on either side of his paper plate. "I can tell you what you need to know."

Her lips parted, but she didn't say anything.

"In the army, they told me I had nerves of steel on the shooting range." Something happened to him when he trained his gun sight on a target. He should have been nervous. He should have had shaky hands or sweaty palms. He should have had to fight to steady his breathing. "They put me through an extra round of psych eval. They thought I didn't feel emotion." Nate didn't look at shooting emotionally.

Duke climbed into the recliner and sighed. The sun was rising, slanting rays from Julie's bright hair onto her untouched eggs. Normal. It was all so normal.

Just not his normal.

Should he tell her who he really was inside? Could he?

Nate started talking before he made up his mind. "After my dad went to prison, we moved to my uncle's dairy farm in the central valley." They'd lived in a tiny home between the main house and the milk barn. "Uncle Paul was convinced once Dad got out he'd come to find us. He said I had to be the man of the house and be prepared to defend my mother and sister. On Sundays, after we milked the cows and went to church, we'd head to a gully near the marshes at the rear of the property. He taught me how to shoot." And how to shoot when all hell broke loose. Shouting, setting off air horns, clanking an old cowbell until nothing unsettled Nate's aim.

"I'm worried for you, as a child," Julie said in a voice that wrapped around Nate's heart and gently squeezed. "Don't stop talking."

Nate almost smiled. "I could stop." He held out his arms. "You can see how the story ends. I survived."

Julie frowned. "But I can't see here." She reached across the table and tapped his chest, over his heart.

"Oh." That was as much intelligence as he could muster. Her touch, her empathy. Uncle Paul hadn't prepared him for that.

She drew back. "I want to know what's in your heart. What makes you...*you*." Those soft gray eyes. They didn't round with pity.

Nate was afraid to name the emotion there, afraid he'd misread her interest and try to steal a base and...

Get a grip, Landry.

All he had to do to push her away, to ensure she never looked at him like that again or asked him to hold her through the night, was to tell her the truth.

He cleared his throat. "A couple of years

later, I got off the middle school bus and there was my dad, sitting on the front steps of our house having a smoke. I was the first one home."

His mother had been at work, waitressing at the coffee shop by the highway. When Mom came home, the first thing she did was check all the hiding places in the house. Molly's elementary school bus wasn't due for another half hour. She still had nightmares and often slept on the floor of Nate's room. Uncle Paul was getting his trailer fixed in town. He was a retired cop who had no qualms about taking on his former brother-in-law. They'd all been gone. Nate had to face his father alone.

Julie's gray gaze was riveted on Nate's face. He wet his lips, but didn't speak.

Dad had flung his cigarette into the hedge and stood. The years in prison hadn't taken the edge off the blades of his father's cheekbones or the sharpness to his black eyes.

Nate had been scared. He'd wanted to run. But he'd also been angry, too. And he didn't want to let his family down.

"I can see you don't want me here," Dad had said, his voice as sharp as the rest of him.

Nate blinked back to the present, to gray eyes that waited for his story to continue. "Dad made me an offer. A shoot off. If I won, he'd leave and never come back."

"Was he a good shot?" Julie's question barely registered above the whisper scale.

The sound of a bullet whizzing by Nate's head on his eighth birthday returned. "He could be."

"You were what? Twelve? Thirteen?"

"I was a mature twelve."

There was a flicker of respect in her eyes.

He sat taller in his seat. "I got out my rifle." The one he'd been given when he was eight. "I led him to the dairy's shooting range with shells and a paper target in my hoodie pocket. It was the longest five minutes of my life."

Uncle Paul had tried to prepare him. He'd paid for self-defense classes. He'd shouted what-if scenarios and obscenities at him until Nate's ears buzzed and he learned not to rise to the bait.

Nate had been silent too long.

Julie touched his hand. "Did he say anything to you?"

"He didn't stop talking. I suppose he wanted to get into my head." He had, but not in the way he'd intended. Nate could still hear his father's voice, loaded with derision and fired with a scattershot approach, looking for any sign of weakness. But every word had an underlying note of uncertainty.

"Your mother's going to be happy to see me.

"Didn't anyone ever tell you a son can't beat his father?

"Somebody's been telling you you're somebody, I see."

"Finally, we reached the gully and I tacked up the target." He'd stepped aside so his father could get a look at it. "Uncle Paul had printed up photos of Dad with target circles around his face." The bullseye was centered between the eyes.

"I see the apple doesn't fall far from the tree," Dad had said, eyes narrowed. "I bet you've got no friends. I bet the girls think you're creepy. I saw you get off the bus. No one said a word to you."

Having walked to the top of the bank during his father's tirade, Nate knew he had more at stake than bragging rights or scoring points in a video game. No wonder he felt like such an outsider with other kids.

He found his balance. He found his center.

"You need to teach those kids to respect you," Dad had said. "Just like I'm gonna teach your mama to respect me."

The ground beneath Nate was soft. The sun

glinted off the stagnant water at the bottom of the gully and into his eyes. The wind pushed at his shoulders. Nate didn't care. He lifted his rifle. He breathed. He adjusted. He drew a bead on the dot between his father's eyes and fired.

Bull's-eye.

"Dang, you must really hate me." Dad had laughed. *Laughed!*

All of Nate's anger. All of Nate's bitterness. All of Nate's fear. All those gut-churning nights when he'd relived the helpless moments his father had caused.

Nate spun and took aim at a live target. Right between the eyes. "I could plant this bullet in your head. I could roll your body to the bottom of this gully and bury you. No one would come looking." *Mom and Molly would be safe.*

His father had raised his hands to his hips. He'd leaned forward. It was then Nate had noticed his knuckles were swollen and bruised. He'd been in a fight. Or he'd stopped by the diner and found his Mom.

Nate's heart lodged in his throat, but he didn't waver. He held the rifle steady.

"You'd kill me?"

"Yes, sir." And in that moment, Nate knew

it was true. He'd kill to make sure the ones he loved were safe.

Dad had rocked back on his heels, something akin to appreciation in his eyes. "I came here to get my revenge, one way or another. But it seems like I've been collecting the Big R the whole time I was in prison."

Nate had no idea what the Big R was. Confusion must have shown on his face.

"Never underestimate the power of intimidation, boy." Dad's smile created a sickening churn in Nate's belly. "If I leave now, you won't know where I'm coming from next or when you'll see me. This'll keep you and your mother on edge the rest of your lives." He'd started to double back. "The Big Revenge." He laughed again. "I've turned you into me."

Nate dropped his arms to his sides, the gun loose in his grip and shook his head.

Julie squeezed his hands. "I lost you for a minute there. What happened? Did you win?"

"He couldn't outshoot me." Not with those swollen knuckles. "But I wouldn't call it a win." The truth of who he was welled up inside Nate's throat. "I drew a bead on him, Jules. I wanted to kill him. What kind of man does that?" Not the kind of man entrusted to raise children.

"He left, didn't he?" Her gaze had become fierce. Her hands left his and sat flat on the table.

"He left, but my mom and Molly left, too." The sun had risen high enough that his side of the table was thrown in shadow. He wished he'd made this confession in darkness. "My mom was horrified." Not proud. Not appreciative. "She told me I was lucky to be alive—"

"You were."

"—and that risks like that would get her and Molly killed." She'd been unwilling to see the young warrior her brother had trained. To his mother, he'd always be the boy who'd hid in the bathtub.

Julie frowned. "That's a bit extreme."

"She left that weekend." Saying the words out loud didn't make them hurt any less. His mother had left him.

"What?" Julie's frown deepened to a scowl. "She left without you?"

Nate nodded. "She took Molly and disappeared. They changed their names and…they were gone."

"But you…" Julie rubbed her forehead as if trying to erase her scowl or his painful past. "You were just a kid."

Nate hadn't been a kid, not when he was

eight. Probably not ever. Kids played and laughed with abandon. That's what he wanted for Duke. "My Uncle Paul stood by me as they drove away."

"It's a thankless job," Uncle Paul had said.

"What is?" Nate had sucked back the tears, trying to act like the man Uncle Paul expected him to be.

His uncle set a hand on his shoulder. "Protecting people."

For the next six years, Nate had one purpose—stay sharp in case his father returned. He'd kept to himself, making few friends— those who didn't mind his silences, especially when it came to questions about his past or his family. And then he'd enlisted. In the military, he'd discovered there were people who appreciated his talents, who were thankful that he helped keep them alive and safe, who didn't care that he wasn't much of a talker.

Julie's hands covered his again. "Your mother should never have abandoned you."

He flipped his palms up and curled his fingers around her wrists. "She was afraid. Having me around didn't make her feel safe. I know she loved me, but that love couldn't stand up to her fear."

"What a cop-out. You were a kid. You stood up to that piece of garbage—no offense—"

"None taken."

"—and you did it for love." Julie was in her element. Her eyes blazed. Her cheeks fired with color. If he said the word, she'd hunt down his mother and tell her what for.

"It's in the past, Jules. Let it go."

"Let it go? Let it… You're not disposable." Julie tugged on his arms as if having him agree with her would somehow make his mother's leaving less painful. "You're not."

"And neither was April," he said gently. "I loved her. And she loved both of us. She knew you needed to confront me to move on." As he said the words, he realized they were true. "That's why April created the Daddy Test."

"You're forgetting one thing." Julie's fingers dug into his skin. "You're forgetting Duke. This doesn't end with me understanding you better and you helping me move past the shooting. We have to decide what's right for him. Together."

"We?" After all he'd told her the past few days, she could still say *we*?

CHAPTER SIXTEEN

JULIE PUSHED THE stroller out of the sheriff's office. "You can't just go dark on me when I want to talk about custody."

"I can." Nate set a brisk pace toward the corner.

"Go, Juju." After that brief command, Duke slurped on the milk in his sippy cup.

Julie obeyed, happy to find she'd regained some of her stamina. She kept up with Nate.

The morning was clear and bright. Gentle breeze, gentle birdsong, gentle clouds in the sky. All that gentleness couldn't make up for Nate's father abusing him and his mother abandoning him. But Julie could. If she ignored the magnetic pull of the pain in Nate's eyes and her corresponding need to shelter him in her arms.

Julie wanted to make things right for Nate. And the only way she knew how to help him was to show him how enriching raising a child was.

"We're going to parent Duke together."

She didn't phrase it as a question, because she didn't want to hear his answer. If they co-parented, she could be Nate's emotional rock, a place he could seek shelter when his memories became too much for him. "You don't have to be afraid you'll be like your father. You're nothing like that man."

Nate was two strides ahead of her.

"Did you hear me?" She had to work to keep annoyance from her voice, if only for Duke's sake.

Nate didn't answer.

"Truck," Duke said, pointing back to Nate's vehicle. He swiveled his arm to a new target. "Tree."

"That's right, little man." At her lowest moment, she'd wanted to drop out of the sheriff's race, but not now. Not when Nate was acting so foolishly. She'd stick with it for the week she'd promised to be here and make him see what she did—that he could be a good father.

If he'd stop walking away from her.

"I'm learning to live with the fact that April deserved better than you could give her. And I'm beginning to understand how you think you don't know how to love someone deeply, including your own child." She picked up the pace when he did, ignoring how each deep breath strained her stitches. "But loving Duke is easy. And you're good at it." Anyone could see he cared for Duke.

It was like someone was propping Nate up, pushing him away from her. He walked so tall, he seemed to have added an inch to his height.

A blond man jogged past them with a woman riding a bike beside him.

"Morning, Nate," the man said, nodding to Julie.

Nate grunted.

Nate was as tangled and tied up as the strand of holiday lights in Julie's crawl space.

"Listen, Einstein." She was getting annoyed now. "Love may be risky, but not with Duke. You'll have years to build a foundation of love and respect before he becomes a teenager and tests both of us."

"Cork it, Jules. You don't know what you're talking about." He looked over his shoulder, catching her reflection in the glass of an empty store window. The warmth she'd seen in his eyes just this morning was missing. He looked trapped and panicky. "I'm not going to parent Duke with you."

A brick facade broke the connection.

Julie nearly stumbled on an uneven crack in the sidewalk. "Not with me." She almost couldn't say the words. He didn't want to parent with her. Rejection clamped around her throat and gave it a good squeeze. She wouldn't be wrapping her arms around him. Not now. Not ever.

"No."

"Is it because of the election?" Because she'd selfishly agreed to run?

"No!" The street was empty and that one word ping-ponged off the buildings.

Duke stopped drinking milk and made a disapproving noise.

"Is it because Duke reminds you of April?" Because he'd been able to walk away from her sister.

"No." Nate's response this time was more contained, as if he, too, realized that he had to be civil to avoid upsetting Duke. He rounded the corner.

Julie was hot on his heels when all she wanted to do was drag hers. She was running out of reasons Nate didn't want to talk and out of gas. "Is it because of me?"

Nate stopped in the middle of the alley and turned. "No." But he couldn't quite meet her gaze and he headed for El Rosal, determined to get there in record time.

They reached the back of the restaurant and

approached the outdoor dining patio corner that opened to the town square.

"Tree," Duke said gleefully, pointing at the lone oak.

"It is because of me," Julie said, unable to praise Duke in her sudden misery. "Because of the things I said when I first came here, because I haven't fully recovered, and I'm your competition."

His shoulders bunched.

Julie swallowed back every lecture Dad had ever given about not being a quitter. "I'll drop out of the race if you want me to, just…just don't send us away. Duke needs you." But she had a feeling that Nate needed Duke more.

Nate stopped, turning slower this time. He closed the distance between them, which wasn't much, and came to stand in front of the stroller.

"Nay." Duke raised his head and grinned at them in turn. "Juju."

Julie mustered a smile. "Even a toddler knows we should do this together."

Nate stared at his son and said nothing.

But Julie knew what Nate was going to say. He was going to reject them the way he'd rejected April. His parents had stripped him of his self-worth, of his ability to trust in love.

"Don't say it." Don't say he couldn't do joint custody with her. Because if he did, then he'd have no qualms saying he didn't want to help raise Duke period. And then she'd have to...

She had no idea what she'd have to do. But she'd have to do something.

Nate raised his gaze slowly to Julie's.

Time slowed. She breathed in. She breathed out. She sent up a silent prayer to April. She willed Duke to keep grinning and look adorable. She sucked in her gut, squared her shoulders and continued to smile.

"It is because of you," Nate said, deflating her hopes and her smile in one fell swoop.

"But..." Her voice sounded very small. "We used to get along."

Nate blew out a deep breath. "A week from now, I'm still going to be the sheriff. You'll go back to Sacramento and pass your psych eval."

Her head rotated from side to side. "And Duke?"

Nate stared down at his child once more, his detached expression softening.

Julie needed to give Nate time so he could think before he blew his chance at a good thing. But she had no idea what to say.

"Julie! Come to the bakery." Doris waved from down the block. She wore a pair of worn blue jeans, a sweatshirt with Chihuahuas prancing through a poppy patch and a scowl for Nate.

Julie had never been happier to see Doris in her life.

"We've got flyers for your campaign," Doris singsonged.

"Flyers?" Julie singsonged back, pushing the stroller past Nate.

"Nate! Nate!" Rutgar waved him over from a table on El Rosal's patio. He sat with Terrance and several elderly gentlemen, including the mayor. "We've got some slogans for you."

"Slogans?" Nate said mulishly, trudging behind Julie.

"We'll continue this conversation tonight," Julie promised, wheeling Duke past El Rosal with the speed of a woman grateful to have dodged an argument.

"Ba-con?" Duke said craning his neck to look for Arturo as they passed the fenced dining area.

"Not today, little man."

Main Street was the main thoroughfare through town. Cars drove past. All the parking spaces were nearly full. People hustled in and out of El Rosal and the bakery.

"I wanted to talk to you alone." Doris met

Julie halfway down the sidewalk. "Without the rest of the campaign committee."

"Go for it." Nothing Doris said could be as heavy as what she'd heard this morning from Nate.

"It's about me." Doris slowed to a crawl. "I used to work at the school cafeteria in town. Thirty-five years. That cafeteria was my kingdom."

Julie could easily imagine how Doris had wielded her command.

"And then the mill exploded." Doris downshifted to a pace slower than a reluctant bride. "Businesses shut down. The school shut down. And the closest place I could find a position was hours away at a school in Dixon."

"I'm sorry to hear it. Work changes can be upsetting." Wasn't that an understatement?

Doris put a hand on the stroller, bringing it and Julie to a halt.

"Hey," Duke said, a pout in his voice. He pushed Doris's hand away. "Go, Juju."

"Just a minute, little man." Julie patted his head. "If you're good, Tracy has cake pops and hot chocolate."

"Pop. Pop. Pop." Duke bounced in his seat, momentarily placated.

"It wasn't the same in Dixon," Doris continued. "They did things their way."

And Doris had been unhappy.

"When I retired from the school system and
returned home, Sheriff Landry had a new way
of doing things. No one used to care that I left
my bass boat on the street. And I used to have
neighbors in their eighties. They couldn't hear
if my dogs barked."

"What you're saying is—" Julie felt a crease
form in her brow "—you want a sheriff who'll
look the other way."

Doris nodded, smiling the smile of a woman
expecting great things. "One who'll look at
things the way Sheriff Borelli used to."

"That won't be me." Julie pushed the stroller
forward at speed.

Doris trotted beside her. "But if you win,
it'll be because of me. I got you in the race. I
deserve preferential treatment."

"If I win—" and that seemed like a long
shot "—I'm more of a stickler for the law than
Nate."

Doris hurried ahead and opened the bakery
door for Julie. "But—"

"No buts. I would've towed your boat to im-
pound by now. And if I was sheriff, I would
give out tickets every time I pulled someone

over." Julie paused in the doorway. "And no one in my town is going to carry concealed without a permit, including you."

For the first time since they'd met, Doris was speechless.

"I became a cop because life should be fair for everyone. No matter their race, their culture or how difficult their past." Julie slanted her head and hit Doris with a hard glance, one that said she'd read between the lines when Terrance had given her a setdown in the bakery the other day. "Think about someone other than yourself for once. This election should be about the bigger picture for Harmony Valley, not how life here can be easier for you."

Julie's words rang with truth. She was afraid it was a truth she needed to look at about herself.

NATE WATCHED JULIE give Doris what looked like a dressing down and leave the woman dumbstruck on the sidewalk.

Why hadn't Julie tossed him to the curb? He'd confessed he had no qualms about the decisions he'd had to make on the job, while she couldn't sleep at night for doing the same. He'd confessed he'd drawn a weapon on his father. Julie should have been doing the math, adding up his deficits and coming up with an answer: *he wasn't father material.*

Typical Julie. She'd figured Nate needed a champion, and had taken the role upon herself, along with the assumption that she was the unacceptable part of a parenting bargain to Nate, not parenting itself.

Nate pulled up a chair next to Rutgar, letting his supporters' excitement about slogans flow over him and glide past.

"Let's get down to business," Rutgar interrupted Nate's thoughts. His gray-blond bushy brows were jumping in excitement. His cane hung off the back of his chair. "Here's my slogan. Vote for Nate. He does good things."

Nate didn't know what to say. Rutgar's slogan was a stinker.

"How about this?" Phil Lambridge's tremulous hands moved more than an orchestra conductor's. Leona's ex-husband was no longer allowed to cut hair at the barbershop-turned-salon, but he was booked six weeks out with color and highlight appointments. "Vote for Nate. He's good enough for me."

Nate raised his gaze skyward. Phil's slogan wasn't much better than Rutgar's.

"Mine's the winner." When the mayor wasn't being neutral, he was nearly as competitive as Julie. He and his buddies were regular contenders in their bowling league in Cloverdale. He tossed his slim gray ponytail over his shoulder and read. "'Vote for Nate. Coooool, man.'" The mayor grinned.

Everyone at the table groaned.

Nate ruled the mayor out. "Although I appreciate the enthusiasm, we don't have time for T-shirts."

"Not to mention it's a conflict of interest," Rutgar muttered. The mayor made a good living selling tie-dyed T-shirts and merchandise.

Arturo placed a coffee cup in front of Nate and tilted his head, the unspoken question being breakfast. Nate shook his head, but he did consider asking the waiter to spike his coffee.

"Mine makes the most sense." Terrance sported a grin the likes of which Nate hadn't seen on him since before Robin had died. "The headline will say I'm Running for Sheriff." He slapped the notepad in front of him and sat back. "And then we'll have a picture of Nate jogging. Brilliant, right?"

The assembled gave it a thumbs-down.

"Why don't you just say A Vote for Nate Is a Vote for Men?" Nate muttered. That's what the election was turning into.

"Brilliant." Phil tossed his hands in the air. "Slogan solved in time for a game of checkers at the bakery." He slumped back in his chair. "Shoot. Doris made Tracy put the checkerboard away."

Rutgar glanced down the street toward the bakery. "And the women banned us from Martin's."

Nate was dumbfounded. Checkers matches had been an institution at Martin's Bakery since it reopened over a year ago. "This is going too far."

"It's the sign of things to come if you don't win," Terrance warned. "Now, pick a slogan."

"I don't want a slogan." Nate wanted life to go back to the way it was before Doris had shown up in town. He liked slow and predictable. He enjoyed watching out for people he knew by name.

But if he turned back the clock that far, he wouldn't have met his son or reconnected with Julie. He wouldn't have helped ease Julie's torment over the shooting. He wouldn't have held her hand or learned the feel of his son in his arms. Those were memories he'd keep forever.

"You need a slogan," Rutgar insisted. "The ladies have a slogan *and* a flyer. They're way ahead of us."

"Let them pass out paper." Mayor Larry had that competitive gleam in his eye again. "We need to think about tonight."

"The pull-over simulation." Terrance nodded, evidently on the same page as the mayor. Each candidate was picking someone in town for their opponent to role-play a traffic stop. "Who are we going to pick for Julie?"

"Oh, ho, ho." Rutgar cracked his knuckles.

"Play nice, fellas." Nate had never realized how conniving the men in town were until this election.

"Nice?" Mayor Larry crossed his arms over his chest. "If we play nice, we choose Mildred or Agnes. And we lose."

"Where's the fun in losing?" Rutgar demanded, finger-combing his beard. "What about me? I can give Julie a run for her money."

"No." Nate scowled at the big man. "We play fair."

"Let's choose Prescott." Phil stood, swaying like Prescott, who was a happy drunk.

Nate steadied Phil with one hand. "Prescott is an extreme case. Remember, Julie's a rookie when it comes to Harmony Valley."

"She's SWAT." Rutgar had a hard-core competitive streak that spoke to a similar vein inside Nate. "Julie is as experienced as they come."

"Remember," Terrance said. "This is a war Doris started, not Julie. We're competing against Doris."

"Doris won't be up there with Prescott." Choosing the town's friendly drunk was the equivalent of stacking the deck in Nate's favor.

But Nate didn't overrule them.

THE FLYERS HAD yet to be seen.

Julie sat at the table in a bakery with her campaign volunteers. There were fewer today with only a handful at the main table where Doris held court. The ladies chattered about life and grandkids. They were sweet women, really. And Julie felt guilty because she'd decided out there on the sidewalk—with Nate looking bottled up, distant and hurting—that she was only staying in the race because it meant she and Duke could stay in town with him. She wasn't going to try to win.

But she wasn't going to throw the race either. She had her pride, just like Doris had hers.

Eunice had crayons and coloring books out today, which wasn't cutting it with the two toddlers. Gregory pushed Duke around the bakery in the stroller. The boys kept stopping by the bakery counter to place pretend orders with Tracy. Or they would have been pretend if Tracy didn't keep giving them miniature chocolate chip cookies.

A woman named Georgia sat to Julie's right. She had thin black hair cut in a bob and a broad forehead that was broken by a sharp widow's peak. "Can we start, Doris?"

"We're waiting for Lilac," Doris said with little grace.

The bakery door flung open and Lilac made her entrance.

"I'm here, I'm here. I hope you didn't start without me." Lilac slid into a seat and unwound the maroon paisley scarf from around her neck. "I'm having a bad hair day. Darn humidity." She peered at her reflection in the bakery display case, finger-combing her sophisticated curls.

"Show me your flyers, ladies." Doris wasn't one to hide her anger well. She trembled with it from her fingers to her short spiky hair. She trembled so much the other women at the table had subtly moved their chairs away from her.

Julie put her elbows on the table and studied Doris the way she would a suspected felon. "I thought you had a flyer."

"Not yet." There came the dog breeder's familiar superior smile. "I wanted the men to think we had a flyer."

"Isn't Doris clever?" Lilac dug in her designer handbag. She unfolded a large sheet and handed it to Julie. "I made this last night."

Lilac's flyer was a page from a craft scrapbook. Julie recognized the paper type because April had been a scrapbooker. The letters Lilac used were peel and press and, although similar in color and size, were reminiscent of ransom notes made by clipping newspapers and magazines because they weren't placed straight.

"'A Vote for Julie Is a Vote for Women.'" Julie read, trying very hard to keep the sarcasm from her voice. "'A Vote for Women Is a Vote for Peace. A Vote for Peace Is a Vote for a Better World.'" She had to give Lilac a smile because it was a nice sentiment. Sexist, but nice.

"I like mine better." Georgia held up a lined sheet of notebook paper. "Vote for Julie! Only Eliot Ness Could Do a Better Job, but It's Not the 1930s and He's Dead." She leaned closer to Julie to whisper, "You do know who Eliot Ness is, don't you?"

"Are you kidding?" Julie's smile came much easier. At least Georgia had some originality.

"You thought I wouldn't know *The Untouchables*?" The movie had been required viewing by her dad, along with every John Wayne film ever made.

"You just earned my vote all over again." Georgia patted her arm.

"Those are both too soft." Doris crushed a paper napkin in her palm. "We need something with strength and power."

"We need something to get the men to vote for Julie." Georgia waved her paper in the vicinity of Doris's face. "The population is split equally between men and women. It's why the Eliot Ness angle will work."

The claws were definitely coming out today and Julie wanted to be long gone before they did any damage. Luckily, Duke had been trying to push Gregory in the stroller, but couldn't quite get the larger boy moving.

"Juju." Duke could say Julie's name with several different tones of voice. This one said, *Help.*

Julie stood. "Ladies, I'm touched you want to help me, but——"

"You don't have to worry about a thing," Doris said, leaning between the tables to clasp Julie's wrist. "Let your campaign team do all the heavy lifting." She lowered her voice. "We get to choose who does the mock traffic stop tonight with Nate. I recommend me."

Julie wouldn't wish Doris on her worst enemy, but if she said that out loud, she'd have her worst enemy in Doris.

"Juju."

"I think I should do it." Lilac adjusted her scarf, avoiding looking Doris in the eye. "Because I have so much experience being pulled over by Nate."

"I agree." Georgia had a contrary look in her eye and a too-innocent smile.

"Me, too."

"I agree."

Doris was being outvoted.

"I'll go with the majority," Julie said sweetly. "Lilac it is."

CHAPTER SEVENTEEN

"WELCOME TO THE second night of sheriff-election activities." This time, Mayor Larry had positioned his podium next to the town council so that he faced both candidates and the voters. He wore a lime-green tie-dyed T-shirt which reminded Nate of margaritas.

A margarita would hit the spot about now.

The empty chair between Julie and Nate served as the pretend vehicle they'd be pulling over. Duke sat in Julie's lap once more, staring out at the assembled with tired eyes. Some of the women sat on Nate's side, which was heartening. The crowd in the church was a bit rowdier this evening, anticipating quite the show.

"The goal for tonight's exhibition is to see how each candidate performs under stress." Mayor Larry winked at Nate. "There will be no interruptions." He gave Julie's campaign manager a stern look. "Doris, that means no objections, no heckling and no offering advice, or you will be removed. This is serious."

Nate couldn't resist a commiserating glance at Julie. Serious? Not hardly.

Julie didn't look his way. In fact, she'd avoided him all day long.

"Here are the rules for tonight's exhibition." The mayor referred to a sheet of paper. "Turns out the two volunteers chosen to participate have been pulled over in the past. I'm going to read the scenario that led up to them being pulled over, and then I'll hand it over to each candidate." The mayor set his notes down. "We flipped a coin and the sheriff will go first. Our volunteer is Lilac."

Lilac had dressed for the part in the show. She wore her Sunday best—a flouncy, flowery yellow dress, low white heels and a blue scarf she'd tied over her short gray hair as if she was driving the Cadillac with the top down. She hurried toward the empty chair on stage the same way he'd seen her cut in line at the Harvest Festival last fall—nose in the air, looking neither left nor right.

Nate knew trouble when it was brewing. Lilac was so concerned with appearances she didn't see the step ahead of her. He leaped up and caught her arm as she tripped.

"Thank you, Sheriff." Lilac rarely blushed, but her cheeks were rosy now. "You're always such a gentleman."

"Oh, Lilac," Doris muttered.

The assembled on both sides of the aisle laughed.

Nate escorted Lilac to the chair in the middle of the dais. She smoothed her skirts, and then held her hands up as if gripping a steering wheel.

"Lilac was pulled over for speeding and reckless driving," Mayor Larry told the crowd. "Take it away, Sheriff."

"Don't forget she also had a hit-and-run." Nate probably shouldn't have added that to her list of infractions, but it was just too good an opportunity to pass up. Lilac took her public image very seriously and, like Doris, always denied any wrongdoing.

Lilac sniffed. "I take back the part about you always being a gentleman."

"And…take it away, Sheriff," Mayor Larry said again, brows waggling with uncertainty.

Nate took pity on him and got the show on the road. "Let's pretend that you've pulled to the curb and I've shown up at your window."

Lilac tossed both ends of her scarf over her shoulders. "I'm ready."

Nate stood next to her, facing the same

way—to the audience. "License and registration, please."

Lilac handed him the imaginary items. "Is there a problem, Sheriff?"

"Ma'am, do you know how fast you were going through town?"

"Of course not." Lilac swiveled her head and her shoulders toward him. "I never look down. I simply get from here to there."

He was grateful she was playing this true to form. It made his job a lot easier. "You were going fifty in a twenty-five."

Someone on the female side of the audience gasped, as if this was news to her. To his left, Julie frowned, because it was news to her, too. And Lilac?

Lilac paused, glancing to Doris. Color crept back into Lilac's cheeks. "Your radar gun must be off. I mean... I...I haven't been in an accident yet."

"Maybe not an accident with another car, but you hit a dog on the east side of the town square."

There were murmurs of disapproval in the crowd. Folks were clearly agitated. Flynn sat in the front row, holding Ian and looking stern. It'd been his nephew's dog.

Lilac had never been subject to public scrutiny before. She squirmed. "Well, the dog didn't die." And she'd eventually paid the vet bills. But she hadn't slowed down since.

"And you nearly killed Chad Healy when he volunteered his time to clear branches from a public street after a big storm."

"Missed me by that much," Chad said from his seat behind Flynn, holding up his thumb and forefinger.

"And you drove away," Nate paused for effect. "Almost as if you didn't see him."

"She needs glasses." Eunice got up from her aisle seat on Julie's side and took a seat on Nate's side of the church, as did a few other women. "She always was vain about her appearance."

Lilac slumped in her faux driver's seat.

"I knew I should've been our volunteer." Doris crossed her arms and glared at everyone.

"Let me remind residents about the rules." Mayor Larry put a finger to his lips. "Shhh."

Nate pretended to flip open his ticket book. "You'll be receiving three tickets today, which will put your license at risk of revocation unless you go before a judge to plead your case, or you sign up for traffic school."

"Traffic school?" Lilac was as indignant now as she'd been for any of her tickets.

Duke appeared at Nate's side. He pointed to Lilac. "Time-out?"

The audience laughed.

"Yes." Nate scooped his son into his arms. "Lilac gets a time-out."

NATE WAS GOING to be hard to beat.

He'd handled Lilac with humor and sensitivity. If Julie pulled over a driver who'd hit a dog and nearly run over a man—and then driven off—she'd have very little respect for them. Not that she gave speeders a chance to talk their way out of tickets. In fact, she'd never let anyone off. She'd had one of the highest ticket rates in the department.

"And now for our second driver," the mayor was saying. "Prescott Driscoll."

There was a murmur in the crowd. Pews creaked as people twisted in their seats to look.

A man near the back of the church stood and made his way to the front. He was tall and slender, wearing cowboy boots, jeans, a tan chambray shirt and a black leather vest. His sparse gray hair was long and thin, and fell over his equally long and thin face. His footsteps rang in the church ominously.

Julie glanced to Nate, who held Duke in his lap. He was looking at the approaching volunteer with something like regret in his eyes. Who had he chosen for her?

Prescott plunked himself heavily in the driver's seat, shifted sideways as if leaning on a car door and held the imaginary steering wheel with one hand. "Ready."

"Prescott was pulled over for drunk driving," the mayor said.

Drunk driving. The goal of the stop was clear to her. Julie needed just cause to check Prescott's blood alcohol level.

Julie slipped on mirrored sunglasses and came to stand next to Prescott the way Nate had done with Lilac. Except she kept a hand at her hip where her weapon would be in a live situation.

But before she could ask Prescott if he knew why he'd been pulled over, he began talking, enunciating as clearly as if he was performing a play. "How are you tonight, Officer?" He glanced up at her with a smile that had decades of charm behind it. "You're looking mighty fine."

"I'm feeling mighty fine." She went with the flow. Was that alcohol on his breath? Had he shown up drunk to a simulation of a drunk driving incident? "How are you feeling, sir?"

"I'm so good, I feel like dancing." He got out

of the pretend car and did a dance that was part tap, part line dance and part disco.

The audience applauded.

Julie flushed with the heat of embarrassment. "Sir, you need to stop." She held up one hand, keeping the other on her imaginary gun.

"Is she going to shoot him?" a woman asked in a concerned voice.

"I suppose you want to give me your tests." Prescott clapped once, and then rubbed his hands together. "I'm ready. Give it your best shot."

Julie glared at Nate. "This is not how he acted when you pulled him over."

"It is."

Nate's mouth slanted toward an apologetic half grin.

It was too late for apologies. She was going to make a fool of herself.

"Welcome to Harmony Valley," someone in the audience said.

She'd been in tough situations before with the odds stacked against her. Julie eased her shoulders back and pushed her sunglasses up her nose. She proceeded to put the old man through his paces. Arms out to the side, alternating touching a finger to his nose. The man didn't so much as wobble. She asked him to recite the alphabet backward. He sang it as ordered, quickly, as if he'd had a lot of practice.

"Wow," Julie said to Prescott, honestly impressed. "I've never actually seen anyone do that."

Doris was practically convulsing with anger in the front row, pressing her lips together in a disapproving flat line.

"I'm ready to walk the line." Prescott slapped a hand against his thigh. "Five, six, seven, eight." He started down an imaginary line. "Step-bump. Step-bump-bump." He swayed his hips to the side on every bump and yet he kept walking in a straight fashion. "Step-bump. Step-bump-bump." He reached the end of the altar, pivoted on his toes and returned the way he'd come.

The crowd hooted and cheered.

Julie's cheeks were hot. She was going to fail the simulation. She'd lost control of the traffic stop. Prescott had given her no reason to administer a Breathalyzer test. She hated losing, but she'd be graceful in defeat. "Well, sir. I've got to admit it. You're a good dancer."

Prescott turned to face her, that charming grin splitting his face. "I'm a good drunk, too. I'm drunk now."

"Aha! I got you." Julie raised her arms as if

she were a referee calling a touchdown. His admission meant she could legally collect his blood alcohol level. She faced Nate. "I did it!"

Nate smiled at Julie the way he'd smiled at Duke the other day in the bakery. Julie's heart bump-bumped.

"You did." Prescott leaned closer, washing her in alcohol breath. "Take me in." He turned to the audience at their thunderous applause and took a bow.

Duke slid off Nate's lap and came to stand next to Julie. He took a bow, too.

Prescott grabbed Julie by her injured shoulder and gave her a bear hug.

Julie's breath caught in her throat as pain sliced through her. Her knees buckled.

And then Prescott was ripped away, leaving Julie staggering for balance.

"Never touch an officer of the law without permission." Nate escorted Prescott to the back of the church, holding the man's arm. "Do you need a ride home?"

"Nope. I walked." Prescott was unfazed by Nate's reprimand and his removal from the stage. "I walk everywhere now."

The audience had grown silent.

Nate returned to the front, boots echoing on hardwood.

"Well," the mayor looked as surprised as everyone else. "That concludes our demonstration. We'd like to thank our candidates and volunteers. Tomorrow, the shooting competition will be held at ten o'clock at the winery."

A subdued crowd began to break up. Pieces of conversation drifted to Julie over the creaking of pews and sound of feet on wood floor.

"Did you see how fast he moved?"

"I never realized how even-tempered the sheriff was. She was getting angry."

"Even when she wins, we lose." Doris tossed her hands and walked out.

"She did fine." Nate swung Duke into his arms.

Julie's skin tingled as if she'd been shocked. She didn't often lose or get outmaneuvered. Her knees locked in place. "You chose Prescott." He'd chosen someone who'd humiliate her.

"Hold that thought until we get home." Nate walked out, leaving Julie no choice but to follow. He waited until they'd crossed the town square and were alone on the sidewalk approaching the sheriff's office before saying anything more. "Someone else suggested Prescott. I could have picked anyone in that church tonight. They're all of the same caliber."

"Soused?" Julie hadn't brought a jacket. The breeze had a chill and it reached to her bones. Or maybe it was how Nate had tried to sabotage her.

"I mean, they all have unusual characters. Like Prescott. He was a dancer in the chorus of community theater in San Francisco." He scanned his surroundings as they walked. "They're all argumentative. And innocent in their own minds. Plus many of them are so independent they refuse to acknowledge they're getting older and are less capable doing everyday tasks, like driving. Two-thirds of the population is over the age of sixty-five. It's not so much about preventing crime as protecting these people from harming themselves."

Julie had to stop herself from saying she had no interest in working in a retirement home, because she didn't want to argue and she didn't want Nate's stupid, stupid job. Maybe if she told herself that often enough, she'd stop being so sensitive about these stupid, stupid events.

"You'll look back on this and smile one day," Nate teased. He even threw her a bone—a half smile.

"Oh, yeah. I'll tell my grandkids about the day I pulled over a drunk and he nearly danced his way to freedom." When she put it like that, it didn't sound like such a dastardly deed.

"See? It stings less already." Nate opened the station door for her.

It was unlocked. He didn't lock the place when he left? How could a town like this even exist?

She led the way upstairs, aware of Nate behind her, of her morning intentions to co-parent.

"Tomorrow we should call off the competition," he said. "You aren't ready to shoot, much less shoot a rifle."

Couldn't he show some faith in her? "I can push through." They'd probably only fire a handful of shots.

He caught up to her at the second-floor landing, crowding into her space as she struggled with the door to his apartment. "What if you freeze in front of all those people? What if the recoil reopens your wound?"

"Dr. Landry, I'll be fine," she reassured him, finally getting the doorknob to turn. "I don't want to talk about this now." She didn't want to talk about her weaknesses, physical or otherwise.

He walked past her to put his cell phone on

the charger. "Then we'll talk about it again tomorrow morning in time for me to call it off."

Julie let him think what he would.

From the kitchen table Nate watched her put Duke to bed. His regard should have been unnerving or made her feel self-conscious. It didn't. His gaze was relaxed and open. She felt the same.

She came to stand next to the table, staring into Nate's dark eyes. He understood this town in a way she didn't. He'd noticed the kittens being abandoned. He knew just how to handle the residents. And himself.

But he didn't know how to handle her.

Julie took him by the hand and slowly pulled him to his feet. She led him downstairs and sat on the bottom step of the sheriff's office, tugging him to join her. Nate was warm next to her. She leaned into that warmth without intending to, lacing their fingers together. "You belong here. And so does Duke. Shared custody. No arguments. I get him on weekends."

He didn't argue. He seemed preoccupied with their joined hands, which made her preoccupied with their joined hands.

She'd forgotten how their fingers fit together perfectly. That fit. His warmth. Her sigh. They were comfortable together. She could almost forget who they were and where they'd been, and sit here in limbo forever.

Well, maybe not forever. She'd never been good about sitting still and keeping silent. "I admit, I'm a little envious of your life here. I've always had to bang down the door to belong."

"You never had to prove anything to me." His voice had the gruff quality of a man who was unsure of himself.

Because of her? Because she held his hand? She gripped it tighter. "I've had to prove myself to you most of all."

"Why?" He looked at her out of the corner of his eye.

Using her free hand, she turned his face to hers. Stubble scraped her palm. "I don't know. But I think it has something to do with this." And then she followed her instincts and kissed him.

He didn't fall back against the wall and demand to know what she was doing.

He didn't push her away.

He didn't do anything, except...kiss her back.

His arms gathered her close, being careful of her shoulder and the awkwardness of being on the stairs. He was always so kind, so thoughtful of others. He must have recognized the spark between them these past few days. He must have fought it the same way she had. She pressed closer, feeling less alone, less unsure of the future.

"Jules," Nate murmured against her lips.

She leaned back and looked deep into his eyes, searching for a mirror of the feeling that threatened to overwhelm her—that this was the right place and the right time and the right person. She should be thinking of April. She should be thinking Nate was off-limits. She couldn't think beyond the feeling that there was a reason their hands fit together so well. And then Julie remembered she was the reason Nate refused to share custody with Duke. "I should drop out of the race."

"No." His hand rested on her hip.

"But you don't want me to shoot tomorrow."

"That's right."

"And you don't want me to win."

"That's right." There was that relaxed partial smile, the one he gave those he was fond of in town. He was fond of her. He cared, just as Terrance had said.

Julie reminded herself to breathe. "But you don't want me to drop out."

"That's right."

Outside, an owl hooted. In the distance, a car honked.

"I don't get it," Julie said mildly, content to be confused if she was in his embrace. "What's the point of staying in the race if I'm not shooting?"

He stared at her so long she thought he wasn't going to answer. And then he said, "You'd leave. You already tossed out the Daddy Test. Why would you stay if you weren't running for sheriff?"

I'd stay for you.

"You are the most infuriating man alive." Nate didn't want her to leave! She was tempted to jump up and do a dance inspired by Prescott. And she might have done so if Nate's arms weren't encircling her.

She slid her hands around his neck. "Kiss me again."

CHAPTER EIGHTEEN

NATE AWOKE IN his recliner thinking about Julie—her tender touch, her gentle kisses, her willingness to quit the race so he could keep his job.

Thinking about Julie made him smile. He kept his eyes closed, content.

Nothing he'd said about his past deterred her from her conviction that he should raise Duke. In fact, it seemed quite the opposite. Almost as if she had complete faith in him—despite years of resentment and hearing about his childhood.

Julie was doggedly determined to do the right thing, to seek out justice, to be as good as anyone else at anything she did. Yet in spite of the competitiveness, she was fiercely protective of April and Duke. And him.

That was the most surprising part of all. After everything that had gone down, Julie seemed to like him. More than like him. They'd kissed. He'd held her close.

Nate wanted to kiss her again. He wanted to

hold her in his arms. He wanted to wake up to the sound of her voice and go to sleep at night knowing she'd be nearby in the morning. He wanted...

He wanted things he shouldn't want. He wanted more than he'd had with April. He wanted...

He wanted a love like Terrance had had with Robin. He wanted the father-son bond Flynn was making with Ian. He wanted to love Julie and have her love him in return.

Was it possible? Or had the kisses last night been something Julie would regret this morning?

Nate opened his eyes.

The apartment was quiet. Most likely Duke and Julie were still asleep. Nate stretched and looked around the room.

Midmorning sunshine streamed through the windows. The bed and the bedroll were empty and in a jumble a few feet away. The bathroom door was open. There were no whispered voices. No tiptoeing feet on the floorboards. No Julie. No Duke.

Julie's notebook sat on the kitchen table. From the recliner he could just reach it. She'd scribbled a note on a page. "See you at ten."

At ten. At the shooting competition.

The clock on the microwave read 9:00 a.m. He'd overslept. Nate never overslept. But he'd had too many long days, too many sleep-deprived nights. It'd caught up to him.

Nate bolted out of the chair. Why couldn't it have caught up to him tomorrow?

Julie hadn't fired a weapon since she'd been shot. If there was a saddle to climb back on, she'd need a safety harness to prevent being bucked off. They were going to use rifles. She was right-handed. She'd have to put the gun stock against her shoulder. Her wounded shoulder.

Rutgar was providing them with rifles to shoot. Who knew how powerful they'd be. And if Julie reopened her wound, she'd need medical treatment, which she should get from the doctor who'd sewn her up. Which meant she'd have to return to Sacramento. She and Duke would leave.

No more early mornings with his son while Julie slept. No more spoiling Duke with bacon and airplane games. No more little boy filling his arms and his life and his heart.

Nate gripped the kitchen counter. He didn't want Julie to go. He loved her. He didn't want Duke to go for the same reason. He loved his son. He wanted to watch him grow and help him be a better man than Nate had been. He wanted him to know his great-uncle Paul, his aunt Molly and his cousin Camille. And he wanted Duke to know his grandmother.

Nate sank to the wood floor. He'd let his mother go long ago, but family was important. Knowing where you came from was worth awkward reunions.

What had happened to his life? Where did he go from here?

He'd kissed Julie last night, but they hadn't discussed anything. They hadn't talked more about April and all the reasons the wedding had been called off.

He quickly showered and changed clothes, only bothering to make the bed because he didn't want Julie to think he was a slob.

"Nate?" Terrance called from downstairs.

And then a louder, *"Nate!"* from Rutgar.

Nate hurried down. He had a lot to sort out in his life, but the first priority was to keep Julie from shooting.

"Today's the day you seal the deal and win this thing." Rutgar stood without a cane. His gray-blond hair looked clean and brushed. And there were no crumbs in his beard.

"What's wrong?" Trust Terrance to notice Nate's agitation. The widower studied Nate's expression like a hawk tracking a possible gopher sighting.

Nate saw no reason to lie. "I'm thinking about throwing the shooting competition."

"Unbelievable." Rutgar dropped into Nate's desk chair, which groaned almost as loud as the big man himself. "I attached myself to a dark horse."

Nate told them about Julie's wound. "I think I should concede, so she doesn't have to shoot."

"Why did you have to have a good reason?" Rutgar buried his head in his oversize hands. "I could have argued with you if you had a bad reason."

"Ignore Rutgar. He doesn't like to lose." Terrance put a hand on Nate's shoulder. It was a supportive hand, and he looked at Nate the way a father should look at a son. "Have you talked to Julie about this?"

"Briefly. She refused to back out."

Terrance sighed and guided Nate into an office chair. "Do you know what women hate more than a man who lies to them?"

"No, but I'm sure you're going to tell me." Nate checked his phone. He didn't have time for one of Terrance's long lectures. "Just be quick about it."

Terrance planted one hand on each arm of

Nate's chair. "Women hate a man who makes decisions without consulting them."

"Julie's not a cream puff." Rutgar lifted his head. "She'll most likely slug you either way."

"Ignore Rutgar," Terrance said again, calm when Nate wanted to shout. "You have to tell Julie why you don't want her to shoot. There's forty minutes until the competition starts."

Nate nodded, drawing a deep breath. "You're right."

But Terrance wasn't done. "And when I say you have to tell Julie your reasoning, I mean you have to tell her you love her."

"How did you…" Of course. Terrance had seen it before Nate had. "No." Nate pushed Terrance's hands off the chair and stood. He couldn't tell Julie how he felt. He wasn't ready. His temples throbbed. "If I tell her…"

"He can't even say the words." Rutgar stood, towering over both men. "Why bother being preventative? I say we bring the first-aid kit and let her shoot. We'll win. We'll patch her up. No serious harm, no serious foul."

"Rutgar," Terrance chastised. "Nate is a gentleman."

"And I'm not." Rutgar shrugged. "I'm okay with that." He came around the desk and dropped his beefy arm on Nate's shoulder. "Shoot today, play Romeo tomorrow."

"He's going to do the right thing." Terrance gave Nate a gentle shove in the back, freeing him from Rutgar's hold. "Knowing Julie, she's going to insist upon competing, no matter what Nate says." Terrance pushed Nate toward the door. "Come on. We need to get Robin's gun. It's designed for a woman, so it won't have the kick of your weapon."

"You own a gun?" A shaft of fear pierced Nate's chest. Terrance had taken Robin's death hard. What if he'd done more than walk around in flannel pants and bunny slippers? What if he'd—

"I know what you're thinking." Rutgar joined the shove-the-sheriff-toward-the-door club. "Terrance ain't no fool. He gave me his guns after Robin died."

"You were shooting Terrance's guns," Nate realized, remembering the bullet-ridden cans at Rutgar's house and the reports of gunfire.

"You've been using my guns?" Terrance's voice simmered with anger.

Rutgar shrugged and nudged Nate forward again, none too gently. "I cleaned them afterward."

"I thought you were my friend." Terrance

lowered his brows and used his hand to guide
Nate toward the door. "Friends don't sneak
shots with their friend's firearms."

"I can't do this." Nate dug in his heels and
spun away from both men. "Not this way."

JULIE COULDN'T REMEMBER the last time she'd
been this happy.

She and Duke were finishing off a breakfast of bacon and eggs. More important, Julie
was finishing off a mug of strong coffee while
Duke tore into a chocolate chip waffle.

She'd woken up in the middle of the night
just as she was beginning to relive the shooting
in a dream. Instead of dipping into the nightmare, she'd opened her eyes and found Nate
sleeping in his recliner a few feet away. Duke
had climbed into his lap, his head resting on
Nate's shoulder.

It was official. Nate had passed the Daddy
Test.

Nate may not have had an idyllic childhood,
but he could provide one for Duke. She could
see the two of them together over the years.
He'd teach Duke how to play sports and shoot.
He'd teach Duke how to drive and the intri-
cacies of tying a tie. He'd stand tall and stoic
when Duke left for college. And then she saw

herself standing next to Nate, her arm looped around his waist, her head nestled against his chest.

Peace settled in her heart.

This was right. *They* were right. She had a feeling April would approve.

She'd closed her eyes and drifted back to sleep for another few hours. And when Duke whispered her name in the wee hours of the morning, she'd taken him to the bathroom to clean up for the day and let Nate sleep.

She was staying in Harmony Valley. She'd find a position on a police force somewhere nearby—Cloverdale or Santa Rosa. She'd go back to patrol. She and Nate would test the relationship waters. Not marriage, because she didn't want to make him bolt as he had with April. She could hope that a wedding would happen someday, but she wouldn't push. What they had between them held the promise of something special, something worth waiting for.

The sun was shining. The coffee was strong. Duke was no longer grumpy in the morning. Her shoulder no longer hurt when she breathed. And when Nate woke up, he'd come find them.

"Juju, pay?" Duke pointed to the town square.

"We're going for a walk after this." To the winery where they'd be shooting.

Rutgar was providing the rifle and ammo. The event would be fun. She was competitive, but she knew Nate was a better shot than she was. She planned to enjoy the camaraderie of being with Nate and doing something they both enjoyed.

"There you are." Doris wore a brown sweater with hundreds of small dancing Chihuahuas embroidered on it. "How good of a markswoman are you?"

"Are you deadly?" Lilac stood next to her friend wearing khaki slacks, a leopard-print blouse and a tan safari hat. The ends of her canary yellow chiffon scarf fluttered in the breeze.

"Of course, she's deadly." Doris had no qualms belittling her friend. "She's on the SWAT team. Tough as they come."

Julie's stomach turned.

"While our sheriff has likely done nothing more than work the system to his advantage."

It was better if they didn't know the truth about either Julie or Nate.

"Are you feeling okay?" Lilac peered at Julie. "You don't look well."

"She's been spending too much time with

the sheriff." Doris tried to stare down her nose at Julie, but she wasn't as good at it as Leona. "That'll upset anyone's stomach."

Rutgar appeared at the wrought iron fence. He had a rifle case slung over his right shoulder and a square ammo bag crosswise over his body. He stood steadily on two feet without crutches. Terrance stood next to him. Neither one of them smiled.

"Are you competing for sheriff, Rutgar?" Lilac put more flirt in her voice than a teenage girl looking for her first date.

"No." Rutgar looked taken aback. "We brought Ms. Smith a rifle."

"Why?" Doris slanted her gaze suspiciously. "Why would you help our candidate?"

"Nate asked us to," Rutgar said in a growly voice. "We're gentlemen." And then he straightened and grinned at Terrance.

"Oh." Lilac looked Rutgar up and down. "So you are."

"The gun was my wife's." Terrance went to Duke and began cleaning his hands with a wet napkin. "It's made specifically for a woman— lighter, more compact and with a top-of-the-line recoil pad." He glanced at Julie's shoulder as if he knew she'd been shot.

They knew? Her hand drifted over her bandage even as her shoulders tensed. Had Nate told them? She rolled the tension away. Clearly, they knew she'd been shot. They'd brought her a weapon.

"Now the sheriff…" Rutgar's voice dropped to smack-talk casual. "He's a big man. He's bringing a big gun."

And it would probably have a big recoil, whereas a gun made specifically for a woman wouldn't. "That was thoughtful. Thank you." Julie's shoulder thanked them. And later, Julie would thank Nate personally.

Doris wasn't convinced of the guys' sincerity. "I smell a rat."

"If you expect a rat, that's what you'll get every time." It was Leona. She stood at the edge of the sidewalk in a blue dress and pearls, clasping her hands as she'd done the night Julie had checked in.

"What are you doing here?" Lilac asked.

"My granddaughter wants me to get out more." Leona shrugged her shoulders, looking more untouchable than ever, until she added, "And I came to wish Julie luck."

"You petty," Duke called out to her.

Nate may have had a half smile, but Leona had an almost smile. When people kept so much bottled inside, any small indication of emotion was like a flower in full bloom.

Julie thanked Leona and gathered her things, ignoring the put-out pouts of Doris and Lilac. "Do you want me to carry that over?" She gestured to the gun.

"Let Rutgar do it." Terrance freed Duke from his high chair and set him in the stroller. "Flynn said Duke could watch the shooting match from the winery's offices. I'd be honored if you'd allow me to take him."

"I'm feeling spoiled now," Julie said, meaning it. Impulsively, she stood on tiptoe and kissed Terrance's cheek.

"Hey. Don't forget the gun bearer." Rutgar tapped his cheek.

Julie gave him a kiss, as well.

Terrance wheeled Duke to the sidewalk where he paused, waiting for Julie to join them.

"We were going to drive Julie over." Lilac hadn't stopped studying Rutgar since he'd arrived. "That's why we tracked her down. Do you know? Doris could be a policeman. She has very good investigative skills."

"No, thanks." Julie tried to hide a smile. Doris knew breakfast was only served at two places in town—El Rosal and Martin's Bakery. It hadn't been that hard to find Julie. "I'd rather walk and loosen up my muscles." Julie left money on the table and hurried to join the older men.

"Good idea," Doris said as if her approval was required. "You'll be a better shot when you're loose."

Rutgar led the way. Duke gripped his sippy cup and kicked his feet happily, sending an occasional smile at Terrance, who pushed him.

Terrance had long legs like Nate, but he tailored his stride to fit Julie's. "Quite an accomplishment to earn a spot on a SWAT team."

Julie flexed her hands, enjoying being stroller-free, looking forward to the morning's events and the warm look in Nate's eyes when she thanked him for the rifle. "Ah," Julie caught on. She stopped loosening up and started paying more attention to her escorts. "You're preparing me for losing to Nate, so I'll appreciate the job I have back home."

"You're a smart one." Rutgar adjusted the ammo bag. "The campaign ends soon. And I predict Nate will still be sheriff. And then you'll be gone. And I might have to write you."

"Rutgar is single and constantly on the lookout for a good woman," Terrance teased. "He has the particular misfortune of finding women who are on the cusp of committed relationships to other men."

"It's a gift," the big man muttered.

"I'm flattered to be letter worthy." Despite their easy banter, butterflies had begun to take flight in her midsection, heralding the nerves Nate had predicted. "You aren't providing me with a defective gun, are you?"

"So suspicious." Terrance chuckled.

"I fired it last week," Rutgar said, earning a growl from Terrance. "The sight is true."

At Martin's Bakery, Eunice sat in the window seat wearing a bright yellow tracksuit that contrasted nicely with the purple tint in her hair. "There's Julie," she shouted. "It's time."

Julie waved as the patrons of Martin's took last sips of their coffee, gathered their jackets or purses and, in some cases, walkers. But Rutgar marched on and so did she.

"Have you ever been married, Julie?" Terrance was quite the talker.

"No." Not even close. "I intimidate men." Policemen treated her like one of the guys. And most men outside the force were put off by her.

"Maybe you're looking at the wrong men." Despite Nate's kisses last night, there was something both soothing and curious about

Terrance's line of conversation. "Strong women need strong men at their side."

"Like me," Rutgar piped up.

"Keep walking, Rutgar," Terrance said, giving Julie a conspiratorial glance. "Back to the topic of strong men."

Julie took a closer look at Terrance's expression. "Are you giving me love advice?"

"I'm trying to." He blushed. "Am I doing it wrong? I have no experience giving advice to women. I only have sons."

"We've got another ten minutes' walk," Rutgar said. "You might as well flap your jaws and she might as well listen."

Duke's grip on his sippy cup slackened. He might be taking a little snooze.

"Ah, yes." Terrance cleared his throat. "Strong men. They aren't perfect."

"I think Nate would be upset to hear you think he's flawed," Julie teased.

"We're all flawed, Julie." Terrance's humility was endearing, even if she suspected he had an agenda. "It's determining if those flaws add to the package or make someone unacceptable."

Cars began passing them, going the same direction. Women waved out their windows and called, "Good luck!"

"Don't listen to Terrance," Rutgar said without turning back. "Perfect men exist. Take me, for example."

"He's perfect, all right," Terrance grinned. "If you like loud, opinionated, rough around the edges. And old."

"You described me to a T until that last part." Rutgar led them over a bridge. "The problem with dating at my age is—"

"Oh, here we go." Terrance rolled his eyes.

"—I can't promise what I'll be like five or ten years from now. Will I be broke? Will I look at the woman I date and remember who she is?"

"Dating is easier when you're young," Terrance agreed. "I'm shocked I finally agree with him."

"We agree because we're friends," Rutgar said simply.

"We're friends because of Nate. I never talked to you much before Robin died." Terrance looked over at Julie. "And now we have a new friend, someone who cares for Nate as much as we do."

More.

"Someone who'll forgive him his imperfections because he has a good heart."

Julie might have dwelled on Terrance's

words longer if they hadn't been met at a driveway by Flynn, who led Julie to where she'd be shooting.

"SO IT COMES down to this," Nate said to Julie as they stood off to the side on the winery property.

He'd nervously awaited her arrival, pacing. Terrance expected him to be honest. But honesty always came at a cost and the words Nate chose in the next few minutes could very well determine what his life was like over the next few years.

Flynn had set up targets fifty yards away where the land sloped gently uphill. He'd chosen a variety of targets—a spinner, a diamond pop-up, soup cans and a traditional paper target on a large tree stump. Someone had provided them with a table with ammunition, a basket of mermaid-shaped sugar cookies and bottles of water. Nate had added a first-aid kit and his rifle to the table. Spectators were about a quarter mile back, lining the road.

Julie walked up to Nate, carrying an ammo bag with what had to be Robin's gun slung over her shoulder. She wore brown cargo pants and a tan button-down. Her blond hair was loose and lively, fluttering in the breeze. She set the ammo on the table and leaned the gun against the edge.

She walked toward Nate with that broad smile he loved so much, the one he'd miss if he messed this up. "How about a kiss for luck?" she asked.

He held her at arm's length. "How about I get a rain check?"

Her smile faded. "A rain check for your good luck kiss?"

"A rain check on all of it—the shooting and the kiss." Nate shook his head. "April and your mother wouldn't want you to shoot, not with your wound so fresh." He didn't like the irate slant to her eyes, but he pressed on. "We can both agree to postpone or I could concede."

"Don't you dare." Julie removed his hands and took a step back. "I know I'm not as good a shot as you are, but my supporters expect me to compete. I'm not going to let them down."

"Don't make a decision based on pride. Think of April, she never took her health for granted." A black rain cloud formed above him, small yet ominous. "Think of Duke and how he'd feel if you had to go into the hospital again."

"April adored you," she said almost absently.

Her arms were twined around her stomach. "And I can see why."

"Yes. April *adored* me." He emphasized the word adore.

"Are you…" Julie paused, a crinkle to her brow. "You're saying she didn't love you. That's not true." Her tone was low and unforgiving. She'd most likely thought they were past discussions of April and Nate and love.

Terrance wanted Nate to tell the truth. But Nate was botching it before he ever got that far. He was in desperate need of a conversation do-over. Or he could consider this a sign that love wasn't meant for him. Anger numbed his heart, his fingers and his hope.

"You want to shoot? Let's shoot." He marched behind the table to retrieve his gun case.

She followed, keeping a short distance behind him. And then she was at his side, leaning over his weapon. "You're going to shoot with that thing? It's too small for you and held together with duct tape."

"My father gave me this gun." Nate looked at the rifle he'd been given for his eighth birthday. He'd taken it out of the gun safe that was built into the floor of his apartment, giving it a brief cleaning. He'd been battling nerves while he waited for Julie, but the moment he held that gun, everything inside him calmed.

"Nate, I'm sorry." Her arm came around his waist. She rested her head on his shoulder. "I hadn't realized this election and me being here would bring back all the painful memories of your childhood. We don't have to shoot."

The cloud over Nate's head thickened, darkened, flashed with lightning.

Maybe she meant to comfort him. Maybe he was projecting pity into her words. And maybe that wasn't anger building in his veins. He had to stop pussyfooting around the truth.

"This has nothing to do with my father." That came out louder than he wanted and they weren't the words he'd planned to say. Nate set the rifle down on the table. "I mean, this election and how I feel about the circus you and I have been roped into has nothing to do with my past."

She tilted her head and studied him. "Explain it to me, then."

Nate drew a breath. The time had come. "I didn't tell you the entire truth about the day April and I were going to be married."

Quicker than a fly evaded a fly swatter, she was angry again. "You said April didn't want to marry you. You said you loved her and that you would've gone through with it. What haven't you told me?" She was staring at his mouth. Unaccountably, her voice softened. "Did you two make some kind of a deal about the marriage and you reneged? I know one of April's last wishes was to be married."

"There was no deal." Nate blew out a breath and ran a hand through his hair. "She asked me a question. Totally out of the blue."

"A question about your father? About your time overseas?" Julie took a step closer, reaching for him. "Come on, Nate. Tell me."

He took her hands. He and Julie were positioned as if they were standing in front of a minister. Too bad they stood beneath a thick black cloud only Nate could see, one threatening a downpour. "April said I didn't love her the way I should, not the way she deserved." He gazed into Julie's eyes, imprinting the soft look of her eyes into his memory because he could tell she was never going to look at him like that again. "She said she could tell."

"And what did you say?" Julie's empathy was draining. He could hear it in her voice.

Nate wanted to hold on to her compassion. He wanted to build on it, preferably into something close to love. But he had to be honest. "I didn't say anything. I knew the day would come when she changed her mind about me." Without meaning to, Nate squeezed Julie's hands as if he couldn't bear to let them go. "Why wouldn't it? I've been a sniper for the military. I've shot bank robbers. I took aim at my own father. What kind of man does that and deserves to be loved? What kind of man does that and deserves a family? A wife." His throat clogged with failure until he had to force the words out. "A son."

Julie thrust out her chin, a fighter to the end. She was fighting the wrong battle. "What did April say?"

"She said I loved you more than I loved her." Nate worked his throat until he could swallow. "And for that...I had no answer."

He'd been broadsided by the accusation. He'd met Julie first. She'd been the more outwardly beautiful of the sisters. She held values and interests closer to Nate's. But he couldn't love her. He didn't know what *love* was. He'd cared for April, but it was a gentle, protective emotion. But because he didn't want to hurt her, when April said she loved him, he'd always repeated the words back to her, knowing admittedly the words were hollow.

Nate felt hollow now. "I could answer her today. I could tell her—"

"Don't." Julie looked upon him as if he'd just told her April had died. Her knees buckled.

Nate kept her on her feet.

"Don't," she whispered.

He had to. He had to tell her everything. "I had no idea what love was back then. I didn't know if April's statement was true or not. And because I didn't answer, April didn't want to get married. I told her I'd go through with the wedding, but she sent me away." He'd done as April wished and left without a word of explanation to anyone.

"That means I caused…" Julie broke free of Nate's hold, horror etched on her face with pale, ghostly lines. "After you left, she told Mom and me…" Her voice was barely a whisper. "And then she turned away. April turned away and… Oh, no." Julie's voice was as taut and off-key as a misplayed violin. "She didn't want to see me. In those days afterward…April didn't want to see me." Julie took a step back, and then another. "I've never put myself ahead of my sister."

"I'm sorry."

Her hand went to her mouth and she made a sound like a stifled sob. "I hate you."

He'd been afraid it would come to this. His chest felt as if it was crumpling in on itself.

"I tried to love her." Just as he'd planned this morning to try to say that he loved Julie.

"Don't make this worse." Her eyes had filled with tears and her voice was as shaky as a dried-out leaf in a late-autumn breeze. "There is nothing you can say that will make me feel better."

He nodded. Once. Briefly.

"I'm leaving today." Julie closed her eyes and turned her head. "I'm taking Duke."

He nodded again, although she still hadn't opened her eyes. He hadn't managed to tell her the entire truth. He hadn't said he loved her. But he'd gotten what he deserved.

And that was loneliness.

She turned away. "Goodbye, Landry." She'd gone two steps when she stopped and turned back. "No." Her chin came up. "I'm shooting. And if there's any justice in the world, I'll beat you."

The black cloud overhead descended.

JULIE DIDN'T WIN.

She couldn't control her breath or her sobs or her shaking hands. She'd wanted to win so badly. She'd wanted to crush Nate the way he'd crushed her heart.

Fool me once, shame on me. Fool me twice...

Julie was twice the fool. First, before she'd ever introduced him to April, she'd thought Nate was her friend. And now...it felt as if someone had ripped her heart out and then reached back in for the rest of her organs.

Nate may have shot better, but he didn't win either. She wasn't going to co-parent with him. She wasn't going to hold his hand through the dark memories. And she was most certainly not going to kiss him.

Julie walked away as soon as she was done. And she didn't look back. She couldn't look back.

April.

Julie owed April a thousand apologies. She should have kept her sister away from Nate. She should have known he was bad news. What kind of man wouldn't let himself smile? Rarely laughed? Didn't talk about his past or his family?

She knew the answers now and it made it that much harder to watch Nate lock down his emotions, to witness him bracing himself for her hurt and her anger.

Do not feel sorry for him.

"What did I tell you about men and imperfections?" Terrance asked gently when she entered the winery's tasting room to claim Duke, who'd been sitting on the floor playing with wine corks.

"How did you…" Julie took inventory of the room. Modern tables, elegant bar, discreet video camera in the corner. She walked around the bar and glanced at Flynn's open laptop. On-screen, Nate sat on the ground, elbows hooked around his knees, head bowed.

Do not feel sorry for him.

Her hands were still shaking and she barely trusted herself to speak. "You filmed this?" she demanded of Flynn.

The winery owner grimaced. "And broadcast it."

Julie slammed the laptop closed and gathered her nephew.

"It only went out to Harmony Valley," Flynn said as if that would make a difference. "We have some voters who were interested in the contest."

Carrying Duke, Julie dragged the stroller out the door. "And all those people lining the road?" All those people who knew, who'd heard, who'd seen Julie make a fool of herself with Nate.

Terrance followed Julie out the door. "Let me help you."

She whirled on the old man, grateful for a new target. "You knew."

He shook his head. "I knew he loved you. I knew he felt he could never be good enough for you."

"He was right." She shouldered the backpack, wincing when the padded strap rested on her wounded shoulder. The gun's recoil made everything hurt. She wanted to get somewhere safe and check her bandage.

"No mad words," Duke said half-heartedly as he climbed into the stroller.

"I can't make any promises." Julie's hands shook so bad Terrance had to strap Duke in.

As soon as the belt clicked, Julie propelled the stroller forward.

Terrance walked at her side. "Nate loves you. I heard him all but say it out there."

"Everyone heard him almost say it. You had a microphone." She couldn't quell the anger in her voice.

"You can't choose who you love, Julie. Imagine how much it hurt Nate to be honest with your sister. Imagine his surprise when confronted with an emotion he hadn't yet acknowledged for himself."

"I don't need to imagine anything. I heard it all." More than she ever wanted to hear. How was she going to tell her mother? What was she going to tell her mother?

"Nay." Duke twisted in the stroller to look up at Julie. "Luv Nay. Where Nay?"

Julie bent over in pain. Duke loved Nate. He loved his dad.

She loved Nate, too. She loved that infuriating, internally scarred, honorable man. Her love... It felt like a betrayal to the sister she loved. When had love blossomed? Was it love on April's wedding day? Or had it grown to love when she'd administered the Daddy Test?

And why was she realizing she loved Nate now when the truth made it impossible to love him?

"Let me help you." Terrance guided Julie's body into an upright position with a hand on her uninjured shoulder and another on her back.

"Nay?" Duke twisted right and left, his dark hair spiraling in the air like antennae in a breeze. "Nay?"

"Nate went bye-bye." Julie choked on the words. Or maybe it was her heart she was choking on.

What if April hadn't been so honorable? What if they'd gone through with the marriage? Would Julie have felt differently if Nate came to her as a widower and said he loved her? Would Julie feel the sharp stab of betrayal?

April was gone and she owed it to her sister to...to...

Forgive.

Julie's steps faltered. She pressed a hand over her bandage, so close to her heart. What if April wasn't just encouraging Julie to forgive Nate? What if she was encouraging Julie to forgive April? For sending her here. For making her promise to administer the Daddy Test. For knowing that Nate loved her and suspecting that given the right circumstances Julie might love him back.

No one was that strong.

Julie's breath hitched.

April had been that strong.

Julie wanted to curl up in a ball and let the pain roll over her. But she had Duke to care for, a career to figure out and a drive on busy freeways to make. She didn't think she could do it.

Love...love was in the way of everything.

Terrance didn't say anything until they were crossing the bridge, mere blocks from the sheriff's office. "You can't drive like this. Think of Duke."

"I am thinking of Duke. I have to get away.

I can't think here." She couldn't honor her sister and forgive Nate in this town.

"Come to my house," Terrance blurted, cutting off her protests. "I won't tell Nate. You can rest. I can watch Duke. And when you're ready, when you're steady, you can leave."

"I'm not running for sheriff." The old man was just tricky enough to try and entice her to go to the vote tonight. "I'm out. Are we clear?"

"Crystal." He took possession of the stroller handles and led her away.

Terrance's house was a memorial to his wife. There were pictures of her everywhere. Wedding pictures. Anniversary pictures. His wife holding babies. His wife cuddling puppies.

Julie slung the backpack off her shoulders and stood in the doorway, uncertain if she wanted to intrude on such overwhelming grief.

Duke had no reservations. He snagged the backpack, ran into the living room and crawled onto the couch.

"You know—" Terrance stood next to her "—I hadn't realized until just now that I might have gone overboard with my grieving."

She looked at him with raised brows.

Terrance laughed. "You're right. I'm not ready to take any of the photos down."

Julie nodded. She understood love and grief. It was forgiveness she struggled with.

"Juju." Duke patted the cushion next to him and then dug in the backpack where she kept a few of his favorite books. "Read."

She sat down, grateful.

Duke climbed into her lap and handed her a book. Except it wasn't a book. It was April's notebook with the Daddy Test.

"Not this one." Julie tried to reach for another book.

"No." Duke shook the notebook in her face. "Read book me."

"Hey. That was three words." A milestone. Milestones should be celebrated. Julie smiled and hugged Duke and looked around for…

Terrance had disappeared somewhere. His wife was the only one to meet her gaze. Everywhere she looked, Robin gazed back. Julie realized she was really looking for Nate.

Disappointment clamped down on her chest. But disappointment with who?

"Let's pick out another book."

"No." Again, Duke shook the notebook as if he was trying to shake all the secrets out of it.

Julie relented, opening the notebook and creating a story from scratch. "There once was a boy named Duke."

Duke clapped his small hands.

"Who had an aunt Julie and a…a dad named Nate."

"Nay," Duke said in a breathy voice. He flipped a page and lay back against Julie. "Luv Nay."

Julie wrapped her arms around him, remembering a conversation she'd had with April months ago.

"How will I know if Nate passes your test?" Julie had asked.

"He'll answer all your questions," April had said, breathless because breathing was a chore. "And although you may not like all his answers, he'll be honest with you. You have to forgive honesty, I think."

"You think?"

"I know," she'd said with one of those enduring smiles.

"Read, Juju." Duke flipped another page in the notebook, one she and Nate hadn't gotten to yet.

April had written: "What will you tell your son about love?"

THE CHURCH WAS crowded for the special meeting called for the election.

Mayor Larry kept announcing that people needed to sit on the side of their candidate.

Nate was distressed to find his side was overflowing.

"Spilling your guts out to Julie was brilliant," Rutgar said when Nate reached the front pew.

Julie and Duke sat at the front of the church on the altar. He knew she hadn't left town because her SUV was still parked in front of the jail, but he hadn't seen her all day. She looked like she'd been through boot camp on little sleep. Her eyes were puffy and her blond hair was limp, and he wished with all his heart that he could make her feel better.

Nate walked over to Mayor Larry and shook his hand. "May I?" He gestured toward the microphone.

"Of course." The mayor stepped aside and then seemed to change his mind and stepped back, leaning in close to ask, "I'm not going to regret this, am I?"

"No." Nate stood behind the podium and drew a steadying breath. "Ladies and gentlemen, I want to thank you for your support over the past few years. When I came here to Harmony Valley, I was in desperate need of a clean slate and you gave it to me."

"The election isn't over," Doris sniped from the front row. The empty front row.

"The election is over," Nate said evenly. "Because someone needs a clean slate more than I do. I'm withdrawing my name from consideration as your sheriff."

The crowd exploded with noise. Some people moved from Nate's side of the church to Julie's side. Others began to shout at Nate. Rutgar howled a loud, "Nooooo."

When he tried to step away from the microphone, Mayor Larry held him fast.

"Hold on. Hold on." Agnes called for order.

"I should go." Nate couldn't bring himself to look at Julie.

"Stay right here." The mayor's grip was unexpectedly strong.

The church quieted.

"Unfortunately, Julie Smith does not qualify for the sheriff's position." Agnes looked like she'd rather be home than broadcasting this announcement via microphone. "As we noted at the meeting where we decided to have an election, the sheriff only qualifies for the position if he or she meets the same criteria as any other elected official. According to our by-laws, a candidate must have lived in Harmony Valley for at least one year prior to running."

The crowd erupted again.

"What? You knew Julie wasn't qualified

all along?" Nate used his outdoor voice and it was picked up by the podium's microphone. He jerked his arm free of Mayor Larry's hold and took a step back, a step closer to Agnes, who he'd used to trust. "You knew and you put Julie through this circus anyway?"

He wasn't alone in his indignation.

"You made Nate think his job was at risk?" Julie demanded.

"That is nasty, Agnes." Doris leaped to her feet. "Just nasty. We should all remember how nasty Agnes is this fall when she's up for—"

Mildred dragged the microphone toward herself. "We wouldn't have been in this position if not for you, Doris."

Not to be excluded, Rose took the microphone next. "And now, unless someone else wants to step up, we won't have a sheriff."

The crowd had a gut reaction, a loud gut reaction.

Duke ran to Nate and hid between his legs. "Nay!"

"I know, buddy." Nate leaned closer to the microphone. "No mad words, please."

The crowd quieted only to have Doris get to her feet and announce, "*I'll* run for sheriff."

The crowd burst forth with protests once more. This time it was boos.

"You don't qualify either," Agnes said, having reclaimed the microphone.

"We need to talk," Julie shouted beside Nate.

He didn't need to be asked twice. "Follow me." Nate picked up his son and led Julie out the back door. "Duke, do you want nachos or ice cream?"

"Nach-cream."

Nate pressed a kiss to Duke's forehead. "You got it, buddy."

"Luv Nay." Duke flung his arms around Nate's neck.

The moment froze in time. The chill to the evening air. The way the oak in the town square was outlined against the night sky. The easy weight of his son in his arms as he said he loved him.

"We need to talk," Julie said again, following him down the sidewalk. "Or maybe you just need to listen. Can you stop?"

"Nope." His son loved him. He'd gladly give him anything he wanted at El Rosal. "I'm a man on a mission for nach-cream."

"Nach-cream," Duke echoed.

El Rosal was empty. Everyone in town was still over at the church arguing about who would be sheriff. Arturo was behind the bar polishing glasses. Nate asked for an order of nachos and ice cream. And then his joy dissolved somewhat as he realized the only *l* word that was likely to come up during his conversation with Julie was *loathe*.

"You can't leave Harmony Valley," Julie said when they'd been seated in a booth. "This town needs you and you need it more than I do."

Nate shook his head. "You need a safer job if you're going to raise Duke."

"I don't plan to return to the force." She selected a straw from a jar in the center of the table and unwrapped it, coiling the empty wrapper around her finger.

"But still. You need Duke." He stopped short of saying Julie needed Duke more than he did. He gazed at Duke with his heart in his throat. He was pretty darn sure his father had never looked at him with love in his eyes.

"These are the custody papers." Julie pulled them from her backpack. She looked at them, looked at Nate, and then she tore them up. "A boy needs his father."

Nate was speechless.

Ice cream was delivered. Nachos were promised next. And still they didn't speak to each other. Duke ate ice cream and they let it drip everywhere.

"Jules." Nate took her hand and slid closer.

"You came here to find justice for April. I'm sorry it didn't work out the way you'd planned." He was sorry he hadn't been good enough for her. But there'd be time enough for self-pity later.

"Let's be clear. I came here wanting justice for myself." Julie looked at everything but Nate. And yet, she didn't yank her hand from his. "April made peace with her feelings the moment she held Duke in her arms. The Daddy Test wasn't for you. It was for me to get to know you."

"But…"

"My sister was a saint. You hurt her and so did I, even if we didn't mean to, even if we weren't in love back then." Julie's gaze slid away, along with the strength in her voice. "Despite that, April knew what she wanted. She wanted Duke to have two parents. She wanted me to fall in love with you." Julie put the worry stone on the table.

"It didn't work." Nate reached for it, letting her hand go. Letting her go.

Julie covered his hand with both of hers. "It did work. I just had to be reminded that loving sometimes involves forgiving. How could I not forgive you when April forgave me?"

Nate didn't dare breathe or speak or move.

Was she saying she loved him? Was she saying there was hope?

Duke used melted ice cream to finger-paint the table.

"Aren't you going to say something?" Julie's words were strong and demanding, but there was vulnerability in her eyes. And there were her hands covering his on the table.

Nate shook his head, and then he blurted, "Everything I said today turned out wrong. Don't ask me to speak. Don't ask me to say anything."

"Okay." A light smile played across her lips. "I'll talk and you listen."

He nodded.

"I had a long talk with Terrance today. Turns out he's not only a well of wisdom about love…" She cleared her throat, casting a bit of doubt on the old man's knowledge. "But he was also a private investigator, which is a career path that helps people obtain justice."

"Sometimes," Nate allowed. No one could guarantee justice.

Julie raised her brows. "Are you speaking or being silent?"

"Silent." He'd never speak again if she gave him a chance to love her.

Julie looked like she didn't believe he could

stay silent and the more she smiled at him, the more Nate was inclined to agree with her. He wanted to talk. He needed to say what he was feeling.

"Duke love Juju." Duke beat Nate to the punch, dragging his ice cream–covered fingers over his face. "Duke love Nay."

"I want to date you, Jules." So much for Nate being silent.

"With your intentions being…" Julie smiled openly now. If Nate didn't know better, he'd say there was love in her eyes.

"My intentions…" Nate hesitated. He'd never said those words out loud and meant them with all his heart. "My intentions are love, honor and marriage."

Julie beamed at his words and said coyly, "I have to tell you, I'm a little gun-shy."

Nate loved it when she made a pun. But until they exchanged vows and signed papers, he wouldn't blame her for doubting him. "We'll go slow. We'll be sure."

Julie nodded. And then she nodded toward the window. "The town council just pulled up. I think they're going to beg you to take your job back."

"They can wait." Nate moved closer to the woman who'd staved off rain clouds. He stroked her cheek with his thumb. "I love you. I will always love you."

"Luv you Nay." Duke wiped ice cream on his hair. "Luv you Juju."

"I love you, little man," Julie said. And then she took Nate's palm and pressed it to her cheek. "I love you, too."

The doors to El Rosal flung open. Loud voices rose above the music. They'd be surrounded by townspeople soon.

Julie knew it. She pressed a quick kiss to Nate's lips, one that promised more to come. "I've been thinking about what kind of wedding I want."

"Really?" Nate hadn't gotten past the joy of the moment to logistics.

She nodded again. "Nothing too fancy or too formal."

Nothing like what he and April had planned. "Whatever you want."

Julie's gaze turned tender. She drew Nate closer. "But I think a bride needs a really great dress."

It was his turn to nod, numbly, because having Julie near and talking marriage had truly silenced him this time.

The leaders of Harmony Valley approached

with conciliatory smiles and determination in their eyes.

Julie pressed her cheek to his and whispered in his ear, "How do you feel about pink?"

* * * * *

If you loved this charming small-town romance from USA TODAY *bestselling author Melinda Curtis, be sure to check out the other stories in her acclaimed* HARMONY VALLEY *miniseries:*

LOVE, SPECIAL DELIVERY
MARRYING THE SINGLE DAD
A MAN OF INFLUENCE
A MEMORY AWAY
TIME FOR LOVE
ONE PERFECT YEAR
SEASON OF CHANGE
SUMMER KISSES
DANDELION WISHES

Available from www.Harlequin.com today!

Get 2 Free Books,
Plus 2 Free Gifts—
just for trying the Reader Service!

Love Inspired®

Get 2 Free Books,
Plus 2 Free Gifts—
just for trying the
Reader Service!

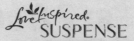

HOMETOWN HEARTS ♥

Get 2 Free Books,
Plus 2 Free Gifts—
just for trying the Reader Service!

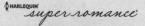

YES! Please send me 2 FREE LARGER-PRINT Harlequin® Superromance® novels and my 2 FREE gifts (gifts are worth about $10 retail). After receiving them, if I don't wish to receive any more books, I can return the shipping statement marked "cancel." If I don't cancel, I will receive 4 brand-new novels every month and be billed just $6.19 per book in the U.S. or $6.49 per book in Canada. That's a savings of at least 11% off the cover price! It's quite a bargain! Shipping and handling is just 50¢ per book in the U.S. or 75¢ per book in Canada.* I understand that accepting the 2 free books and gifts places me under no obligation to buy anything. I can always return a shipment and cancel at any time. The free books and gifts are mine to keep no matter what I decide.

132/332 HDN GLWS

Name	(PLEASE PRINT)
Address	Apt. #
City	State/Prov.	Zip/Postal Code

Signature (if under 18, a parent or guardian must sign)

Mail to the **Reader Service:**
IN U.S.A.: P.O. Box 1341, Buffalo, NY 14240-8531
IN CANADA: P.O. Box 603, Fort Erie, Ontario L2A 5X3

Want to try two free books from another line?
Call 1-800-873-8635 today or visit www.ReaderService.com.

* Terms and prices subject to change without notice. Prices do not include applicable taxes. Sales tax applicable in N.Y. Canadian residents will be charged applicable taxes. Offer not valid in Quebec. This offer is limited to one order per household. Books received may not be as shown. Not valid for current subscribers to Harlequin Superromance Larger-Print books. All orders subject to approval. Credit or debit balances in a customer's account(s) may be offset by any other outstanding balance owed by or to the customer. Please allow 4 to 6 weeks for delivery. Offer available while quantities last.

Your Privacy—The Reader Service is committed to protecting your privacy. Our Privacy Policy is available online at www.ReaderService.com or upon request from the Reader Service.

We make a portion of our mailing list available to reputable third parties that offer products we believe may interest you. If you prefer that we not exchange your name with third parties, or if you wish to clarify or modify your communication preferences, please visit us at www.ReaderService.com/consumerschoice or write to us at Reader Service Preference Service, P.O. Box 9062, Buffalo, NY 14240-9062. Include your complete name and address.

READERSERVICE.COM

Manage your account online!

- Review your order history
- Manage your payments
- Update your address

> ***We've designed the Reader Service website just for you.***

Enjoy all the features!

- Discover new series available to you, and read excerpts from any series.
- Respond to mailings and special monthly offers.
- Browse the Bonus Bucks catalog and online-only exculsives.
- Share your feedback.

Visit us at:
ReaderService.com

Get 2 Free Books,
Plus 2 Free Gifts—
just for trying the Reader Service!

HRLP17R2